HONOUR AND EMPIRE

Recent Titles by Philip McCutchan from Severn House

THE FIRST COMMAND
SOLDIER OF THE QUEEN
CAPTAIN AT ARMS

CAMERON'S CONVOY
CAMERON IN THE GAP

HONOUR AND EMPIRE

Philip McCutchan

This title first published in Great Britain 1999 by
SEVERN HOUSE PUBLISHERS LTD of
9–15 High Street, Sutton, Surrey SM1 1DF.
Previously published 1972 in Great Britain and the USA
as *The Gates of Kunarja* under the pseudonym *Duncan MacNeil*.
This title first published in the U.S.A. 1999 by
SEVERN HOUSE PUBLISHERS INC of
595 Madison Avenue, New York, N.Y. 10022.

Copyright © 1972 by Philip McCutchan

British Library Cataloguing in Publication Data

McCutchan, Philip, 1920-
  Honour and empire
  1. Great Britain. Army – Fiction
  2. Ogilvie, James (Fictitious character) - Fiction
  3. India - History - British occupation, 1765-1947 - History - Fiction
  4. Historical fiction
  I. Title
    823.9'14 [F]

    ISBN 0-7278-2293-4

Printed and bound in Great Britain by
MPG Books Ltd, Bodmin, Cornwall.

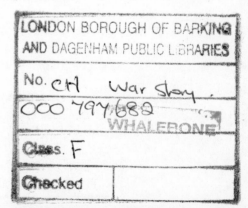

1

To SEE LONDON again, after four years of mainly active service on the North-West Frontier of India, had been splendid fun; to have, for a while, his own unregimented rooms in Half Moon Street off Piccadilly, had been a delicious relaxation, the more so as Mary Archdale had, to his parents' fury, accompanied him by train from Peshawar and then by the P. & O. steamer from Bombay to Tilbury. But when, after a month of London—and even though prudence had dictated that Mary should remain behind— Captain James Ogilvie had left Kings Cross aboard the Flying Scotsman for Edinburgh, where he would change on to the slow line for Aviemore and Corriecraig, he had felt for the first time that he was really coming home. For a little over four hundred years the Ogilvies had occupied Corriecraig Castle; from its keep and battlements, once garrisoned by its private army, they had throughout the more democratic centuries set out to their various wars, to fight in all corners of the world for monarch and country and ultimately for Empire, as Lieutenant-General Sir Iain Ogilvie was currently doing in India, as soon James his son would once again be doing; and the grip of Corriecraig, of its wide-flung holdings, of its inherited responsibilities, was strong and binding. The traditions were entwined in James Ogilvie's very being; he had been a part of Corriecraig from birth, and it had become a vital part of him in its turn, moulding him into a life of service and high endeavour, predestining him, as the only son of his father, to enter what had become the family regiment, the 114th Highlanders, the Queen's Own Royal Strathspeys, into which the eldest son always went...

The stations, the landmarks to Scotland, came up and fell behind: Huntingdon, Peterborough, York ... Durham, the platforms high-perched by the tall viaduct, with a splendid view of the cathedral and the castle as dusk fell over the North; Newcastle upon Tyne, with mist wreathing around the station lanterns and the gaslights; and then at last Edinburgh and the Scots accents of the porters as they loomed up ghostlike in the light from the carriage windows, and bustled aboard to take hold of the trunks of the ladies and gentlemen in the First Class coaches.

"Corriecraig, is it, sir? You'll be wanting the train for Perth and Inverness, or are you staying overnight in the hotel?"

Ogilvie smiled. "I'll be going on, porter. I'm going home, you see. All the way from India!"

"India, is it, sir? Then welcome back to Scotland. If you'll follow me, sir, I'll put you on the train north. You have twenty minutes just."

*   *   *

James Ogilvie was met at Aviemore railway station—met by a large, clanking monster in the charge of a young man wearing a soft-crowned peaked cap and a dark blue tunic buttoned to the neck beneath a heavy greatcoat. The mechanical contrivance upon which this man attended was the centre of much attention from the railway station staff and the few passengers who had alighted with Ogilvie.

"What the devil!" Ogilvie said as his trunks were lifted into the back of the four-seater beneath the glare of gas lamps. Curiously, he walked round the motor-car; it was beautifully kept, with the brass lamps gleaming with much polishing and the paintwork spotless; it was not the first mechanical carriage he had seen, but he was surprised at his uncle having acquired such a thing. "What's my uncle doing with a contrivance like this? Who're you, by the way?" he

6

asked the object's guardian.

"MacNab, sir. The admiral's chauffeur, sir. This . . ." MacNab patted the bonnet lovingly. "She's a Panhard-Levassor, the very best, sir. Since the man with the red flag was done away with last year, the admiral's made more use of her than he has of horses, sir."

"Well, I'll be damned! Does it really go?"

"Indeed she does, sir, though with the weight of your trunks she'll not make so much speed."

Ogilvie nodded, and, cautiously, climbed aboard the Panhard-Levassor. MacNab did something to the controls and they moved off, noisily and with a warm smell of oil. Ogilvie shook his head in wonderment. Uncle Rufus, fairly recently retired from the Navy as a rear-admiral and currently tenanting Corriecraig Castle in Sir Iain's absence overseas, was not only his father's younger brother, he was also an old shellback of an admiral who had detested, and most bitterly resented, the advent of steam propulsion in the Queen's Navy and its attendant abortion, engineers. *A dirty race of black devils*, he had written to James Ogilvie's father. *Quite impossible people ... God alone knows what the Service is coming to.* Logically, James Ogilvie would have supposed, internal combustion would have ranked on a par with steam in the mind of a man hitherto accustomed, when ashore, to the saddle.

*   *   *

"You're looking damn well, my boy, damn well," Rufus Ogilvie said over whiskies by a roaring fire in Sir Iain's study. "India suits you—hey?"

"Well enough, Uncle Rufus."

Blue eyes, sailor's eyes, ran over him critically. "Plenty of action?"

James nodded.

"Wish to God I was still serving. Kicked me out, the buggers—*I* didn't want to go! Age—that's the trouble. I didn't quite make vice-admiral in time, you see. They'll have your father out soon, and what'll that do to him? Break his heart, I shouldn't wonder. Oh, the buggers!" Rear-

7

Admiral Rufus Ogilvie lifted his arms with his fists clenched, and waved them violently in the air, his round red face deepening in colour to a dangerous purple. He was standing up, while his nephew sat. He was standing very straight, very square; he was not a tall man like his brother and nephew, but he was robust and solid, the sort to face a gale like an abiding rock. James often wondered how his uncle had ever fathered a son such as cousin Hector the Civil Servant, largely desk-bound in Whitehall—ruling India by remote control, from a sea of paper and a tidal wave of regulations and minutes and semi-decisions arrived at by committees. Uncle Rufus would have a very short way with committees...

"Why the petrol carriage, Uncle Rufus?" James asked curiously after some moments of silence.

"What's that?"

"The petrol carriage—the, what's it, Panhard. I always thought mechanical—"

"Ah—yes, yes. Well now, my boy, call it a hobby. Oddly enough—your aunt's hobby rather than mine. Call it un-womanly if you like, but that's the truth." There was something in the admiral's expression that told James it wasn't quite the truth: but it was a convenient enough face-saver for a sailing-navy man. "As for me, it gives me an engineer to bully—"

"Chauffeur?"

"Damn silly frog name! Engineer. I make him keep it spotless, even the tyres."

James grinned. "I don't believe you really bully him, Uncle Rufus."

"Perhaps not, perhaps not." Rufus Ogilvie gave a sudden deep laugh. "Did I ever tell you what I did to my confounded fleet engineer once—"

"Yes, you did—"

"When he was slow to give me the speed I wanted—"

"Yes—"

"I picked him up with my own two hands," the admiral continued obstinately, for he was fond of this story, "and I threw him over the bridge rails, right into the sea. That cool-ed him and cleaned him, by God! I let him wallow before I

8

sent away a boat." Suddenly, he sat down facing his nephew; in that moment he looked, Ogilvie thought, older and less sure of himself. He said, "D'you know, James, I've thought from time to time since, that *could* have been why I wasn't promoted. I still think it was worth it, though. One has to make one's protest." He pulled a heavy gold watch from his waistcoat pocket, and looked at it with his head held back and eyes narrowed. "Dammit, it's late, very late. Something I wanted to talk to you about, but it's too late and it'll do in the morning. Before your aunt's up. You an early riser, my boy?"

"Fairly."

"Very well, we'll have a bright and early spin in the Panhard. I'll have you called at six bells ... seven o'clock."

They went together up the great staircase and parted on the landing, after a warm handshake. James Ogilvie went to the room that had always been his since he had left the nursery. It was a room to come back to, a room that was full of memories, a room that was home, an anchorage in a somewhat nomadic life. Here there were no reminders of the regiment or of India, unless the silver-framed photograph of his father in his uniform when he had, as a lieutenant-colonel, commanded the battalion, could be considered as such. The memories here were of childhood days, and schooldays, and Sandhurst days; he had not been home since just after he had been gazetted from Sandhurst to the 114th Highlanders as a second lieutenant. And so—moustached now, and tanned, and with a hardening line to his jaw and a very military bearing—he moved around the things of the past and felt a wrench of nostalgia as he did so. A tennis racket, a pair of ice skating boots, a cricket bat, some fishing tackle, a moth-eaten and useless set of bagpipes ... all these had had their niche and they all brought back vivid scenes of what now, to Captain James Ogilvie, seemed the very long ago. So much had happened in between. India, the fighting outside Jalalabad in Afghanistan, the terrible march under Bloody Francis Fettleworth to the relief of Fort Gazai, his wanderings in the wild hills of Waziristan on attachment to the Political Service, the terrible death of Jones, the arms salesman from Birming-

9

ham. And Mary Archdale. Mary, who at that moment would be lonely, and thinking of him, in her quiet hotel in South Kensington. Mary who, James Ogilvie was certain, was to be the subject of the forthcoming early-morning talk with his uncle.

Talk? Lecture, more like!

Restlessly, suddenly ill-at-ease, Ogilvie swung away from the well-remembered cupboard into which he had been staring. His eye was caught by a crudely-coloured picture, framed, at his mother's insistence, upon the wall: a childish painting executed, with immense pride, by his young sister years ago, a young sister that a mother could not bear to see hurt. James Ogilvie as a child had been cruelly critical of that lovingly done painting, furious at being made to hang it, ashamed of it before his friends. He had always been critical of his sister; now, he saw the picture through different eyes, saw it for what it was and had always been, a genuine expression of devotion. He moved away, subject to a little guilt, went towards a window and pulled aside the heavy curtain, and looked out over the courtyard of the castle and beyond the walls to the Scottish countryside bathed in bright moonlight—unobscured moonlight was rare enough in Corriecraig and Ogilvie had the feeling the clouds had withdrawn to allow him a welcome home. Looking across towards distant mountains and hearing a faint sighing of the wind from the North Sea, he thought of India, and Murree, of his father currently commanding the Northern Army half a world away, his father and mother who belonged here and had scarcely seen their property in the last seven or eight years. Except when, as in the case of Uncle Rufus, a member of the clan took temporary possession, Corriecraig was left to his father's agent to oversee and administer and maintain. That Sir Iain loved Corriecraig no one could ever doubt; but James guessed that he loved the regiment and the army more. He was a born soldier; the son, a little less so. There had been a time indeed when James Ogilvie had hated the army life; that time had passed, and with added years and responsibility and maturity he was content enough. But his first loyalty was to Corriecraig; and he could not understand how, when his grandfather had died, his father could have remained on in the army rather than send in his papers and come home to Corriecraig to take upon his shoulders the mantle and duties of the laird. James Ogilvie had no doubts as to what he himself would do when the time came.

*   *   *

She hadn't really wanted him to come north, though she had not precisely said so and certainly had not put any obstacles in his way. Still—he knew. Knew, regretted, but understood completely. She, the widow of an officer killed in action in India, was very much on her own in London and without an escort found her horizons sadly circumscribed: ladies did not go about unaccompanied, never rode alone in hansom cabs and, of course, could not possibly —no more could a gentleman, indeed—travel by omnibus.

Ogilvie had suggested as companion a Mrs. Gleeson, also a widow, also young, also resident in Mary's hotel; but this had led to a pout and a flat and spirited rejection.

"*That* silly woman! Oh, dear, James, no thank you! Besides, she wouldn't."

"Why not?"

Mary laughed; they were in his rooms, and she nestled her head down against his chest. "My dear, you're no more perceptive than most men. She disapproves of me. I see far too much of you. She's as stuffy as a bath bun, James, and I hate her. I've always hated respectability, as you very well know. Letitia Gleeson, though in all conscience I wouldn't dream of ever calling her anything but *Mrs.* Gleeson, is *very* respectable. Her husband was a barrister. Old, I've gathered—like my Tom. But at least Tom was a soldier, even if not a very good one." She laughed again. "Oh, James, do you remember his field lavatory, and the bum-havildar?"

"Of course."

"That's the sort of thing one could never mention to Mrs. Gleeson. She'd choke. No, it's no good, I represent Sin to her. She even hinted the other day that my Captain Ogilvie was very *young* ... the inference was obvious enough." She brought her head up and looked into his

11

eyes, searchingly. "James, I don't look all that much older, do I? Please tell me truthfully. Seven years *is* a long time."

He took her face in his hands and kissed her, passionately. "Darling, I've told you so often, you don't look it and it doesn't matter anyway."

"It does to your parents ... and the old trouts in Peshawar. Not all female trouts either."

"Well, don't let it spoil things. Mrs. Gleeson's not in the least important."

"How true! But don't ever suggest her as a chaperon again, James dear. Don't suggest *anyone*. There's simply no one in what I suppose you could call my circle, which after years in India hasn't much of a diameter, that I've the smallest thing in common with. India changes people, love. Changes them a great deal. It's so narrow in some ways, so wide in others. Women like me are aliens in their own country. Just to mention one thing ... I've become used to a *chota peg* at sundown. I shouldn't, but I have. Even in Peshawar it wasn't quite the done thing for a lady, but here in London ... love, it would make Mrs. Gleeson give birth!" She gave a sudden rather wicked gurgle and nestled into his chest again, her hands roving lightly. "Talking of that, love, since you're off to the highlands so soon..."

"Mary," he murmured into the soft hair. "Mary, my dearest." That had been in the afternoon, the respectable English afternoon when the ladies of London were calling and leaving cards upon other ladies who sighed but put a well-bred good face upon the intrusion, the entirely predictable intrusion, into their peace. That evening Ogilvie took Mary in a hansom cab to dine at the Café Royal and after that to a music hall—the Canterbury, in the Westminster Bridge Road. She much preferred that to a West End theatre. As they went in the newsboys were tearing out their lungs, shouting the late news, running with their flapping posters beneath a chill drizzle: unusual, for late summer weather. There was something about India, and the Frontier, and a border flare-up. There was always a border flare-up, but Ogilvie bought a paper and when they were in their seats he read the reports. It was nothing much, but there was mention of the Division at Peshawar and Now-

12

shera, and of its commander, Lieutenant-General Francis Fettleworth. Even in a London music hall, an officer on leave couldn't remain unaware of Bloody Francis, Ogilvie thought with irritation.

Mary's hand touched his arm. "What is it, love?"

"Oh, nothing much. Some patrols have been fired on and there've been some wounded. No ... nothing much. All the same..." He hesitated.

"Well, love?"

"We tend to be forgotten, in India ... till something big is in the air. The home papers—"

"Not tonight, James dear. Forget Peshawar, *please!*"

He smiled, and pressed her fingers. "All right, Mary." It was not possible, however, entirely to forget; there were many uniforms in the audience—bluejackets, infantrymen, guardsmen in their scarlet tunics, riflemen in dark green; and there were plenty of patriotic songs: songs like 'Soldiers of the Queen', and 'By Jingo If We do'. Ogilvie sang with the rest, and with a will, and thought inevitably of the Frontier.

> We don't want to fight,
> But, by jingo, if we do,
> We've got the ships, we've got the men,
> We've got the money too!

One way and another, it was an enjoyable last night in London. The memory of it was in Ogilvie's mind as sleep came to him in his old room at Corriecraig, and his subsequent dreams were of Mary. But he woke refreshed and on the instant when, sharp on seven o'clock, there was a loud bang on his door and his uncle's own servant came in with tea.

"Good morning, sir. It's a fair bright day, sir. The admiral's up already."

"Thank you, Morrison, and good morning to you. What's that you have there—apart from the tea, I mean?"

"A flask, sir. A drop o' whisky works wonders, sir. The admiral always takes one." Morrison, late coxswain of the admiral's barge, unscrewed the top of the flask.

"Not for me, thank you, Morrison," Ogilvie said with a smile. "It's a kind thought—but no. India teaches one to have a care!"

"It's just as you like, sir, of course." The flask was slid back into a capacious pocket; it would very likely come out again in a couple of minutes if the floridity of Morrison's face, accented by the fringe of white whiskers, was anything to go by. The coxswain left and Ogilvie drank his tea and dressed quickly. When he reached the courtyard his uncle was tinkering with the Panhard, his hands covered with oil. There was no sign of the 'engineer'.

"Good morning, Uncle Rufus."

An intent face looked up from the bonnet. "Morning, James, morning. Damn thing's sulking." He went back to his work.

"I'm afraid I can't help," James said, going to the admiral's side. "Why not leave it to what's his name, Mac-Nab?"

"Stuff-and-nonsense, I know as much about it as he does." The admiral prodded and fiddled and very obviously had no idea what he was doing. Nevertheless, something happened; Rufus Ogilvie covered his surprise pretty well when the vehicle heaved and spluttered and vibrated and a spout of vapour issued from somewhere. "Get aboard, boy!" he shouted. "Get aboard before she changes her mind!" James did as he was told; his uncle steered somewhat erratically across the courtyard, heading towards the road beyond the main gatehouse. Soon they were going along at around ten miles an hour and the admiral was holding on to his hat. The air was wonderful, fresh and keen, really invigorating, and Ogilvie took a succession of deep breaths, filling his lungs with the good highland morning. The colouring on the hills was superb. The road was a white dusty ribbon, curling away into far distances.

"I dare say," his uncle observed, "it reminds you of Afghanistan."

"Yes."

"Quite a place, so they tell me—Peshawar."

"Peshawar's not exactly in Afghanistan, Uncle Rufus."

"Dammit, I know that! Never said it was."

"I'm sorry." Ogilvie felt his heart sink; his uncle was being a shade obvious, in his blunt seafaring tradition. The mention of Peshawar indicated that he was approaching his point, bows on and with good steerage way. Ogilvie had no wish to discuss Peshawar within the context which his uncle so plainly intended to probe. Guilefully, he expressed an interest in the mechanics of the Panhard.

The admiral was pleased. "Very simple—I'll explain it. I wonder you don't get one, James. It would be very useful in India, I imagine?"

"My Colonel, I think, would scarcely approve!"

The old man nodded sagely. "I can see that, of course. Horses ... just like sail ... *horses* are for gentlemen. I concede that point. To become too mechanical is to place oneself in the hands of the lower classes to a great extent— unless one takes steps to learn the ins and outs, as I have done. But in, say, Peshawar—"

"Uncle Rufus, you were going to explain—"

"So I was, so I was! Nothing to explain really, James, and anyway I'm sure you younger men don't need on old buffer like me to tell you about modern methods of propulsion. Mind you, the steam cars were—are—a good deal simpler in many ways. Several advantages, too. The motion of the piston, you see, being produced, as it is, by the direct application of steam pressure, gives a wonderfully strong starting force—and it's tremendously useful when climbing hills. More suitable for Scotland really—but I didn't fancy the idea of *stoking* going on around me. As a matter of fact I believe they did produce something that was virtually automatic in action, but I don't know ... damn things can explode, I believe."

"Explode?"

"Yes. But a man called Serpollet or something, a Froggy, invented the flash boiler back in '88 and that makes it a great deal safer. Instead of heating up all the damn water at one go, just a small quantity is fed into a hot coil at each engine-stroke and—and turned into superheated steam. Yes, much simpler than internal combustion." Rufus Ogilvie, who seemed in fact not to know very much about internal combustion, cleared his throat at this point and somewhat briskly turned the conversation. "I forgot to say, there's breakfast in the back. Cold ham, bread, toast, marmalade, flask of coffee. We're not in a hurry, are we? I thought you'd like to have breakfast down by the loch, James."

Ogilvie nodded and looked pleased. It would be grand, he told his uncle. To the Ogilvies at Corriecraig, 'the loch' meant Loch Rannoch, though in fact there were nearer lochs. But there was something about Loch Rannoch that appealed strongly, especially to James Ogilvie, and this his uncle knew well. In a not untuneful voice the old sailor began singing, as the wild highland miles rolled back beneath their wheels, that old Scots air of 'The Road to the Isles'.

> By Tummel, and Loch Rannoch,
> And Lochaber I will go,
> By heather tracks wi' honey in their wiles...
> If you're thinking, in your inner heart,
> Braggart's in my step,
> You've never smelt the tangle o' the Isles.

They breakfasted by that glorious loch, set in the physical heart of Scotland's history of wars and fierce loyalties; breakfasted beneath a climbing sun and a mist now clearing from the water to leave it with a face that reflected the blue of the sky. The very presence of the Panhard seemed to James Ogilvie an insult, a sacrilege, a spoliation of nature and of God's peace; he could understand the bitter hatred of his uncle and men like him for the clanking monstrous engines that had sullied the grand old sailing navy's spread canvas and roared their rude, uncouth, oily songs at the great winds of the world. Soon perhaps, he thought as he drank strong coffee by that peaceful lochside, there could be another of these mechanically propelled vehicles in the district, and then a third, and a fourth. The roads would become hideous. The appeal of such picnicking lay in the fact that, organised shoots and so forth apart, you were the only ones doing it on any particular day...

"You'll want to be meeting old friends," his uncle said

with sudden abruptness. "You're being asked after, James. The Duncrosses, the Blairs, the Campbells from Glen Lochay—"

James laughed. "Oh, I've no doubt I am! If I have them in the right order—Miss Elspeth, Miss Hester, and Miss Lorna."

Rufus Ogilvie stared at him squarely. "Well? They're nice gels, all of them. Families are old friends of your parents. What's wrong with that, boy?"

James shrugged. "Nothing."

"Then?"

"They're all looking for husbands, Uncle Rufus, as well you know!"

"I call that uncharitable—ungentlemanly. Ungallant."

"The drift from the highlands—"

"And downright rude to your father's friends!"

"In the Navy, don't you call them the Fishing Fleet?"

The old man saw the spark of humour in his eye, and laughed. "Not on their own territory, James. When their mamas drag them down to Southsea, and Plymouth, and Chatham—then, yes! Poor gels, they're flung to the wolves at one ball after another, largely to become wallflowers, with some admiral's or captain's wife working her guts out to fill their programmes tactfully. But up here, James, it's not like that. Never was."

"You didn't choose Aunt Katharine from a local family, Uncle Rufus."

"True. But who's talking about *you* choosing anyone?"

James grinned. "You are, Uncle Rufus."

"Balls and bang me arse, I'm most certainly not, though it's a matter you'll have to give thought to before long. I merely made a suggestion that you do your social duty, that's all. You can't neglect old friends, James."

"I won't, don't worry. I know my manners! Is that all you wanted to say, Uncle Rufus?"

There was a short hesitation, then the old man said gruffly, "Why, yes, James, that's all. That's all!"

Ogilvie knew very well that it was not, but guessed that his uncle shrank from spoiling the morning, the first morning back by the lochside, with argument that could, and would, become bitter. For his part, though he very strongly resented the smallest hint of interference, however well-intentioned, in his personal affairs, and was deeply angry at the very thought of hearing Mary Archdale discussed probably disparagingly, he kept his temper and refrained from precipitating anything that he might later regret. They talked of other things, making plans for his stay at Corriecraig, plans that, magnanimously on his uncle's part, included learning to drive the Panhard. They enjoyed their breakfast, and then a brisk walk by the loch, and then they returned to Corriecraig and the start of the social round that awaited an officer of Her Majesty's Service on leave from active duty. Ogilvie spent the month of September at Corriecraig; and the day before he was due to return to his rooms in Half Moon Street, with another fortnight yet to go before he would embark at Tilbury for Bombay, his uncle retailed, as the two of them breakfasted alone in the great armour-strewn dining-room, some items of news that had reached him in the morning's post. The originator of the news was cousin Hector. It seemed that Hector's long nose, prodding deeply as usual into the web of gossip enmeshed about his room in the India Office, had snuffled up the fact that three newly-commissioned subalterns, green ex-Sandhurst Gentlemen Cadets, had been gazetted, during Ogilvie's absence, to the 114th Highlanders in garrison at Peshawar; and Hector's letter contained a reminder that his father had met one of them—a certain Alan Taggart-Blane.

"By God I have," the admiral said. "He really needn't have reminded me! Taggart-Blane—the elder brother—was one of my lieutenants, or rather one of my Flag Captain's lieutenants, in the 4th Battle Squadron. Eighteen months ago, that was. The brother came aboard in Portsmouth, for a wardroom party. He cheeked me—I happened not to be in uniform. Thought I was the ship's cat or something. Tight as a drum! Disgusting, not that I normally mind drink. No, it was something else, James."

"Yes?"

The admiral pursed his lips. "I shouldn't pass remarks. I should leave you to form your own judgments. But having gone so far, perhaps it's only fair to warn you."

18

"Well, go on, Uncle Rufus, I'm feeling tantalised!"

"So long as that's all you feel," the admiral said grimly. "Once—years ago when I was a lieutenant myself—my ship was guardship in a North African port and I was on duty as Officer of the Guard. A Greek warship entered ... it was our job to board all vessels entering and to wait upon their Captains to pass them all the port regulations and special orders. So it fell to me to go aboard the Greek to represent my own Captain. I've always remembered what my Captain said when he gave me my orders. 'Ogilvie,' he said, 'bear in mind that it's a Greek ship and we all know what these damn dagoes are like. If you'll take my advice, you'll wear tin pants and stand with your backside hard against a bulkhead.' That was what he said. Now, Taggart-Blane's no Greek, but possibly you get the drift?"

James nodded. "I think so, Uncle Rufus. By God, though —I hope you're wrong!"

"So do I. I may be—I may be, no man's infallible. But I'm damn sure I'm *not* wrong, all the same." He perused his son's letter again. "Now, here's the next piece of backstairs information, and it's rather more interesting. There's some sort of trouble with the Ghilzais." He looked up. "Does that mean anything to you, boy?"

"Yes. The Ghilzais are a Pathan tribe, living in Afghanistan ... they more or less control the passes into India."

"The Khyber?"

"Among others, yes. They're a warlike bunch, but so are all the Pathans. They've been friendly enough so far, though."

"It seems that's not going to last, James. Hector says they're likely to lose some subsidy or other and they're reacting badly against the British. Hector thinks it likely your Division will be in action shortly. You're a damn fortunate young man, James. There's nothing like a good war for promotion!"

2

THE INDIA-BOUND P. & O. pulled away, slowly, from Tilbury beneath a mid-October drizzle, taking its leave-expired contingent of officers and civilians back to their far-off places of duty. It was a melancholy scene, as the sailing of a ship to distant seas always was; the poignancy of parting to another long spell in the sub-continent was heightened by the liner's band, playing 'Auld Lang Syne'. James Ogilvie carried with him the image of Mary Archdale, waving a white handkerchief from the quayside, a dwindling figure soon to merge inextricably with the figures of the other God-speeders. Mary was spending a few months longer in England, bowing to a necessary discretion, and had promised to return to India, if not to Peshawar, in due course. She would not be lonely as she had been during Ogilvie's stay at Corriecraig; some old army friends had come back into her life, by a chance meeting in London, and they had invited her to regard their Cambridgeshire house as her home until she went back to India. Ogilvie, however, in spite of the social life of the ship, missed her company more and more as the liner steamed south for the Gibraltar Strait, and on through the Mediterranean for the slow, hot passage of the Suez Canal.

*   *   *

"Captain Ogilvie, sir! Welcome back, sir!" There was

a stamp of boots and a swinging salute from Regimental Sergeant-Major Cunningham, first of the regiment to greet Ogilvie in cantonments. Cunningham was obviously delighted to see him back. "I trust you enjoyed your leave, sir?"

"Very much, thank you, Sar'nt-Major. It's nice to see the old faces again, all the same. Yours especially," he added as he shook Cunningham's hand warmly. "How's your good lady, Sar'nt-Major?"

"Well, thank you, sir."

"And the regiment?"

"In good heart, Captain Ogilvie, in good heart considering." The R.S.M. paused. Despite his words, he had sounded unhappy. Looking away across the parade-ground where the drill-sergeants were shouting at squads of highlanders, away to the distant foothills of Himalaya rearing upward through light cloud, he went on, "Not that the men haven't grown a shade too idle, a shade too much fat on mind and body, sir, from a long spell of quiet along the Frontier."

"No action, Mr. Cunningham?"

"None, sir—none to speak of. Just patrol activity. But that's a situation that's due to change, and I'll not be sorry!"

Ogilvie nodded. "I've read the papers, of course—up to the time I left England. And I gathered from the *Times of India* in Bombay that the Ghilzais are none too happy."

"That's it, sir. They've been upset by Calcutta."

"By the Civilians?"

"Aye, sir, by the Civilians."

"What's it all about?"

"Money's at the bottom of it, sir, though I don't know the ins and outs." Looking over Ogilvie's shoulder, the R.S.M. stiffened. "The Colonel, sir."

Ogilvie turned smartly, standing at attention and lifting his topee as Lord Dornoch came up, swinging his kilt around his knees.

"Well, James. I'm glad to have you back with us, I must say, though I've no doubt you have mixed feelings! How's Scotland?"

"As good as ever, Colonel."

"I'm sure it is. There are times when I can't wait to see

21

it again, but when I do go home, I expect I'll feel the same about India. That's life, is it not, James?"

"Yes, Colonel."

"Did you call on the depot when you were at Corrie-craig?"

"Yes, Colonel. Invermore's not changed."

"So I've gathered. We have three new subalterns from there—you'll meet them shortly, of course." As the R.S.M. saluted and, on the Colonel's nod, about-turned and marched away to his various concerns, Lord Dornoch laid a friendly hand on Ogilvie's shoulder. Together they walked across the dusty parade-ground, in a coldish wind coming down from the Himalayan snow-line: the winter season was now upon the district of Peshawar and the air was fresh. Farther west, in Afghanistan, the passes would soon be heavy with snow and ice. Dornoch said, "James, you've only this minute rejoined ... it's possibly unfair to give you news that may not be entirely welcome, but I feel trouble blowing up and there may, for all I know, be little time."

"Yes, Colonel?"

They walked on, slowly, Ogilvie matching his step to Dornoch's. "The fact is ..."

"The Ghilzais?"

"Why yes, indirectly. But there's something else, James, and it's this: a native infantry regiment, sepoys—the 99th Rawalpindi Light Infantry to be precise—they've been just recently brigaded with us as replacements for the Connaught Rangers, who've gone to South Africa to finish their spell of foreign service. It seems they're a slack lot—indeed I've seen it for myself. Poor quality officers—the usual mixture of British and Indian, of course, but definitely not up to standard. Orders have come through from Division that they're to be brought up to active service standard at once. They're to have a ramrod."

"Yes, Colonel?"

Dornoch gave an involuntary sigh. "The ramrod's you, James. You're to be seconded to the sepoy regiment with effect from tomorrow. You're not going to be happy on parade with the short Light Infantry step—it doesn't suit tall men! I'm sorry—you're not *my* choice. I don't mean

22

I think you can't cope, for I know very well you can—that's not my point. My point is that I don't want to lose you! But the order originated from General Fettleworth himself, so there's no more to be said." The Colonel smiled. "You may take it from me, a lot *has* been said already—but, regrettably, to no effect at all. Well—how d'you feel about it?"

"It's a disappointment, Colonel."

"Only a temporary one. I'll see that you come back to us the moment the sepoys are brought up to scratch—so work on them hard, James, in your own interest. Look upon it as added experience, which of course it is. A native regiment is a very different kettle of fish from one of ours, but I can promise you one thing: win the trust and respect of the sepoys, and you'll get a very steadfast loyalty in return." They had reached the door of the Mess by this time, and the Colonel halted. "There's one thing more: I've also been ordered to send a subaltern with you, name unspecified. Well, I've made my choice, and I've made it because I know you're a good soldier and you can do a lot for the young gentleman who's going with you—and whom I do *not* consider is at this moment quite up to the standard of the Royal Strathspeys. His name is Taggart-Blane."

Ogilvie said, "Oh."

"D'you know him?"

"No, Colonel, but my uncle has met him."

"Your uncle, the admiral?"

"Yes, Colonel."

"And did he venture an opinion?"

Ogilvie said with some hesitation, "He was not entirely in favour, Colonel."

"I see. Well, I'll not enquire what exactly he said—we must not prejudge any man. Nevertheless, I have a shrewd suspicion and frankly I'm somewhat ... but never mind, never mind. Form your own conclusions. It's by far the better way."

"Yes, Colonel."

Lord Dornoch went off to his office and Ogilvie entered the anteroom. Surgeon-Major Corton looked up from behind the *Times of India* and greeted Ogilvie warmly. The

23

atmosphere of the Mess, of a way of life, at once enfolded him; as at Corriecraig, he had the sense of homecoming. It was as though he had never been away from the regiment. He slipped straight back into the past without effort. Going along a little later to his room, he found that his servant had already unpacked his trunks and that everything was in its familiar place. On his chest-of-drawers was the silver-framed photograph of his parents, together with his silver-backed hairbrushes. On the other side of those brushes there now stood another photograph—of Mary Archdale, taken in an exclusive London studio against a fake background of potted palms and marble columns and font-shaped stone receptacles containing a profusion of flowers. She was in a daringly low-cut dress, and the expression of the eyes was provocative and mischievous. She was very, very lovely; Peshawar would not be the same without her. Since the day the regiment had first arrived on Indian service, she had been there: now there was a vacuum, to be filled, no doubt, by intensive work on the slack sepoys and the un-satisfactory Alan Taggart-Blane: poor substitutes both!

Ogilvie stared, devouringly, at the photograph. It was an excellent likeness, but as insubstantial as all photo-graphs: somehow, the more you looked, the more the reality escaped you. But looking, Ogilvie's thoughts went back to Corriecraig, where ultimately his uncle had spoken out, unburdening himself of what he had hesitated to talk about that early morning by Loch Rannochside. The admiral's words had hurt, and the hurt was still there, but so was the resolve that had been strengthened rather than shaken by what the old man had said. Rufus Ogilvie had left the matter until all but a week of his nephew's stay was up; and then, with the two of them alone over brandy and cigars after dinner, he had brought the conversation round to the question of marriage, though he had not at that point spoken the name of Mary Archdale, Scarlet Woman—or so one would have believed her, from the ponderousness of an elderly approach. In the end James had forced the issue. "Uncle Rufus," he had said shortly, "please, for God's sake, say what you want to say. You've heard from father, haven't you?"

24

The admiral had looked disconcerted at that; he had blown out his cheeks and then said mildly, "Well, yes, I have, it's true. I'll not deny it. The fact is, your mother's in a tizzy."

"And she made father write?"

"I dessay she had some influence." Rufus Ogilvie studied his cigar, frowning and ill-at-ease. "As a matter of fact, y'know ... I somehow read into his letter that *he* rather liked the lady. Nevertheless, he's under no illusions as to the effect it could have on your career. No more have I—hence this pi-jaw, James."

"A career isn't everything." James waved a hand around the great dining-room, around the portraits of Ogilvies dead and gone, around the family silver on the table, and, by inference, around the Ogilvie lands beyond the old grey castle walls. "One day—and may it be a long time coming, Uncle Rufus—one day, this part of Scotland is going to have a need of me. The need could be more pressing than that of the regiment."

"Yes, I understand that." Rufus Ogilvie took a mouthful of brandy and swallowed with slow appreciation. "I do understand, James, truly. I loved the Service, you know that. I loved travel, I loved the ships, I grew attached to the men—simple fellows, rough and ready, often enough foul-mouthed, but real men and as honest and straightforward as the day. Like so many of our highland crofters. I loved, I suppose, the sheer *power* I wielded. It was literally life and death! They say, don't they, that all power corrupts, and absolute power corrupts absolutely. True up to a point, but nonsense when applied to gentlemen. Gentlemen—"

"Uncle Rufus, I—"

"Please don't interrupt me, James. Gentlemen are *not* corrupted, because they always put their duty first—their duty to their ship, their regiment, their servants, their tenants, whatever it may be. *That* is the mark of a gentleman, boy—*service*. There's a new breed now, of course, based upon trade. They're not gentlemen yet, they're not accepted by the county families—but they will be, they will be one day! That won't make them true gentlemen, and they'll weaken the breed, James. They'll have no sense of duty, and they'll be corrupted, they'll serve their own ends, but because they will have become accepted as gentlemen, we'll all be tarred with their dirty brush because people will have forgotten what a true gentleman was." He jabbed his cigar towards his nephew. "It's up to people like us to keep the breed pure, don't you see? Do what we damn well can anyway! But where was I?"

"You loved the Service," Ogilvie said grimly.

"Ah, yes. Yes. It doesn't fall to the lot of younger sons to inherit ... otherwise I might well have been drawn back to Corriecraig when my father died. I think I would have sacrificed my Flag to that! And damme, but I'm downright *glad* to know you feel like that about the old place, James." The admiral pulled out a vast coloured handkerchief like a string of bunting, and dabbed at his face with his cigar-free hand. "Nevertheless, certain basic facts remain. You, as the heir, need an heir of your own. I understand the lady—"

"*Is* a lady, Uncle Rufus—"

"Yes, yes, don't misunderstand me, I've never suggested the contrary. I was going to say, I understand the lady is older than you by seven years, no less!"

James gave an irritated laugh. "Don't be absurd. One is not past child-bearing at the age of..."

"Go on."

"Thirty-one."

There was sympathy in the old man's face but he said quietly, "You spoke that age with a certain hesitancy, James. Thirty-one's not old, God knows, but no more is it the first full flush of youth, and you should one day have a bride of nineteen or twenty. Childbirth in the thirties is not easy for the mother. You must bear this in mind, James—for the sake of Corriecraig and the Ogilvie line." He hesitated. "There are other things. The lady has been married before—"

"Yes, and is widowed—not divorced!"

"Quite, quite." The admiral waved his cigar. "But you know Scotland well enough! You know the Presbyterians— oh, and as far as that goes, the Church of England too, to some extent, it's not just us Scots! Remarriage—whilst, of

26

course, obviously *permitted*—is not looked upon well by the strictly religious. The flesh remains as one in their eyes, even after death. The resurrection of the body raises certain practical difficulties in the hereafter ... James, my dear boy, I don't exaggerate in the very slightest when I say that for various reasons many of the older and more God-fearing tenants of Corriecraig would regard Mrs. Archdale as living in sin with you, were you to marry her!"

"Am I answerable for my conscience, and my life, to the tenant farmers of Corriecraig, Uncle Rufus, and to the Bible-thumping hypocrites, the sanctimonious maiden ladies of the manse?"

The old man laughed; but cautioned, "Not so loud, not so vehement—if the servants should overhear, you'd be tarred with the devil's brush, boy! Of course you are not *answerable* to them, but you have a duty to them nevertheless. Remember one thing to your dying day and don't treat it lightly: we Ogilvies are God and the Queen in their eyes, all rolled into one! They set their standards by us, and they use us as an example to their children and their children's children. You cannot ever let them down. The hurt would be so immense, so immense. It's a very great responsibility, James, to be an Ogilvie." He added, "And it's one you can't lay down. You can send in your papers, leave the regiment—but you can never resign from being an Ogilvie!"

"Is there anything else you want to say, Uncle Rufus?"

"Yes, there is one thing," the admiral said. "Now, don't take this the wrong way, for it has to be said. Once said, it'll not be repeated by me, and that's a promise. But you must face it, and face it square. You said, and rightly said, that Mrs. Archdale was not divorced. But there has been talk, James—"

"You mean, this talk says that she might as well have been divorced?"

"Yes. I'm more than sorry, my boy, more than sorry. I'm fond of you—always have been. You're a damn sight more my sort than my own son is. But I'm an Ogilvie too, and Corriecraig means just as much to me as it does to you. Corriecraig *must* have a suitable mistress once your mother's in the Dower House." The admiral was looking thoroughly uncomfortable now but was clearly backing his words with deep and genuine feeling. "I ask you to ponder all this in your own time and in your own way, James."

Coldly James asked, "Was it my father who told you of this—this talk?"

"No, it was not. My brother was never a tittle-tattle. And because of the respect and love I have for both him and your mother, I must for their sakes confess that my inform-ant was your cousin Hector." He reached out a hand, clumsily. "I'm very sorry, James, very sorry. Hector can be such a nasty little bugger at times, and I have frequently to restrain my boot from hard contact with his arse. But he has many links, naturally enough, with Peshawar and the Frontier as well as with the Government in Calcutta. If he keeps his ear closer to the ground than he really needs to, well, I can't prevent it. Neither, in everyone's interest, can we shut our ears entirely to what he—er—reports. You know as well as I do that there is an interchange of military society between Scotland and India—that the world is a small place on occasion, and that gossip has a very long tongue. I repeat—I'm sorry."

Memories! Resentful ones; and regretful ones that, back in London again, he had been short with Mary when she had questioned him about his stay at Corriecraig; for he had preferred to remain silent as to his uncle's remarks. This in turn had led to disharmony. There had been a passionate row, healed only just in time for her to come to Tilbury to see him off.

*   *   *

There was a full muster of the officers of the battalion in the Mess that night; and before dinner, the talk in the anteroom was all of the possible action that now looked like becoming necessary against the Ghilzais. It was Surgeon-Major Corton who, with Rob MacKinlay, back from his staff course to resume command of a company, filled in the detail for Ogilvie. Corton said, "It's all come down to money again."

"So Cunningham suggested. What's the story, Doctor?"

Catching MacKinlay's eye, Corton grinned and said, "It seems it's all due to dear old Fettleworth. Bloody Francis may have rather badly overreached himself this time, don't you think, Rob?"

MacKinlay nodded and said, "I fancy so. His panacea's come unstuck, James."

"What panacea?" Ogilvie was bewildered.

"Well, James, since you went home on leave certain matters of high politics, as high as Fettleworth anyway, have become fairly common knowledge. Someone on the Staff has been guilty of an indiscretion, apparently, and when Bloody Francis nails the culprit, if ever he does, then a head on a charger is going to be demanded!" MacKinlay laughed, and signalled the mess waiter to refill the officers' glasses. "Put very simply, James old boy, it's this: the Ghilzais have never been exactly keen on British influence in Afghanistan, they've been one of the more troublesome tribes in the main—"

"Yes, I know that—"

"Of course. And we've held them in check, haven't we, kept an eye on 'em, maintained our good old British vigilance, our iron hand of Imperialism for the benefit of the Raj—"

"I say, steady on, Rob," Corton murmured. "Aren't you sounding just a little like that fellow Marx?"

"Sorry!" MacKinlay grinned. "It wasn't my intention. It was just that I was about to enlighten James on the point that the iron hand hasn't been quite enough—as, it appears, Bloody Francis knew from the start—"

"This," Corton said to Ogilvie, "is where the money angle comes in, if you haven't guessed already."

MacKinlay said, "Bribery. Fettleworth's been diving his hand into his contingency account or whatever it may be— Government funds, anyway—and doling out the largesse to the Ghilzais. To be more exact, to their leader, Jarar Mahommed. Jarar's become dependent on this subsidy—it's a pretty big one, by the way—"

"Was Fettleworth acting off his own bat, Rob?"

"Not entirely. It was his idea in the first place, but he got Calcutta's backing, via the Commissioner—he hasn't done

29

anything illegal or against orders—but this backing was not supposed to become too overt all the same. Bribery's never been an *official* policy of the Raj—not even when it's called a subsidy—so a decent discretion has always been observed. Now, however, times are changing. I dare say you can guess the rest?"

"Sorry, Rob, I can't."

"Excesses whilst on leave have clearly dulled your brain, old boy. Calcutta's instituted far-reaching economies. The India Office wallahs have been concerning themselves with matters of finance, James. The home Government sees too much money being poured into the Indian Empire, I think. Something like that, anyway. So Fettleworth's access to the cash has been politely cut, and he's been told to withdraw Jarar Mahommed's—er—subsidy. Well, you can imagine how badly Jarar's feelings have been hurt!"

"And more so, his purse?"

"Exactly. Our Divisional Commander's a very worried old gentleman, James! His responsibilities have grown irksome and onerous—I don't suppose you know, he's been acting in the room of the Commissioner for some months—Fordyce is on sick leave and no one's been appointed. Mind you, I give Fettleworth his due—he has a knack of doing the right thing in the end, even if for the wrong reasons very often, and he's never shirked a fight. But, and it's a big but, he likes having the leisure to be the lion of Peshawar society. And this time there's something more pressing agitating his mind, so it's said: he can't risk being walloped by the Ghilzais. For that matter, none of us can."

"Ha! That's scarcely likely—"

"Come now, James, you've had quite enough experiences of the Frontier to know the fighting worth of the dear old Pathan! And when trouble comes," MacKinlay added, "it won't be the Ghilzais alone. Things haven't been entirely happy since those religious devils stirred up the Malakand rising, you know, and our march on Bajaur. The whole concept of the Durand Line could so easily be upset." He paused. "It's not just that either. It's us!"

Ogilvie's eyebrows lifted. "Us, Rob? How's that?"

MacKinlay shook his head and smiled. "You're only just

back from a long home leave. You'll not have seen yet how a lengthy spell of inaction has affected the men. They've grown *slack* in the interval, James—"

"And of course *they've* had no home leave—"

"Exactly. Inaction gives 'em too much time to think about home, however hard the R.S.M. and the N.C.O.s chase 'em on parade and on exercises—not to mention the Colonel at Defaulters! Look, old boy ... it's 1897, they've been out here a long time, they're fed-up, apathetic, and bloody unhappy. In addition to that, the Connaught Rangers have gone, as you know. Instead of them, we have the sepoy outfit—your outfit now—the worst bunch I've ever seen! You make sure you lick 'em well into shape, James, before the fun starts!"

"Ours isn't the only brigade in Northern Command."

"True. But it's a large part of Fettleworth's Division, and the others are in no better heart. We've all been too ruddy long in India, that's the thing, James."

"But if action's coming, won't that buck them up, pull them together?"

"Yes, of course, up to a point. The trouble is, the rot's set in and it's never easy to eradicate. The current state can't be helping poor old Fettleworth's ease of mind. In fact it hasn't. There's been a stream of bumph issuing from Division lately, all designed to pep up the Commanding Officers and get 'em to put the guts back into the men. All it's achieved is to cause immense irritation and ill-feeling. I'm sorry to depress you, James; but I believe you'll see what I mean when you join your natives tomorrow. Their officers are a terribly crummy lot, though for God's sake don't quote me on that." MacKinlay looked across the anteroom, caught someone's eye, and beckoned. "You've not met our fresh-from-Sandhurst contingent yet, have you, James?"

Ogilvie confirmed that he had not. Two young subalterns came up and were introduced to him as Alastair Macfarlane and Roger Renshaw. MacKinlay asked, "Where's young Taggart-Blane got to?"

Macfarlane said, "I'm sorry, Rob, he's not feeling well."

"Before dinner? *Already?*"

The two subalterns looked awkward but didn't answer.

Coldly MacKinlay said, "I suppose you've taken him to his room."

"Er ... yes."

MacKinlay scowled. "Oh, all right. Just see he stays there." He nodded a dismissal, and the two young officers moved away. "A bad start, James. I'm sorry. You're going to have to work very hard on that young man. He's not doing his reputation any good at all, or his health either, what, Doctor?"

"Or his health either," Corton agreed, and added, "The Colonel doesn't know the half of it, James. Soon it's going to be either a Court Martial, or invaliding home at the very least."

"How's it been kept from the Colonel?"

"I didn't say it *all* had," the Surgeon-Major corrected. "A good deal of it, though."

"What about the adj?"

"Black?" MacKinlay laughed without humour. "Black's the reason for the Colonel's innocence! Black still likes his whisky too, just as much as ever, and since both he and Taggart-Blane are in the same unpopularity bracket, they've been known to sozzle in each other's company."

Corton said drily, looking into his glass, "And I hope that's all ... for the sake of the regiment."

"I don't think we should go into that."

"Maybe not, but I think James should be warned."

"Let him see for himself, Doctor!" MacKinlay laughed, but seemed embarrassed. "In any case, whatever one thinks of Andrew Black, he..."

"I've heard things about Taggart-Blane already," Ogilvie said. "I'm not prejudging anyone—but if a certain thing is true, and appears to be so obvious, how the devil did he ever get through Sandhurst?"

Corton said briefly, "He has connections. And, who knows, possibly even someone in the War House..." He shrugged.

MacKinlay said, "God forbid!"

"Aye. But such things happen, Rob. It was not until this Queensberry affair that people—"

32

"Yes, yes, I know. I'm not a babe in arms. But it's still rather horrible, isn't it?"

*　　*　　*

Next morning, B Company of the 114th Highlanders was paraded for a final inspection by James Ogilvie before he left them. He was not, as he said, going far—merely to the adjacent lines—or, he hoped, for long. But he took a personal farewell of each man, and gave them news of home. Talking to the Scots soldiers, his eyes noted the truth of what MacKinlay had said the night before in the Mess: they were largely sullen, with heavy looks. Many appeared unfit, as though the heavy drinking had not been confined to Black and Taggart-Blane—indeed, by the very nature of a soldier's life, it would not have been; but in too many of these faces were the signs of a gross excess. Even Colour-Sergeant MacTrease showed signs of bleariness and an aching head. They were not insubordinate, but they were woodenly polite, almost studiously so, as if they were making a conscious effort to remember their stations. There was no eagerness, no real regimental spirit. Ogilvie was saddened; there seemed to be a crack coming in a fine regiment, the best. Even the fact of a subaltern like Taggart-Blane being gazetted, and accepted ... Ogilvie caught himself up sharply: he had scarcely as yet met Taggart-Blane, just a brief introduction after breakfast in the Mess. Taggart-Blane had only too obviously been suffering from a hangover, which probably accounted for the greenish pallor of the face and the dark shadows beneath the eyes, haunted eyes they had seemed to Ogilvie. The face was puffy and the body slight and thin, with sagging shoulders: not a pleasant specimen physically, but there had been something in the man's face that seemed to indicate bitter self-knowledge and a desire to make something better of himself. Ogilvie could be no more precise than that; but on the whole he was not really so displeased with his new assistant as he had felt he would be. It was very early days and much remained to be discovered. One thing was certain: Alan Taggart-Blane was different from the usual run of infantry

33

officers and possibly had very much more below the surface than most of them. Ogilvie reflected wryly that indeed he must have had *something* in order to make his way through Sandhurst to Her Majesty's Commission, something beyond the lewd and disgusting desires of some fat old major-general in the War Office, as the doctor had seemed to suggest...

*　　*　　*

"Captain Ogilvie, sir, and Mr. Taggart-Blane, from the 114th Highlanders, on secondment."

"Ah yes, yes, thank you, Captain Scrutton. Thank you, that is all." Lieutenant-Colonel Rigby-Smith of the Indian Staff Corps, commanding the Rawalpindi Light Infantry, half lifted his scraggy frame from his chair, then let it drop back again. He looked cagily at the two highland officers as his adjutant left the room. His face was red and beaky, overhung by heavy white eyebrows and bisected horizontally by a drooping walrus moustache, mainly white but yellowed at the trailing ends. He left his new acquisitions standing while he addressed them in a hoarse voice.

"You come from a smart regiment," he said.

"Yes, Colonel."

"Colonel?" The eyebrows rose.

"In the 114th—"

"Yes, yes, I am aware of your regimental customs. In my regiment, I am addressed in the more normal manner, Captain—er."

"Yes, sir. Ogilvie, sir."

"Ah yes, yes, Ogilvie. I trust you will enjoy your time with us, gentlemen. And profit by it—whilst also profiting me. It will, I would venture to say, broaden your experience. A sepoy regiment is very different from a British regiment— *very* different, as you will find! You are now part of the Indian Army, not the British Army in India."

Why rub it in? Ogilvie thought. He said, "Yes, sir."

"You sound disparaging—"

"I'm sorry, sir, that was not my—"

"But it so happens that the boot is on the other foot,

34

gentlemen!" Rigby-Smith's protuberant eyes seemed to rake the Scots with fire. "The Indian Army is by the very nature of its existence better equipped to understand the Indian, and better equipped to fight on Indian territory."

Ogilvie felt Taggart-Blane stirring at his side. The subaltern asked, "And on Afghan territory, sir?"

Colonel Rigby-Smith's mouth dropped open. "What? What d'you mean, sir?"

"I gather most of the fighting, when it takes place, takes place on the *other* side of the Frontier, sir."

"Then you gather wrong, sir, you gather *damn* wrong!" Sweat broke out in beads on the Colonel's forehead. "I, for my part, gather that you are newly arrived from England?"

"Yes, sir, that's—"

"Then shut your mouth, sir, and speak only when addressed."

"Very good, sir."

"I am aware, without your telling me, that my orders are very good. Kindly do not use that expression again, d'you hear me?"

"Yes, sir."

"Thank you!" Rigby-Smith simmered down. "Now, Captain Ogilvie. As I was saying, we of the Indian Army have extremely high standards. I shall expect you to observe them—observe our traditions and customs also." He dabbed at his face with a handkerchief. "You and I both know precisely why you are here and I shall make no bones about that. I *asked* for officers to be appointed from another regiment—*asked*—this was *not* imposed by Division—specifically because I have recently been sent new drafts of untrained sepoys straight from the fields of their fathers—and they must be licked into shape. My own officers, both British and native, have enough to do as it is and my havildars need supervision as in any other regiment or corps. I don't deny that you will have a somewhat difficult task, difficult because it is bound to be, to some extent, invidious. You will have no company of your own, you will act generally, and you will be responsible only to me personally, whilst at the same time, of course, being fully attentive to both my

35

second-in-command, Major Fry, and my adjutant. You understand?"

"Sir!"

"You must be most tactful in your dealings with my native officers—my subedars, of whom there are one to each company, and above all be *scrupulously* correct in regard to my Subedar-Major—Subedar-Major Mulim Singh, who has served in the army for almost fifty years—since the days of the East India Company, before the mutiny. In this connection I must point out that, although I myself have made use of the word, 'native' is an untactful term to use in the presence of sepoys or Indian officers, and has indeed been so since the mutiny." Colonel Rigby-Smith blew out his moustache and glanced at his clock. "I shall expect you to draw up a training programme, Captain—er—Ogilvie, in consultation with Major Fry and my adjutant, and the Subedar-Major. I should like to see this on my desk within forty-eight hours, when we shall talk again. That is all, gentlemen."

Ogilvie and Taggart-Blane saluted and turned about smartly. Outside the door Taggart-Blane let out a long breath. "Phew, I say! This isn't going to be a bed of roses, is it? How the merry hell do we steer a safe and tactful course between all the people he talked about?"

"I don't know yet, but I'm not too worried, Alan."

Taggart-Blane laughed and said, "Hadn't you better use the jolly old surname?"

"What's that?"

"We're not in the 114th Highlanders any more," Taggart-Blane said in a clever take-off of Rigby-Smith's hoarse, bombastic tones. "When in Rome. . . ."

"We'll not take all that too literally! We're still part of the family." Always the 114th had prided themselves on the family feeling, the family tradition. They were as brothers; and as brothers even the raw subalterns used Christian names off parade to all officers in the regiment below Major's rank. It was one of the differences, one of the departures from the norm that marked out the Queen's Own Royal Strathspeys. Ogilvie, as they made their way towards their new Mess, added, "You were a shade tactless, though, to take Rigby-Smith up on what he'd said about Indian fighting."

"Yes ... wasn't I?"

Ogilvie gave him a sideways look and a word of caution. "Take this seriously," he said. "It's a job like any other. You're so new out here you're still wet behind the ears. A lot of your future is going to depend on how you shape in the next few months. Remember that!"

"Oh, I'll try. By the way, I've been meaning to ask you ... a brother of mine who's in the Navy, served under an Ogilvie. Remotely, that is. An admiral. Any relation?"

"My uncle."

"Oh, really? That's interesting." Taggart-Blane lost his interest quickly, however. "Look, I say ... do you believe the Colonel was speaking the truth, when he said he'd *asked* for us?"

"Something else for you to remember," Ogilvie said as they reached the Mess. "One always believes what the Colonel says! Especially so in this sort of situation."

"Which means you *are* rather worried after all."

Ogilvie didn't answer that. They went in. A handful of officers sat around, the majority of them seedy-looking and paunchy. Not one got to his feet in welcome. They all stared insolently at the newcomers; one of them gave a loud, ungainly yawn. Ogilvie felt coldly angry at such incivility. He took in the furnishings of the anteroom: dingy, bare, almost sordid, dusty and untidy. This was not a rich man's regiment. Of itself, such was of no concern to a soldier; what was important was the obvious lack of pride and the equally obvious slackness in the supervision of the Mess servants.

The future seemed far from inviting. With a sinking heart Ogilvie advanced into the general unfriendliness.

3

It was a difficult and unpleasant period for James Ogilvie. He and Taggart-Blane were made to feel, in a very positive sense, that they were interlopers. This hostility came principally from the British officers; the subedars, the Indian officers holding the Viceroy's commission, were more friendly, scrupulously polite, and on the whole anxious enough to please. The old Subedar-Major, Mulim Singh, was a tower of strength and an excellent man to turn to for advice. He had served with better regiments than this one, and though with the loyalty of his kind he never once criticised his present unit, he was as keen as Ogilvie himself to bring about an improvement.

"I'm going to ask you to be frank with me, Subedar-Major Sahib," Ogilvie said after he had been a couple of days with the regiment. "I have formed the opinion that the officers are given little help and encouragement ... that the trouble starts at the top, shall I say?"

The Indian shrugged. "Is this not always the case, Ogilvie Sahib?"

"Why is this, do you think?"

"You ask the question generally, or in particular?"

"In particular, Subedar-Major Sahib."

They were marching up and down the parade-ground, with Ogilvie adjusting his step to that of the elderly Indian. The old soldier pulled at his beard for a few moments and then said, "I believe the Colonel Sahib is a tired man. There is slackness because of this, and also as a result perhaps, there is much drinking in the Mess."

"More than in other regiments?"

"More than I myself have observed in other regiments, Ogilvie Sahib."

"Why is this?"

"How can I say? Perhaps it is a simple case of events following one another in a circle. I believe the British officers have become apathetic, that they see no point in trying to tighten the slackness of the rein ... and that this feeling of hopelessness leads to more drinking, and this in turn leads to more slackness."

"Yes, that's quite likely. But I've seen for myself, you have potentially excellent havildars and naiks."

"They would be excellent if they were given backing— backing by the British officers. I am sorry to say this, Ogilvie Sahib."

"I wanted the truth, Subedar-Major, the facts."

"Yes. Another fact is this: the sepoys and their N.C.O.s see the drinking, and the effects of it. This is bad for discipline. There is no energy, no initiative, left in the officers, you understand? The day plods on easily beneath the sun, and when the sun is down, then the drink flows again, and another day closes. Day after day, it is the same."

"Then it'll have to stop!"

The Subedar-Major turned his head, and smiled at Ogilvie. "You have a saying in your country, it is easier said than done. This you will find. The ingrained habit of drink is discarded only with great difficulty!"

"Yes, but officers can be replaced."

"A word of advice, Ogilvie Sahib: do not run before you can walk. The cure you suggest is too drastic to be even considered yet. In the meantime, you and I, we shall see what can be done to improve matters. I promise you my support, Ogilvie Sahib, in full."

"Thank you, Subedar-Major Sahib, I value that very highly."

"As I value the army and the British Raj, Ogilvie Sahib. In both lies my whole life's work. This will be my last posting, my last regiment. I shall wish to leave it, when the time comes, with pride, as you would wish to leave your own regiment of Highlanders."

"Yes, indeed, Subedar-Major."

They parted company soon after this; Ogilvie spent the morning watching the havildars drilling their squads of sepoys. No other British officer was present on the parade-ground, apart from Taggart-Blane. It was very noticeable that the sepoys smartened up considerably when they saw they were being watched. The moral of that was obvious enough. So was something else: Taggart-Blane wilted more and more as the day wore on, and Ogilvie wondered how he would stand up to the summer's heat next year. In the privacy of his room that night, he talked pointedly to Taggart-Blane about what the Subedar-Major had said in regard to the drinking.

"There's plenty going on at this moment," Taggart-Blane said, with a somewhat injured air at being withdrawn from it himself. "Quiet, but steady."

"That's the insidious kind. No one minds the occasional binge. Don't get pulled into it yourself."

"Why d'you say that?"

"I've got eyes."

Taggart-Blane studied his finger nails and pursed his lips. "Well, I can take it, you know—"

"Can you? Honestly?"

"I never pass right out."

"The night I rejoined from leave, you'd been taken to your room."

"But I hadn't—"

"All right, you don't pass right out—but you can make a damn silly exhibition of yourself all the same, when it begins to approach that stage. I'm no teetotaller, far from it, but you and I have simply got to keep our noses clean and that's all about it."

"A straight gentleman, very straight, but serious and a shade stiff."

Ogilvie stared. "I beg your pardon?"

"Oh, I was just quoting," Taggart-Blane said with a shrug.

"Quoting who?"

"The R.S.M.—our R.S.M., old Bosom Cunningham. The R.S.M., referring to you in conversation with one of the Colour-Sergeants. I just happened to overhear. He was right, wasn't he?" A grin was lurking around the subaltern's mobile mouth.

Ogilvie had flushed. Irritably he said, "I really don't know, and I'm not particularly interested. And don't change the subject, which happened to be your drinking habits. You'll lay off—understand?"

"Is that an order?"

"Yes."

"Oh, all right, then. You won't find it so easy to stop the others, though!"

"No, you're right, but I'm going to have a word with the Colonel all the same."

Taggart-Blane gave a nervous laugh, a high sound. "And put it to him that his British officers are a lot of boozers, and a bad example to the natives?"

"More or less, yes. It's not the sort of thing you can wrap up, is it?"

"I suppose not, but sooner you than me, James. By the way, you seem pretty friendly with old Mulim Singh."

Ogilvie nodded. "He's a good fellow. Sound as a bell, utterly loyal."

"To what?"

"Why, the Raj, of course, what else?"

"What *else*?" Taggart-Blane laughed again, this time with a touch of derision. "I wonder how his own countrymen regard his loyalty?"

*   *   *

"Damned if I don't think I should order a full-scale review," Lieutenant-General Francis Fettleworth, Divisional Commander, said to his Chief of Staff. "Those damn Ghilzais ... why the devil can't *they* economise as well?" Angrily, he blew out the ends of his moustache. "A show of strength ... damme, it works wonders on the Pathan mind!"

"Not invariably, sir."

"H'm? What d'you mean, not invariably?"

41

"Well, sir, not *last* time. It didn't stop that crazy *sadhu* from Waziristan—the 114th Highlanders did that if you remember—"

"Yes, yes." Fettleworth rocked irritably in his chair. He always had his panaceas in order, and a show of strength came first in his priorities. The enemy apart, it did *him* good to see the regiments and the corps paraded before him, to hear the skirl of the pipes, and the thunderous brass of the English regiments, to see the dust rise as his cavalry, the Guides and the Bengal Lancers, rode past in column of squadron beneath their splendid guidons, the riders, with their lances, lifting with the grace of ballerinas from the shabracks. Yes, it was very splendid, very moving, reminded him sentimentally of the good old Queen at Windsor and put the fear of God into the damn natives when the word of it spread through the Khyber. This time, however, something the Chief of Staff had just said sent his mind off at a tangent.

"The 114th," he murmured. "Barbarous lot, but good soldiers. Queer fish—the Scots. Uncouth in many ways—their Colonel's rather a rude man. Lord Dornoch ... he's the feller that's supplied two officers to that bunch of natives, isn't he?"

"On your order, sir, yes."

"Quite."

"Captain Ogilvie being one of them."

"Yes. We seem to hear rather a lot of that young man one way and another, don't we, hey? Too uppish. Comes of being the Army Commander's son, no doubt." Fettleworth sniffed.

"There's absolutely no connection, sir," the Chief of Staff said coldly. "If you remember, Ogilvie was the officer who dealt with the trouble in Waziristan—on his own in the first place. And before that at—"

"Yes, all right, all right! What I was going to ask before you interrupted ... how are those natives getting along? What are the reports?"

"If you refer to the Rawalpindi Light Infantry, sir, the reports from Brigade indicate some improvement. They've been smartened up considerably by Captain Ogilvie, and a strict training programme has been put in hand, including rifle practice, rout marching, co-operation with artillery—"

"Artillery! I don't trust the guns any more than ever I did, frankly. Are they practising forming square, tell me that?"

"I doubt it, sir."

"Find out, Lakenham, find out! I may sound old-fashioned, but the square has proved its worth continually —continually! Who's their Colonel?"

"His name is Rigby-Smith, sir."

"Ah, yes, yes. When was he first commissioned?"

The Chief of Staff crossed the room and brought out an Army List from a bookcase. He flipped the pages and said, "In 1859, sir, to the 14th Foot."

"Then he's bound to be in favour of squares. See that he's informed of my own wishes, please. And tell him something else at the same time: I'm giving him another fourteen days, if the damn Ghilzais allow us that long, then I'm advising Brigade I wish to carry out a full and personal inspection of his regiment, and I'll be dining in his Mess that night. I'll expect to see a fully fit fighting force in first-class trim and spirit or I'll have somebody's guts for garters."

*   *   *

"I agree entirely with the General, Captain Ogilvie," Colonel Rigby-Smith said coolly, moving his heavy white eyebrows like antennae. "Even if I did not, his wish is his order and I must obey. So must you. Squares there will be."

"But—"

"There are no buts, Captain Ogilvie. The British square has stood the test of time, and what better test than that, may I ask? I—"

"Sir, with respect, I consider this a complete waste of time—"

"Hold your tongue, sir—"

"—we may not have long to bring the regiment up to scratch—"

43

"Damn you, sir, are you attempting to suggest that my regiment is *not* up to scratch—"

"It was not I, sir, who first suggested that. It was the General."

Rigby-Smith's face grew mottled. "You insult me, sir! Remember what I said when you first joined us. You accuse me virtually of lying!"

"I—"

"Get out, sir. Get out of my sight!"

"But, sir—"

"*Get out!* Get out or I'll have you in arrest, under the charge of a damn nigger!" Colonel Rigby-Smith, whose passionate anger had caused him to rise to his feet, fell back into his chair as Ogilvie saluted, turned about, and marched out of the room. Colonel Rigby-Smith, whose shout had been loud, realised that he would be considered guilty of a remarkable indiscretion if the word nigger happened to have reached the sepoy lines or the flapping ears of his subedars. And God damn Ogilvie! The man was a cad. With shaking fingers Colonel Rigby-Smith seized paper, pen and ink and scrawled a message to Brigade. He then rang a bell loudly and a sentry came in. The sentry was sent post haste to find a runner. Ten minutes later James Ogilvie was informed by the adjutant that his dismissal back to his own regiment had been requested by the Colonel and would become operative the moment Brigade's confirmation came through. He was advised to tell his servant to pack his belongings, which he did light-heartedly enough; but by the time the Officers Dress for Dinner call was sounded upon the bugle, his servant was once again unpacking. For Colonel Rigby-Smith had received peremptory instructions from Division, via Brigade, that the services of Captain Ogilvie, having been ordered in the first place by the Divisional Commander himself, were, again on the General's own order, to be retained whether the Colonel of Sepoys liked it or liked it not. Indeed, there had been, though naturally Ogilvie didn't know this, more than a touch of the tantrums in the message. That night, Ogilvie went early to bed, leaving behind a good deal of the quiet, steady drinking of which he had not as yet spoken to the Colonel. Now, he feared he had left it too late. After this day's little contretemps, the C.O. would scarcely be in any mood to listen.

Next day Ogilvie and Taggart-Blane diligently set the sepoys to the business of training in square formation. With blood-chilling howls and yells the attacking companies fell upon the compact squares and failed dismally to penetrate. Taggart-Blane was incredulous at the whole spectacle; Ogilvie, whilst still regretting the waste of time, was less so.

"Our Divisional Commander," he said, "is rather set in his ways. What was good enough for Wellington ... no, this doesn't really surprise me, Alan. One must admit, too, that the usefulness of the square did outlast Wellington for a devil of a long time! I dare say its days aren't quite over even now, if used in the proper place and at the proper time."

"The Sudan?" Taggart-Blane suggested, with a smirk.

"Well, not quite! But the Fuzzy-Wuzzies, my dear chap, were the only people that ever *did* break a British square, remember!" He turned as the havildar-major came up, halted and saluted smartly. "Yes, Havildar-Major?"

"Sahib ... the Colonel Sahib, at the edge of the parade-ground."

Ogilvie looked; Colonel Rigby-Smith was impatiently tapping with a riding switch at his brightly-polished boots. "Thank you, Havildar-Major," Ogilvie said. With Taggart-Blane at his side, he marched across the parade and halted in front of the Colonel. "Sir?"

"I merely wished to say, Captain Ogilvie, that I don't care for my officers gossiping on the parade-ground like a couple of old women in the market-place."

Ogilvie flushed. "I'm sorry, sir. I—er—"

"Yes, what is it?"

"I see no other of your officers, sir—with respect, I think they should be present when—"

"Dammit, sir, you're impertinent!"

"I'm sorry, sir."

"My officers are seasoned in Indian fighting. They need no instruction from you, Captain Ogilvie."

"As you say, sir. But if they were to be seen to impart their knowledge to the sepoys, sir, and more importantly their interest, then my presence and Mr. Taggart-Blane's might not be necessary!" Ogilvie had spoken hotly, more so than he had intended. He added, "I say that with great respect, sir. I have noticed that the sepoys—and they're first-class material—have responded well to the presence of officers on parade."

Rigby-Smith's mouth opened and shut again; he looked furious. Without another word he turned on his heel and stamped away. Ogilvie was in a state of suspense all the rest of that day; but nothing further was in fact said, and next morning there was a satisfactory, if angrily reluctant, attendance of the British regimental officers at the training programme. It was a victory for Ogilvie, but he was very well aware of the hostility.

* * *

"Pariahs," Taggart-Blane said, "that's what we are. Well, to hell with them, James. I'm not going to lose any sleep over it!"

"You have to see their point of view, you know." Ogilvie reined in his horse, and leaned forward to pat its flanks. The two of them had left cantonments just before sundown, riding in the keen evening air, trying, at Ogilvie's suggestion, to ride unpleasantness out of their systems. "We're an ever-present reminder of dear old Fettleworth's displeasure, after all!"

"You'd think they'd appreciate that we've a job to do, one we didn't exactly *ask* for."

"I agree. The thing is ... Alan, India tends to warp a man's judgment after a long time stationed here. You know what I mean—little things loom big and one's sense of values goes. They're not bad fellows at heart."

"Their hearts are buried very deep, then!"

Ogilvie looked at Taggart-Blane's face keenly through the gathering dark. "Don't sound so bitter. I thought you said you weren't going to lose any sleep over this."

"Yes, well." The outlines of the subaltern's face looked very young to Ogilvie, young and guileless, but the droop of his shoulders seemed more than ever pronounced; there

46

was some worry deep inside him, one that had not yet emerged and which, Ogilvie was becoming more and more convinced, was not wholly connected with their shabby treatment in the Mess. Watching, he had seen a twitch in the face, a flinching away when in contact with the British officers; Taggart-Blane seemed much more at ease with the subedars, and even with the sepoys when occasion arose. Taggart-Blane was currently learning the dialect and Ogilvie had noticed the different look that came into his face when he tried his prowess, often with funny results, on the sepoys. He didn't in the least mind the amused smiles that spread over those native faces. Rather, he seemed to respond to them. For his own part Ogilvie found the natives easy to get on with too, though there was a difference between his and Taggart-Blane's approach: he was beginning already to find that he was getting from the sepoys that respect of which Lord Dornoch had spoken. In Taggart-Blane's case, he fancied, it was less a case of respect than of a curious kind of sympathy, a mutual recognition of a degree of common under-doggery; this, if carried to any extreme, could result in the very opposite of respect and the consequences of that to Alan Taggart-Blane might well be serious. But of course, the difference in station between a British officer and a mere sepoy was so immense that contact was inevitably on the smallest scale ... Ogilvie gave himself a mental shake: like the long-service officers to whom he had referred earlier, he could be in danger of losing his own sense of balance!

"Come on," he said briskly. "I'll race you to that hill— see where I mean?—then we'd better get back to cantonments. All right?"

Taggart-Blane nodded and Ogilvie touched his spurs to his horse's flanks. He was still not a brilliant horseman, though India had improved his riding a good deal; Taggart-Blane, on the other hand, whatever else he might lack, was a skilful rider. He beat Ogilvie hands down, and was waiting for him as he came up.

"Nicely done!" Ogilvie said with a laugh. "You should apply for a transfer to the Guides, old boy!"

"Oh, I think not. It's pretty beastly, isn't it?"

47

"What is?"

"Why, horses being made to go to war and get mangled. It's not their concern, is it, when men fall out?"

"No, I suppose not. But even in the infantry—"

"Oh, I know we take horses into action too, but not so many as the cavalry. They're not a basic and essential part of our armoury, as it were. No, James, you can keep the Guides!"

They cantered back to cantonments, across the rough terrain with the moon starting to lift above the sky's black rim. They were warm from exercise, but the air was cold now and growing colder. This was a different Peshawar from the oven-hot one that Ogilvie had left a few months before on leave. As, approaching the regimental lines, he heard the harsh notes of the bugles reminding the officers of dinner, he found his thoughts flying back across the wastes of land and sea to London, and that leave with Mary Archdale. They had gone one day to watch the guard being changed in the forecourt of the Palace. Ogilvie had, he recalled, tended to be a shade superior over the elegant Guards officers as they marched in pairs up and down the great forecourt, two with drawn swords, two with the regimental colour. It had been a fine sight, of course, with all the scarlet and blue, and the crimson sashes, but there had been a sense of unreality about it, for these splendid socialite officers fought, in the main, nothing more lethal than the good matrons of Berkeley Square and Belgravia—and that merely for the hands of the debutantes of the London season. There was no glittering jewel of Empire here, at least not in any military sense. Mary, with her memories of the North-West Frontier, had agreed with him, though she had been loyally sentimental about the old Queen— sentiments with which, naturally, James Ogilvie had felt no disagreement—and then, soon after the Old Guard, found that day from the Coldstream Guards, had slow-marched in their stately fashion through the gates, they had walked away in the sunshine, along the Mall, beneath the shade of the trees; and they had been passed by a squadron of the Life Guards in a jingle of harness and a rhythmic rise and fall of red tunics beneath gleaming breastplates,

48

and of plumed helmets. It had been then that Mary had said something similar to what Taggart-Blane had just come out with.

"Aren't we brutes," she'd said, suddenly clutching his arm. "I'm sure those poor horses loathe all that ceremonial. They'd be so much happier in a field!"

"Oh, come, Mary, they love it!"

"Well ... but not war if ever they see it. We *are* brutes, James, really we are. Look at poor Tom and that beastly pig-sticking he was so fond of!"

"Pigs is pigs," he had said with heavy solemnity.

"Oh, don't be silly! Besides, the horses break their legs often enough, don't they? I think ... I think India *makes* men cruel and heartless."

There was some truth in that; in India, the life of men and of animals was held very cheaply. Nevertheless, as they walked their mounts into the lines and handed them over to the grooms, James Ogilvie reflected that it was a woman's sentiment, a woman's way of looking at things; and it was a sentiment that—at any rate in regard to horses—was evidently shared by Second-Lieutenant Taggart-Blane.

"We'll ride again tomorrow evening," Ogilvie said as they went to their quarters. "Same time, Alan?"

"Oh, I ... if you don't mind, old man, I can't ... not tomorrow."

"Something else on?"

"Well, yes, I've an appointment with the *munshi*."

"Studying the lingo?"

"Yes ... yes, that's right."

"Oh, well, some other time then."

"Yes, of course, I'd love to, and thanks."

Ogilvie went into his room and washed and changed into Mess kit. Taggart-Blane had seemed embarrassed and ill-at-ease, and Ogilvie wondered why. Next evening he rode out alone; and, returning to the lines, happened to see Taggart-Blane emerging from a harness room at the side of the square. The subaltern seemed caught off guard for some reason or other. Ogilvie called out, "Hullo there, Alan. Riding after all?"

"No, no. I've just finished with the *munshi*. I ... I just

49

went along to the harness room to check on some of the leather equipment—that's all."

Ogilvie nodded. "All right, all right, I only thought you might have changed your mind."

"Well, I hadn't."

Ogilvie grinned. "Look here, I'll stand you a *chota peg* before dinner if you cut along and get changed quickly."

"Thanks very much."

* * *

Lieutenant-General Fettleworth rode at a solemn walk down the ranks of the Rawalpindi Light Infantry. Behind him, in procession, went the Chief of Staff, the A.D.C., Colonel Rigby-Smith, the adjutant, James Ogilvie, and the appropriate Company Commander, while the subedars in charge of half-companies remained at attention in front of their sepoys, waiting to receive either praise or condemnation from their General—praise or condemnation that would filter down to them from the Colonel by way of the adjutant, of Ogilvie Sahib, and of their own Company Commanders; and, in the military tradition, would be handed still farther down until, by way of the havildars and the naiks, it would descend on the meek shoulders of the sepoys themselves.

In point of fact Bloody Francis kept his own counsel until the very end of the inspection; and then, slowly turning his horse to run an eye up and down Colonel Rigby-Smith, he said loudly, "Well, I'll be damned!"

"I beg your pardon, sir?"

"I think you heard what I said, Colonel, so I'll not waste my breath by repeating it. Now I'll tell you *why* I said it."

"Sir!"

"I said it because your battalion looks damn smart, that's why—"

"Thank you, sir—"

"*Looks* smart, I said! Appearances can be deceptive, can they not, Colonel Rigby-Smith?"

"Indeed, sir, but I—"

"Proof of the pudding's in the eating, what? Let's see

'em in action! Fall out the parade, if you please, Colonel. Dismiss your men and set 'em about a demonstration of what they've been learning—hey? I'm sure you've laid on some sort of show for me, haven't you?"

"Yes, sir, I—"

"Good, good!" Fettleworth chuckled. "I expected no less! What's it to be?"

Colonel Rigby-Smith caught Ogilvie's eye and a small flicker of triumph was apparent as he said, "Forming square, sir, and withstanding an attack."

"Really—really? Well done, Colonel Rigby-Smith, you are most sedulously attentive to my wishes, to be sure! Pray proceed. Captain Ogilvie!"

Ogilvie approached the General and saluted. "Sir?"

"You'll kindly wait upon me closely whilst the training programme is demonstrated." Fettleworth blew through his moustache. "We'll see what you've managed to achieve, Captain Ogilvie."

"Yes, sir."

Squares were formed, and duly attacked. Most of the attacks, fortunately, failed; but one square collapsed as a company of excited sepoys charged through it full belt, and this annoyed Fettleworth considerably. From that moment on, praise turned to bitter sarcasm and complaint. The men moved too slowly, their fighting spirit was not sufficiently apparent especially in defence, their marksmanship was poor; their bayonet drill appalling. Appearances, it seemed, had certainly been deceptive. Ogilvie came in for a good deal of personal criticism, so did Colonel Rigby-Smith and his officers. Fettleworth, however, was not basically an un-just man; and it was noticeable that he let the Indian officers down lightly and also that his attention, when that night he was dined at his own order in the Mess, was much upon the British regimental officers. Ogilvie believed that a long overdue shake-up, and a number of very necessary replacements, would shortly be forthcoming from Division.

The sands, however, were running out; and it was while Fettleworth was in the anteroom after dinner, and doing stout work upon the brandy, that a Staff Officer arrived from his headquarters and asked, as a matter of urgency, to speak alone with the Divisional Commander. After a brief talk in Rigby-Smith's office, during which Rigby-Smith himself was sent for, Fettleworth bustled back into the anteroom and held up a hand for silence. "Gentlemen," he said. "Your full attention, please. Jarar Mahommed's shown his hand. His damn Ghilzais have risen and are moving into the Khyber Pass. All the signs are that the rising will spread unless it's nipped smartly in the bud." He paused, weightily, running an eye over his audience. "Gentlemen, I have instructed your Colonel to prepare the regiment to march as soon as possible and, by Gad, he's got an uphill task in front of him!"

4

NEXT DAY FEVERISH preparations were put in hand, and not
only in the lines of the Rawalpindi Light Infantry; adjac-
ently, the 114th Highlanders were also preparing for action,
as were two other battalions of infantry and a regiment of
cavalry. Ogilvie, busy with his duties in supervising the
overhaul of the sepoys' war equipment, had no time in
which to visit the Royal Strathspeys, but Taggart-Blane
slipped across during the morning and came back to report
to Ogilvie that the prospect of action was having a good
effect on the Scots.

"We're a bloodthirsty lot, aren't we, James ... though
I'm not so sure *I* am," he added.

"You will be, when the fighting starts. Listen, Alan. Just
face the fact that you're going to be scared until it *does*
start. It's no disgrace, you know. We all go through it."

Taggart-Blane stared across the busy parade-ground. "I'm
not scared. At least, I haven't been before."

"You've not seen action yet."

"I had some experience of patrols before you rejoined,
James."

"Yes, true. Well—keep your mind occupied until we meet
the Ghilzais, that's the best thing. There's plenty to do here
so you needn't feel under-employed! I want a painstaking
inspection carried out of all rifles and machine-guns, and—"

"They were all inspected before Fettleworth's parade,
James."

Ogilvie nodded. "I know. But we aren't going to a parade this time, we're going to war, and there's a difference. Generals like rifles to be clean, and come to that, so do I, but a clean rifle isn't *always* synonymous with a rifle in tip-top working order. So, if you value your life, you'll carry out that inspection with the minutest eye for detail that you've used since birth!"

* * *

Later that day fresh intelligence reached Division concerning Jarar Mahommed and the rebelling Ghilzais, intelligence that to some extent negated the earlier report and tended to reduce the immediacy of the general situation: the Ghilzais had indeed risen, but were not as yet in fact marching on the Khyber Pass. So far, they had contented themselves with laying siege to the house of the British Resident in Kunarja, a town some twenty miles south-west of the Afghanistan end of the Khyber. It was through the agency of the Resident, a Major Gilmour, that Jarar Mahommed's bribe, or subsidy, had hitherto been paid.

"This puts a slightly different complexion on the matter," Fettleworth announced, having read the fresh report.

"I don't know that I agree, sir," Brigadier-General Lakenham, the Chief of Staff, said. "In my view, it'll not be long before they *do* move to cut the Khyber. Anyway, in the meantime, what do we do about Gilmour?"

"We send in a force, naturally." Fettleworth got to his feet and went across the room to study a large wall map. "The thing is, Lakenham, it won't be necessary to go in in full strength. In the circumstances, I'd prefer merely to extract Gilmour, or anyway throw a defensive ring around his house, rather than deplete the Peshawar garrison and thus possibly lay us open to probes from elsewhere—you know what the damn tribes are like, after all! Bound to take advantage, blast 'em! Also, I happen to know that's the view Calcutta's likely to take. There's another aspect, too: to enter in strength means we've precious little reserves to throw in if needed—and I do like to have a strong reserve in hand. It always routs the natives, when you suddenly

54

throw in fresh troops. It rattles 'em, you see. You need to *understand* the native mind out here, Lakenham."

"True, sir, true. Yes, I take your point. I dare say one battalion would be enough at this stage."

"That's what I thought." Fettleworth returned to his desk, and sat in the swivel chair behind it.

"Who's it to be, then?"

The General drummed his fingers on the desk-top. "I'll send Rigby-Smith's battalion of sepoys. It'll do 'em a power of good. I've never seen such a bunch of officers, Lakenham, quite appalling, not a gentleman among 'em! Merchants' sons the lot of 'em. Not that I was so poorly impressed by Rigby-Smith himself—he has quite sound ideas, especially on tactics, but the rest of 'em, poof!"

"Then d'you really think it's wise, sir?"

Fettleworth looked irritated. "Yes, of course I do, otherwise I wouldn't have decided upon it, would I? Do try to remember, my dear fellow, that my responsibilities are not only to poor Gilmour in Kunarja, but also to my command as a whole. One of my duties is to see to it that the men get appropriate action experience—and also to pull a degenerate battalion up by its boot-strings!"

*   *   *

"We have been accorded the honour, gentlemen— accorded the *honour*, I say, by the General himself personally—of proceeding through the Khyber to the relief of the British Resident in Kunarja. We alone shall carry out this task, and we shall carry it out successfully!" Colonel Rigby-Smith spoke with hoarse pomposity: he was really preening himself, Ogilvie thought. Even the crowns and stars on his shoulders seemed to have gained a new shine, a new and vigorous sparkle. He seemed to be spoiling for the fight; whatever else he was, he was no coward. Ogilvie, as the Colonel continued, looked around at the faces of the assembled officers, British and Indian. The Indians seemed mostly grave and non-committal, and the British officers gave little hint of eagerness: a long, hard march through wintry conditions faced them now and, coming as it did

55

within sight of Christmas, the prospect was not a happy one. The Mess, the life in cantonments in Peshawar, with all its peaceful diversions, appealed far more than a tussle with, as it were, General February, to say nothing of the affronted and impoverished Ghilzais embattled in Kunarja. Irreverently, Taggart-Blane caught Ogilvie's eye, gave him a nudge and whispered, "If only Queen Victoria could see them now, what?"

Rigby-Smith stopped in mid-sentence. "Who was that who spoke?"

"It was I, sir. I'm sorry, sir."

"Do you normally, in the 114th, interrupt your Colonel when he is speaking, Mr. Taggart-Blane?"

"No, sir."

"Then kindly accord me the same courtesy." Rigby-Smith, standing with his behind to the fire, nicely warm, rose and fell upon the balls of his feet. Ever since the General's visit, Rigby-Smith had tended to become an echo of Fettleworth, upon whose lengthy monologues he had on that inspection day most diligently attended. "Now, then! As I was saying, gentlemen ... I am ordered to be in every respect ready to march at first light the day after tomorrow—Thursday. To this end, you will all make yourselves fully acquainted with your various duties, under the overall orders of Major Fry and Captain Scrutton, and ensure that your companies and sections are brought to a first-rate standard of efficiency and readiness by four o'clock tomorrow afternoon, at which time I shall carry out a thorough inspection of the battalion. If there should be any deficiencies, the officer responsible will incur my very severe displeasure. I think I need go into no greater detail. You all know your duties. Captain Ogilvie?"

"Sir?"

"You and Mr. Taggart-Blane are from henceforward relieved of *your* particular duties, which will be no longer relevant to a fighting force upon the march."

"Yes, sir. May we take it that we shall rejoin our regiment?"

"You will do no such thing, sir! Why, sir, does the thought of action frighten you?"

There was a sycophantic laugh from the assembled officers; Ogilvie felt the blood rush to his face. "By no means, sir. I've seen plenty of action the last few years, and in any case I have no doubt that the 114th will soon be coming through the Khyber behind us."

"Why so, Captain Ogilvie?" Rigby-Smith's voice was sharp and hostile.

Ogilvie shrugged. "It's possible reinforcements will be needed, and it would be logical for the General to despatch the rest of the brigade, sir."

"H'mph." There was suspicion in Rigby-Smith's face, suspicion that a veiled suggestion had been made that his regiment would not be able to cope on its own; but evidently he decided to let it pass. "Well, Captain Ogilvie and Mr. Taggart-Blane, I have other work for you to do. As no doubt you are aware, I have some of my British officers absent on leave and on Staff duties. You, Captain Ogilvie, will therefore take charge of E Company as acting Company Commander, with Mr. Taggart-Blane to assist you. You will quickly acquaint yourselves with these duties, and see to it that E Company does not lag behind the others in their readiness tomorrow afternoon." He blew out his cheeks in a Fettleworth gesture. "That is all, gentlemen. You may disperse about your concerns."

Rigby-Smith, relinquishing the fire to a wider distribution of its heat, strode from the anteroom. There was a buzz of conversation after he had gone, and the second-in-command, Major Fry, came across to Ogilvie. "A word in your ear," he said, taking his arm. He led Ogilvie to a corner of the room, and they sat, in sagging leather armchairs, by a window overlooking the square. Fry, a squat and gloomy-looking man, bald, with bad teeth and a poor colour, bent his head towards Ogilvie and spoke in confidential tones. "I've a feeling you've never been made very welcome in the Mess," he said.

"I've noticed an air of reserve myself, Major," Ogilvie said with a grin.

"I'm sorry, Ogilvie. Very sorry."

"Oh, it's understandable—"

"Decent of you to take it like that. Thing is—what I wanted to say, you know—that's in the past now. We're glad to have you with us, Ogilvie, very glad."

"Thank you, Major."

"It's not good to be short of us British officers in action. Of course, I'm saying nothing against the natives, the subedars, you know. Nothing."

"No."

"They're first-rate chaps. But we *British* ... well, you know what I'm getting at, I don't need to put it all into words, do I? Yours is a fine regiment—you Scots are fine soldiers, Ogilvie, we all of us know that." Major Fry pulled at his moustache and looked worried. "Thing is ... well, it's awfully difficult to say this, but I'd better come straight out with it. I gather young Taggart-Blane's not been long with your lot, has he?"

"No, he hasn't, Major. Why d'you ask?"

Fry, stroking his bald head, gave a slightly embarrassed cough. "How's he going to shape up in action, Ogilvie?"

"I've never seen him in action. But I've absolutely no reason to doubt that he'll shape just as well as anyone else. After all," Ogilvie added drily, "he's *British*—isn't he?"

"Yes, of course. Yes, indeed. It's merely that he's totally inexperienced, not only in fighting as such, but more importantly in the ways of the Frontier." Major Fry hesitated, coughed again, and looked up at the ceiling. "There's—ah, um—something else, too. It's hateful even to mention, but—" He broke off, pursing his thick lips and frowning.

"What is it, Major?" Ogilvie, knowing what was coming, determined to knock it smartly on the head.

The second-in-command, bringing his gaze down from the ceiling of the anteroom and his face even closer to Ogilvie's, murmured, "Perhaps—yes, perhaps we may put it this way. He—ah—has a nickname among certain of us. . . ."

"What nickname?"

Again Fry's eyes moved to gaze upon the ceiling, and he moistened his lips with the tip of his tongue before saying, "Yes, the nickname—it's—ah—Oscar Wilde."

58

"Oscar Wilde?"

"Indeed. The Marquess of Queensberry—"

"Yes, thank you, Major Fry, I'm well enough aware of that story, and I fully understand the implications of the name, Oscar Wilde, Major." Ogilvie's tone was crisp, coldly angry. "Am I to understand that you have actual grounds for pinning this nickname, this label, upon Taggart-Blane?"

"Oh no, no, no, no! Indeed not!"

"Then why pin it?"

"Ah."

"Dangerous—I would have thought."

Fry's tune had changed considerably. "It's just an impression we've got. Nothing more."

"I see. Then in that case I suggest, with all respect, Major Fry, that you keep your opinions and your nicknames to yourself entirely—and see to it that your friends do the same!"

"Really! I consider that impertinent in an officer of Captain's rank when speaking to a Major, Ogilvie—"

"I'm sorry, but there is a point of principle here. I'm still an officer of the 114th Highlanders whether or not I'm temporarily attached to this regiment, and so's Taggart-Blane. To that extent at least, while we're with you, he's my responsibility. There are such things as the laws of slander, Major, and if you or anyone else makes it necessary, I'll not hesitate to make a report to my Colonel the moment we come back through the Khyber. And as I think you must be aware, Lord Dornoch is an officer of immense influence— and one who is immensely proud of the good name of his regiment! I don't believe I need say any more?"

"No, you need not. I understand—*perfectly!*" Major Fry bounced to his feet and hurried away, fat and furious; but not before Ogilvie had seen the scowl and the suddenly renewed hostility—or before Ogilvie had read into his final remark all that he had been intended to read. Furious himself at the implication, Ogilvie left the anteroom. The second-in-command had been correct enough in calling his words impertinent; but Ogilvie had felt, and felt still, that he owed that much to a young subaltern who, in terms of Indian life and Indian station intrigue, was no more than

59

a babe in arms. Loyalty still ranked high in the Ogilvie order of priorities.

* * *

The bugles, rousing the men from sleep, sounded out clear into a chill morning. Within minutes the regimental lines came alive, alive with hurrying, still half-asleep men, with the shouts of the havildars and the naiks, the neighing of horses from the horse lines, the stamp of hooves, of human feet, the hither-and-thither scurryings of the camp followers, that oddly assorted collection of depressed humanity, scourge of all the native units, that would accompany the regiment through the Khyber into Afghanistan, and if necessary into action, the camp followers that would be concerned with the sepoys' commissariat on the march, and whose backs would supplement those of the mules and the carrying capacity of the wagons.

Dressed and ready, Ogilvie watched for a while from the windows of the Mess as the servants prepared an early breakfast for the officers. The wind was going to whistle round men's bodies once they entered the Khyber Pass, Ogilvie thought with a premonitory shiver—would tear right through the heavy greatcoats of the officers, the scantier wrappings of the sepoys. But this was what he had come to India to do—and they would not have to face conditions as bad as, for instance, those in the Koord-Kabul Pass farther north; in all conscience it would be little colder than Corriecraig in winter! Ogilvie wondered how his uncle's smelly mechanical contrivance, the Panhard-Levassor, would behave under winter conditions of snow and ice and high, bitter winds. He smiled to himself; one day, perhaps—though such a thought would bring horror to the hearts of Colonels—an army might move to war in motors! Ogilvie would have welcomed such a foot-saving means of transport through the Khyber Pass, at all events, had it been even a remote possibility; but men's feet and the commissariat mules' hooves and the simply-constructed wagons were surely the only things that would ever move through that terrible cleft in the border mountains, where every high crag held likely death from the sniper's bullet, where every blind turn in the track, or what passed for a track, held the possibility of an ambush....

He turned from the window as he smelt hot coffee, a smell that sharpened his hunger though he had woken to a headache and a furred mouth after some celebratory drinks the night before—celebratory of forthcoming action, for an unwelcome inebriation among the officers had temporarily dulled their dislike of leaving cantonments for the snows and the bullets. Some of them, he thought grimly, would be feeling pretty bloody this morning! For his part he had had a sleepless night, worrying about Taggart-Blane and the insinuations of Major Fry. It was a thoroughly unpleasant business, and Taggart-Blane would have to watch his step and give no possible ammunition to anyone—but it was scarcely a matter on which he could be explicitly warned. There was, really, nothing to be done....

"Morning, Ogilvie."

Ogilvie looked round; the adjutant, Captain Scrutton, had come into the Mess, looking preoccupied rather than eager to march. "Good morning, Scrutton," Ogilvie said. "How's your company?"

"Oh, in good form, I'd say."

"You've been along to them this morning, have you?"

"Yes."

"Keenness, that's what I like to see!" Captain Scrutton smiled thinly, managing to look not in the least keen. Ogilvie was beginning to see what the old hands meant by saying, as they had said—R.S.M. Cunningham had virtually said it about the 114th—that a few actionless months played havoc with morale. Without further speech, the adjutant sat down at the table and called for strong coffee and no food.

* * *

They moved out in column of route to the accompaniment of the drums and fifes of the battalion and a few cheers from the neighbouring lines. As he led his company past the quarters of the 114th Highlanders Ogilvie saw the Regimental Sergeant-Major standing at the salute with his pace-stick held rigid beneath his left arm. Beside him a solitary piper played 'Cock o' the North', the tune that always played the Royal Strathspeys into action. It was a nice gesture and one which Ogilvie much appreciated. He returned Cunningham's salute and as he did so he felt a lump come into his throat; it was strange to be marching towards action and leaving the regiment behind—strange and unwelcome, a feeling of alienation. For one thing, quite apart from the comradeship of his own kind, he would miss the robust singing of the British Army songs along the route to Kunarja.

*   *   *

Colonel Rigby-Smith rested the battalion by the old Sikh fort of Jamrud, eight miles to the west of Peshawar, with four more miles to go for the eastern entry to the terrible Khyber Pass. As they fell out, Taggart-Blane said this was the nearest he had yet come to the Khyber; as he said this, he gazed westwards, shivering, his face looking drawn and anxious.

"Well, don't worry too much," Ogilvie told him, noting his expression. "Plenty of people have been through before, and come back again. Me, for one!"

"Yes, I know." Taggart-Blane's inward eye was seeing, more sharply now that they were so close to the pass, the numberless British dead, the officers and men who had made the entry and had not come back again to Jamrud. So many had died through the bitter years of Frontier fighting, died that the British Raj might live. This was a very different form of soldiering from the routine occupations of gentlemen in garrison at Portsmouth and Colchester, Edinburgh and Chatham and the Curragh. With sympathetic insight, Ogilvie knew that all this was passing through Taggart-Blane's mind.

"Don't worry too much," he said again. "I'll be surprised if Jarar Mahommed mounts any attack in the Khyber, Alan—"

"Why?"

"I think he'll wait and see what the Colonel brings with him—apart from the battalion, I mean! After all, he could be bringing terms of some sort, couldn't he, some kind of offer from Fettleworth? Jarar's bound to have the possibility in mind, anyhow."

Taggart-Blane stared up at him dolefully. "D'you really think so?"

"Yes, certainly I do. And you don't kill the goose, do you —not till you're quite certain it's not going to lay any more golden eggs!"

Taggart-Blane nodded but seemed no happier. "Well, yes, I suppose that's true, but all it means is, if we don't get attacked going in, we'll surely be attacked coming out, that is if they ever let us get away from Kunarja, after we've failed to produce any of those eggs of yours!"

Ogilvie laughed, but there was a touch of irritation in his laughter. "Oh, damn it all, we're a regiment of the Indian Army, going in to cut out the British Resident from under the noses of a bunch of rebels. There's bound to be *some* element of risk, isn't there? You don't succeed in *any* mission if you insist on counting the cost all the way through—"

"You don't seem to take any account of the possibility we mightn't succeed at all, do you?"

Ogilvie said with vigour, "No, I damn well don't! Of course we're going to succeed. And don't you think any different—the Raj wasn't built up on thoughts of failure and the sooner you realise that, the better!"

"You're a bit of a jingoist, aren't you, James?"

"What if I am?"

Taggart-Blane grinned. "Oh, nothing, I suppose. But what's it all going to matter in the end ... when you're sitting in some ghastly hotel lounge in Cheltenham?"

"No Cheltenham for me, thank God." Ogilvie was thinking again of Corriecraig. "But for those of us who do one day foregather there, it's going to be mighty important that they've done their duty!"

Soon after this, word came down the line from Colonel Rigby-Smith to resume the march. Men, as yet untired, got once again to their feet and, with the camp followers, some two hundred of them straggling along with their bundles and the commissariat carts and mule-trains in rear, covered the remaining four miles to the Khyber in good time. The distance from Jamrud to Torkham at the Khyber's Afghanistan end was no less than fifty miles: from now on there would be much forced marching, and an increasing weariness, and, despite James Ogilvie's encouragements to Taggart-Blane, and despite the irregulars of the Khyber Rifles garrisoning Landi Khotal, there would be a continual apprehension of sniping from the crags and of sudden ambush along the steep sheer drops where the track, beneath its snow and its slippery ice-covering, ran above the deep, rock-strewn valleys of a basically very hostile terrain.

5

THERE WAS A general mêlée outside the Residency in
Kunarja, with the crowd shouting insults and imprecations
and waving fists and knives as they were held back by Jarar
Mahommed's ragged, wild-looking soldiery. A heavy chunk
of hard-packed earth broke against a shuttered window.
Major Gilmour put an arm about his wife's shoulder, holding her close.

"It can't go on, my dear. It can't last."

Shaking violently she said, "It's only a matter of time, that
I know! What will happen to us?"

"I didn't mean that. I meant only that the troops will
come in soon now," he told her gently. "Fettleworth'll not
leave us to face this, you may be sure!" Releasing her, he
went across to the window, listening through the slats of the
shutter, his hand on the revolver-butt in its holster. The
sounds were menacing enough—were, frankly, terrifying
when one had women to consider. If Fettleworth didn't
come, if, perhaps, the message had never reached Peshawar
at all, their future was indeed a mere matter of time and its
content didn't need to be spelled out to anyone familiar
with Afghanistan. The usual routine would be followed:
the break-in by the mob, the overwhelming of his personal
guard, now for some while withdrawn inside the Residency
itself; the pillage and the plunder, the rape of his wife and
daughter, and then a terrible death in view of the ravening
tribesmen. So far, Jarar Mahommed's soldiers, though as

wild as the tribesmen, the Pathans and Afridis from whom they came, had kept the mob strictly outside the Residency garden; but of course the moment Jarar gave the word this situation would change dramatically and the building would be stormed. A matter of time? And when, and if, that time should come ... Gilmour's hand felt the hardness of the revolver-butt once again. Death, for all of them, would come more quickly and more easily at his own hand. *If it should come to that*...

In point of fact, the outcome was now entirely in Fettleworth's not-very-capable hands.

The reason for Jarar Mahommed's holding off the killing mob was, of course, perfectly clear and none of the Gilmours had any doubts at all that they were being used as hostages, pawns to be used in the forcing of Jarar's financial demands on Lieutenant-General Fettleworth. Naturally, Jarar must know he faced the danger of an expeditionary force being sent in to rescue the Britons; but he would know equally well that a dead Resident and family would of a certainty bring a punitive expedition, while the dead could scarcely have any hostage-value. The current real danger to the Gilmours, which they also recognised quite clearly, was that very soon Jarar might lose control of his hysterical, death-demanding mob. Judging from the sounds outside, this might well happen before a relieving force could arrive.

Gilmour, a small and perky man with bird-bright eyes, turned away from the shuttered window, his face grim but at the same time desperately sad. Here in Kunarja lay much of his life's work; his ambitions—ambitions for harmony between the tribes and the British Raj, ambitions to improve the lot of the natives—had been large ones, possibly too large for fulfilment in any man's lifetime. But progress had been made, and now the clock was moving backwards into pillage and death and all he had striven for was about to be destroyed. As he strode across the darkened room in a bitter frame of mind, a new sound came: a trumpet call, a tinny sound from the distance that was accompanied by a sudden diminution of the shouts and insults of the mob. Then there came the sound of drums—not British, but native.

"It's Jarar himself," Gilmour said wonderingly. "Now, what the devil does he want?"

"Do you think he's coming here?" his wife asked.

He gave a short, humourless laugh, his nerves on edge. "Where else?" His hand closed over hers, gripping it tight. He looked at her face, worn and yellowed and lined far beyond her age by Indian service—service, as his had been, for the Raj. With his other hand he reached out to his daughter, Katharine. Together they waited. The drums and the trumpets drew closer, and they heard the beat of horses' hooves on the hard ground beyond the Residency garden. There was a lump in Gilmour's throat as he looked again at the two women. Life had been hard for them. In this wild outpost, surrounded by mostly hostile, or at least semi-hostile, faces life had not been the customary round of pleasure that was the memsahibs' lot in British India, in the garrisons of Nowshera and Peshawar and Rawalpindi, of Murree and Ootacamund, or in the Simla hills. If this was to be the end, they could scarcely be blamed if they were to hold him responsible for bringing them to a life of hardship and one without apparent point, and then to a lonely and violent death. A moment later they heard horsemen moving up the short drive, and soon after this, there came a heavy and peremptory banging at the locked and bolted main door of the Residency.

*   *   *

"Damme," Colonel Rigby-Smith said disconsolately. "I don't understand it. Don't understand it at all! There's been neither sight nor sound of anyone. I don't like it. What d'you think, Fry, what d'you make of it?"

"Well, sir, it's disquieting, I'll not deny. Most disquieting." Major Fry put up his field-glasses once again, and stared around the high peaks rearing above the track. A few vultures wheeled and cried, and that was all. The pass appeared totally uninhabited except for the regiment itself and its camp followers. All along it had been the same; even as they had come below the fort at Ali Masjid, and again at Landi Khotal—even as they had straggled, chilled

67

and weary now, beneath the fortress guns—they had seen no humankind at all. It was eerie, and it was menacing, for it was utterly unlike the Khyber not to be under the obvious surveillance of native scouts, unlike the Khyber for not even a solitary sniper to send a bullet hurrying down on passing British troops.

"Where's the Subedar-Major?" Rigby-Smith demanded for the hundredth time since entering the Khyber. "Have him sent for, Major Fry, and quickly."

Turning in his saddle, the second-in-command gestured for a runner. When the elderly Indian officer came up, Rigby-Smith catechised him as to his thoughts, but he could offer no help other than to suggest, as he had suggested so often already, some deeper purpose behind the apparent peace and quiet.

"Yes, but *what* purpose, Subedar-Major?"

"Colonel Sahib, I cannot say. I cannot read the mind of Jarar Mahommed."

"Ambush—some trap in Kunarja—or a desire to placate the Raj? No, you cannot say, Subedar-Major, and no more can I. We must hope for the best, and at the same time prepare for the worst." Colonel Rigby-Smith gnawed worriedly at the ends of his moustache. "You cannot, perhaps, see just a little way into the mind of the Ghilzai, Subedar-Major? Think you it could be a trap in Kunarja? If you were in Jarar Mahommed's place, would not such a trap appeal to you?"

The Indian inclined his head. "Yes, Colonel Sahib, I think it would."

"The General must surely have had such a possibility in mind, don't you suppose, Major Fry?"

"Most probably, sir, most probably."

"I trust he will be ready with a reinforcing column if necessary." The regiment, halted for a brief rest, was moved on again, to stumble wearily past the jags of rock, along the bitterly cold track over which a keen wind funnelled, sighing like all the devils of hell released in fury on the British interlopers, though no fresh snow had fallen. They were allowed all the rest of the way through the Khyber without incident; when they emerged at last into a prospect of the

plains of Ningrahar their only casualties had been four
native soldiers, some mules and stores and camp followers,
lost in death falls into the deep, rock-strewn valleys that had
lain below the slippery ledges. Much more seriously, the
tents brought for the officers had all been lost in one of the
drops into a gorge.

After leaving the Khyber itself the going was a little easier
and there was still no snow. Two days after entering Afghanistan the Rawalpindi Light Infantry approached the gates
of Kunarja, marching without hindrance towards the town
behind their drums and fifes, an earnest of the intention of
the Raj to maintain under all circumstances the safety and
wellbeing of its emissaries. Once again the officers were
puzzled; they marched, so bravely and so ostentatiously, into
a total lack of opposition. Mobs there were—hostile, im-
precatory ones, with the natives leaning forward to shake
fists and wave long knives and jezails; yet even so it was
anticlimax. This could, of course, be the trap, but if so, it
was not to be sprung yet. Passing through the gateway into
the old walled town, Colonel Rigby-Smith was met by Jarar
Mahommed in person—an imposing figure, tall and well-
built, with a hooked beak of a nose, and black eyes glittering
with sardonic humour beneath a turban of peacock-blue.
He was mounted and surrounded by his fighting men—but
with an apparently peaceful intent. The jezails—the old-
fashioned long-barrelled muskets—were not carried in war,
were not pointed at the Feringhees. Jarar Mahommed's
right hand was lifted in salute, and he was smiling.

He called out, "Welcome, Colonel. Welcome to Kunarja,
if you come in peace."

"You are Jarar Mahommed, leader of the Ghilzais?"

"That is so, Colonel Sahib."

"Very well." Colonel Rigby-Smith's fingers tightened on
his horse's rein; he cleared his throat noisily as he looked
around him, at the silent but threatening mob, at the
motionless figures of Jarar Mahommed and his personal
mounted guard. "I am Colonel Rigby-Smith, commanding
the 99th Rawalpindi Native Light Infantry, in the name of
the Queen-Empress, Her Majesty Queen Victoria."

"And you come in peace, Colonel Sahib?"

"I come in peace," Rigby-Smith said in a faintly hector-ing tone, "so long as I am met in peace, and so long as the accredited representative of the Empress of India has not been harmed. I refer, of course, to Major Gilmour Sahib, the British Resident. And to his wife and daughter."

"Who are all well, and unharmed."

"I may see them, Jarar Mahommed?"

"But of course, most certainly." The Ghilzai spread his hands wide.

"Then if I may be allowed to pass with my regiment, to the Residency—"

"Gilmour Sahib is at the Residency no longer. He is my guest, in my palace. I have offered, and he has been pleased to accept, my protection."

"Protection against whom, Jarar Mahommed?"

"Against my people, justly angry with the British Raj, Colonel Sahib, because of the poverty which they now endure. I, of course," Jarar Mahommed went on blandly, "know in my heart that the British Raj is generosity itself, that its wishes have been misunderstood, and that you, Colonel Sahib, have come to Kunarja to talk, to make an offer, to relieve our terrible distress! Is this not so?"

Rigby-Smith's mouth opened and shut again, closing hastily on a flat denial, a simple statement of the truth: no offer had ever once been discussed and he had come in war to extract Major Gilmour and his family. But now he had a feeling that the time for the truth had not yet come; the mob was close on all sides, and its members looked pretty ugly, and very greatly outnumbered the sepoys of the Rawal-pindi Native Light Infantry. Instead of committing himself to speech, therefore, he made a vague gesture with his hand.

Jarar Mahommed, who was still smiling, said, "It is not always possible to make one's more fanatical elements understand the facts, Colonel Sahib, as you will naturally appreciate, and I regret that because of this the British Residency has been attacked—"

"*Attacked,* Jarar Mahommed? Attacked? To what extent, may I ask?" Rigby-Smith was safe, at this point, in putting on a show of anger and dismay.

"It has been razed to the ground, Colonel Sahib—"

70

"Good gracious—"

"A pity, for it was a magnificent building and the cost of replacement will be immense. My personal intervention saved Gilmour Sahib and his wife and daughter, who have not been harmed. Have not *as yet* been harmed, Colonel Sahib."

There was a heavy silence; Rigby-Smith broke it by asking, "Pray what do you mean by that, Jarar Mahommed?"

"I mean that it will be in the interests of everyone, Colonel Sahib, if terms are quickly discussed—and then quickly agreed. Do you understand?"

Rigby-Smith looked around once again; the mob was watchful, intent, still silent. It would need no more than a gesture from Jarar Mahommed to send them and their razor-like knives at the throats of Rigby-Smith's sepoys; there would be great slaughter on both sides; with the regiment hemmed in as it was currently, the sepoys would not have a proper chance. A better time would come. Rigby-Smith, drawing himself to his full height as he sat his horse, said stiffly, "I make no promises, Jarar Mahommed. Lead me to Gilmour Sahib, at once."

The Ghilzai inclined his head fractionally, then turned his horse. "Follow," he said looking back over his shoulder. "You and all your men." He moved slowly along the narrow way, between market stalls, past the hovels of his people, deeper into the varied smells of the town, with the mob crowding along beside the sepoys, watching their every move, hostile and suspicious. Ahead of E Company, James Ogilvie could almost feel the fear eating into the minds of his sepoys. This kind of situation was very different from open fighting on the plains of India or even in the Afghan passes; there was no elbow-room at all, here in Kunarja. It was a feeling of claustrophobia, and there was the stench of death and failure already.

6

DEEPER NOW INTO Kunarja, they came under another gate-way, this time into a stronghold, Jarar's palace, a high build-ing of white stone, with towers and minarets, that rose commandingly above the mean, clustered dwellings of the poor. With Colonel Rigby-Smith at their head, they marched into a wide courtyard around which the palace lay, curled and watchful with many windows looking down.

Ogilvie shook his head. "If we weren't in a trap before, we certainly are now, Alan."

"What's the Colonel up to?"

"I don't suppose he had much option—not once he'd entered the town. Better, really, to have stayed outside and waited for Jarar to come to him."

"But all that time, Jarar could have been attacking the Residency, and the orders—"

"Yes, I know." Ogilvie glanced over his shoulder; behind him, the companies were bunching. Ahead, the subedars were marking time and looking worried, as well they might. In Ogilvie's opinion, Colonel Rigby-Smith had acted with crass stupidity in marching his regiment into such confine-ment. As he looked back, he saw a movement behind, over the entrance through which they had just marched: the slow descent of a vast metal grille like a portcullis.

He yelled a warning to Colonel Rigby-Smith, and himself ran towards the gate, pushing through the milling sepoys. He had almost got there when a native, one of the denizens of the palace, dropped like a snake from a window, landing on his shoulders and bringing him to the ground in a winded heap, and remaining astride him. Looking towards the gate, he saw that they were now neatly and totally sealed within the courtyard.

Rigby-Smith looked angrily at Ogilvie, still flat on the ground. "Kindly order the release of that officer," he snapped at Jarar Mahommed, his face reddening.

"And if I do not, Colonel Sahib?"

"I shall—I shall...." Rigby-Smith's voice trailed away; he had just seen the grille for himself. Jarar, laughing insultingly, called an order and the native removed himself from Ogilvie's back.

"Are you all right, Captain Ogilvie?" Rigby-Smith called out.

"Yes, sir." Ogilvie got to his feet and dusted down his uniform. He was somewhat bruised, but no more than that. "I was trying to stop that portcullis coming down—"

"Thank you, Captain Ogilvie. I congratulate you on your alertness. Now, Jarar Mahommed, I wish, if you please, to see Major Gilmour."

Rigby-Smith was keeping nicely cool, much more so than Ogilvie would have expected; he was showing no sign of fluster to the Ghilzai leader, even though he must now know that he had done something remarkably stupid. As Ogilvie looked on, Jarar Mahommed dismounted from his horse, spoke for a moment in low tones to a dignified, turbaned native, a bearded man who salaamed low to his leader; and then went into a great doorway that, as Ogilvie was to find, led into a high-ceilinged entrance chamber off which led many corridors and a fine staircase. Soon after this Rigby-Smith was sent for and taken into the palace; and a few minutes after this again, the remainder of the officers, both British and native, were escorted into the building as well and bowed ceremoniously into one of the smaller rooms leading off the great hall. The sepoys were left outside with their havildars, under the long-barrelled rifles of the tribesmen at the surrounding windows.

*   *   *

"You'll have to go back on it," Gilmour said. "You'll have to, Colonel!"

"But really, I—I can't possibly! The British *always* tell the truth!"

"Well, I'm awfully sorry, but this time you'll have to say you didn't, you told a lie. God knows *why* you told it—but you did! You've seen the error of your ways, Colonel!"

Rigby-Smith lifted an eyebrow. "The error of my ways, Major Gilmour? I call that damned rude."

"I'm sorry, but you must forget all the regimental niceties now—damn it all, you know India and the Frontier! We're not talking about some old ladies' bun-fight in Peshawar now! I tried to warn you, to convey what I wanted you to say—but you didn't seem to understand."

"Winks and nods and such things...."

"It was all I could do," Gilmour said impatiently. The two men were pacing up and down a small open space, a kind of terrace that had been allocated to the British Resident and his family during what amounted in fact to their imprisonment in Jarar Mahommed's palace-fortress; off this terrace led two rooms with small barred windows looking down directly on to the stinking dirt of Kunarja's crowded streets of hovels. One room was for the use of Major and Mrs. Gilmour, the other was for Katharine their daughter. The Gilmours had been quite well treated; and Jarar Mahommed, at the recent interview with Rigby-Smith, had insisted that he had never had any intention of harming the representative of the Raj. Gilmour went on now, "You know, Rigby-Smith, I consider Fettleworth to have been high-handed over this. Or anyway—Calcutta. I suppose Fettleworth has to follow his orders, the same as the rest of us, though in all conscience..."

"Yes, Major Gilmour?"

"Well, I was going to say—one grows accustomed to this kind of thing with Fettleworth, doesn't one? No need to answer that, if you'd rather not! After all, he's your Divisional Commander—not mine, thank God." Gilmour gave a quiet chuckle. "But he does seem to, well, attract misfortune and—and a general ambience of mishandled situations.

Like a magnet! He should have been much more insistent, much firmer with Calcutta. These people really have come to depend on that subsidy, you know." He looked hard at Rigby-Smith. "*Do* you know that?"

"I do now."

"But before?"

"Er ... no."

"Neither did you care?"

"Frankly, no." Rigby-Smith's tone was stiff.

"Neither does Fettleworth, in my opinion! That's the whole trouble. To him they're just damn natives who have to toe the line, and when they don't, you go to war."

"I don't know that that's entirely fair—"

"Possibly not, but it's fair rule-of-thumb. To get back to what I was saying, Rigby-Smith: you've come with power to discuss terms—"

"But I have no such power, Gilmour, no such power at all!"

"I accept that—"

"Well, then!"

"Yes, but you've got to *invent* the power! I tell you, it's vital, or we're all done for. You came here to extract me and my family, or protect us, and I'm terribly grateful, believe me. But you're not going to be very much use at that now, I'm afraid, with your sepoys all so nicely rounded up." Gilmour gave a cough; he could have been indiscreet in pointing out the only-too-obvious. While Rigby-Smith and he had been fencing verbally with Jarar Mahommed, reclining on silken cushions in the banqueting hall of the palace, the 99th Rawalpindi Native Light Infantry had been firmly and insultingly disarmed. While still, so far, nominally under the charge of their own havildars and naiks, and physically unmolested, they had been rendered utterly impotent and wide open to rifle and machine-gun fire, should it be used, from the windows that dominated the courtyard. It was a position of great indignity that was currently infuriating the British and Indian officers. Gilmour murmured, "I'm terribly sorry, Rigby-Smith."

Colonel Rigby-Smith refrained from comment, and Gilmour went on, "So, you see, some other way has to be found.

That way is subterfuge. Terms, my dear fellow—terms leading to a safe conduct through the Khyber into India, for all of us!"

"Lies, falsehoods?"

"If necessary."

"Not very sporting."

"Oh, for God's sake!"

Rigby-Smith said stiffly, "You know what I mean, Gilmour. We British have a reputation for speaking the truth, for playing the game come what may. One hesitates ... one bears in mind what may happen in the future, to other people, if we should act so as to destroy faith in our veracity. We cannot act only for ourselves, you know."

"I've had a good deal of time to think about this," the Resident said quietly. "As you know, word of your coming reached us ahead of you. Jarar Mahommed was convinced you would bring terms, something to discuss. He's not such a bad ruler, you know—as savage, as bloody *cruel* as the rest of 'em, but not so bad as some tribal leaders—and he feels let down."

"Yet you propose telling him lies?"

Gilmour shook his head. "Not exactly. If necessary, then yes, I would—for the greater good, Colonel. Think: if we should be massacred, or even simply kept in confinement, then Calcutta's hand would be forced. A full-scale expedition against the Ghilzais would become essential—public opinion, if nothing else, would demand that. There would be many casualties, and the Ghilzais would be broken—or Jarar would, at the very least." He smacked a fist into his palm. "I don't want to see that, Colonel. I've spent a good deal of my life working for the benefit of the frontier tribes —and I don't want to chuck all those years away!"

"My dear Gilmour," Rigby-Smith said disparagingly, "that is something men are doing constantly in the Raj, or in any other part of the Empire, are they not?"

Gilmour gave a short laugh. "In other words, in your view, natives are natives?"

"Certainly!"

"Then we know where we stand, at least! Now, Colonel Rigby-Smith. Let me repeat—you have, after all, come with

76

terms. You and I will discuss together what these terms are—"

"But I have *not*—"

"*Then you shall dissemble!* I assure you, it is our one and only hope. There is no other course. I've said Jarar Mahommed is a reasonably good ruler. He is—I stand by that. But when things go wrong for him, when he doesn't get his own way, he is no different from all other Pathans. I repeat, he can be cruel and vicious—I needn't elaborate, Colonel." Gilmour was still speaking quietly, but with insistence and sincerity. "*You* have a regiment to consider—*I* have a wife and daughter. It's a big responsibility."

"I still dislike the destruction of *trust* ... trust for the years ahead."

Gilmour smiled. "This needn't necessarily follow. Fettleworth, remember, is a vain man ... a very vain man. If *he* could settle the Ghilzai problem, Colonel, what a feather in his cap *that* would be, would it not?"

Rigby-Smith stared at him, his brows creased into a frown and his lips pursed. "You mean—"

"I mean you could commit Fettleworth in advance. You and I will settle the terms with Jarar Mahommed, subject of course to the agreement of Calcutta, and then we will return to Peshawar under a safe conduct—this safe conduct to be an essential preliminary to the possible granting of any terms at all—and once we're in Peshawar, Colonel, we present Fettleworth with a *fait accompli!* He must press Calcutta for agreement, for the word of a British officer and gentleman will have been given, and given, moreover, in his name—Fettleworth's name." Gilmour pulled at his moustache. "Since, in my opinion, there must be a settlement with Jarar Mahommed whatever happens, we shall be handing Bloody Francis the wherewithal for another decoration! He's bound to see that, given time! You'll find him perfectly amenable, I promise you."

"Possibly, possibly." Rigby-Smith's tone was full of doubt and anxiety. "By God, Gilmour, I don't like this in the very least."

"You'll come to love it, when we're marching out for

77

Peshawar! Now—let's discuss the terms we're going to propose, Colonel...."

* * *

The room where the officers were confined had, like Gilmour's accommodation, a window, barred and set high up in the wall; it let in light and it let in the smells of Kunarja, and the sounds of the crowded streets, but it gave no available view since it was well out of reach. Ogilvie, having paced the room for hours, was now sitting on the floor with his back to a wall, with Taggart-Blane next to him. Taggart-Blane, who had not stopped worrying for an instant, asked for the hundredth time, "What's going to *happen*, James?"

Ogilvie stifled a sigh. "We can only wait and see, can't we? Do try to be patient."

"Patient!" The subaltern's voice was high; soon he could become hysterical. There was decided softness there and Ogilvie couldn't see him lasting the course in India. Meanwhile, inaction and uncertainty were preying on Ogilvie's own mind as well. Some while earlier Major Fry had been sent for, and escorted by wild-looking guards from the room, to the presence, apparently, of Jarar Mahommed. He had not yet returned; when he did, the situation might clarify a little.

Taggart-Blane said suddenly, "I can't take much more of this, I'll go mad—"

"That's enough—"

"Rigby-Smith's a bloody fool, he led us into this—"

"Shut up, Alan!"

"He's not *fit* to command a battalion, and you know it. You bloody well know it, and so do I!" Taggart-Blane's body was shaking like a jelly. Ogilvie heard Captain Scrutton, the adjutant, getting to his feet, and saw him stalk across the room scowling bleakly.

"All right, Scrutton, I'll deal with this," he said.

Scrutton faced him, his eyes cold. "The little blighter's insulted my Colonel, Ogilvie. D'you expect me to stand for that?"

78

"I'm sorry. It was inexcusable. I apologise on his behalf, Scrutton, but—"

"I'd like to hear his own apology, thank you, Ogilvie."

"Can't you leave him alone? Can't you see he's—"

"Acting like a girl? Oh yes, Ogilvie, I can see that very well indeed!" Scrutton loomed over the subaltern, one hand on his hip, the other holding a riding-crop. "Now, if you please, *Mr.* Taggart-Blane—your apology for your damned insults!"

Ogilvie caught Taggart-Blane's eye and shrugged; there was nothing he could do—Scrutton was well within his rights and no decent officer could have been expected to behave otherwise. Ogilvie said, "Come along, Alan. Do as he asks."

Taggart-Blane seemed almost in tears. Without facing the adjutant he muttered, "Oh, all right then, I'm sorry, I apologise. Is that *abject* enough for you?"

Scrutton gave a snort and turned away contemptuously, going back to his own side of the room. Taggart-Blane sat in silence after that, staring at nothing, worrying about his current situation, his face twitching with his inner fears and imaginings. He was probably, Ogilvie thought, visualising torture; if so, he was not being too fanciful by any means. Torture was still part of the Pathan way of life. While the other officers talked among themselves Ogilvie, still the outcast Scot, listened to the sounds coming through the window. The cries of market stall-holders, of itinerant beggars, gusts of sudden laughter, all mingled with the more threatening sounds of the mob still milling around the walls of the palace, waiting, no doubt, to be told by their lord and master, Jarar Mahommed, that the British had agreed to start paying the subsidy again—or, in default of this, were to die in the full view of the populace.

It was long after the day's light had faded from behind the grille that the waiting officers heard the footsteps approaching; and then the door of the room was thrown open and two of Jarar Mahommed's retainers were seen in the doorway, outlined in the light of a lantern carried by a third man in rear.

"Highness wishes to talk with Ogilvie Sahib and Subedar

79

Gundar Singh," one of the men announced. "You will come, please, at once."

Ogilvie scrambled to his feet and approached the door, where he was joined by Gundar Singh, a stout man with a heavy beard. "What does Jarar Mahommed want?" Ogilvie asked.

"Sahib, Highness will tell you what he wishes you to know."

"Is the Colonel Sahib with him?"

"Yes, Sahib."

Ogilvie left the room and the door was at once secured behind him. He followed the man with the lantern, ahead of the armed escort, with the subedar beside him and breathing heavily, towards the staircase that he had seen on arrival. It was a splendid staircase of marble, rising to a half-landing and then parting to either side and climbing again in graceful curves to right and left. The lantern-bearer led the way across a wide space with tall columns lifting towards a high ceiling and a great dome; and turned along a thickly carpeted passage which in turn led direct into a lighted chamber at its end. Here, lolling on his silken cushions, lay Jarar Mahommed; sitting rather more stiffly, with crossed legs, and looking white and tired and strained, were Colonel Rigby-Smith, Major Fry, and the British Resident.

"So this is Captain Ogilvie?" Jarar Mahommed asked, running an eye over the kilted Scot. "From those terrible soldiers dressed as women, the ones who go into battle with a most terrible screaming instrument of torture, so as to terrify their enemies before the fight begins?"

Ogilvie gave a half smile. "It is usually effective, Jarar Mahommed," he said.

"That is so, indeed. I myself have seen it. I honour a brave opponent, Ogilvie Sahib, and I myself have fought these wild mountain-dwellers from your land. My father also. The 42nd and the 44th Regiments are mountain-dwellers, is this not so?"

Ogilvie nodded. "Yes, that is so."

"Good, my memory plays me no tricks!" Jarar gave a thick chuckle, a sound deep in a powerful throat. "Have that much in mind, gentlemen," he added, turning to Rigby-

Smith and Gilmour. "My memory is long ... as also is that of my people. Treachery, if such should be indulged in, will never be forgotten. For so long as the British Raj remains in being, the Ghilzais would spit upon the flag of England ...should there be treachery!"

"If there is treachery," Rigby-Smith observed stiffly, "it would not come from *us*, Jarar Mahommed."

"Then you accuse *me* of possible treachery?"

"No, he doesn't," Gilmour hastened to say before Rigby-Smith, who was looking thoroughly angry, could get his word in. "The Colonel Sahib was merely stating what you must surely know to be no more than a fact—that the Raj deals in no lies and no treachery. In any case, the matter is pure hypothesis. There has been no treachery, and there will be no treachery."

"Rigby-Smith Sahib was not anxious to enter into any discussions in the first place, Gilmour Sahib, this you cannot deny?"

"No, I don't deny it, but he has explained that he was under orders to talk first with me, Highness—and British officers are inclined to obey their orders whatever happens! And now..." Gilmour spread his hands, and smiled at the Ghilzai leader. "Now there has been discussion! I think all will be well now, Highness."

"So long as your government in Calcutta honours the agreed terms of settlement, Gilmour Sahib."

"Of course. Have no fear, Highness. Now, Captain Ogilvie, your Colonel wishes—"

"Thank you, I am able to speak for myself, Major Gilmour." Rigby-Smith, Ogilvie thought, sounded upset about something or other, upset and bloody-minded too, as he sat on the silk cushions with two fingers tugging at the neckband of his winter uniform. "Captain Ogilvie ... His Highness, Jarar Mahommed, has agreed to a safe conduct through the Khyber Pass for Major Gilmour and his family—Mrs. and Miss Gilmour. He will also permit one company of my regiment to be re-armed and to march as escort, as a protection against what he calls unruly bandits and elements not subject to his control, which *I* consider—" He broke off as he met Gilmour's warning glare. "However ... what was I saying? Ah, yes. One company, Captain Ogilvie, will therefore accompany Major Gilmour and his—er—caravan. That company will be yours, and you will yourself command it, assisted by Subedar Gundar Singh. You will be answerable for the safety of your charges, Captain Ogilvie. I trust you understand?"

"Perfectly, sir. I have one request to make."

"Well?"

"I would like to take Mr. Taggart-Blane with me."

"Oh, really? Really?" Rigby-Smith's eyebrows lifted disdainfully. "Why—*why*, may I ask?"

"Because, sir, he is a good company officer and a good soldier." Ogilvie was disinclined to give his real reason, which was, that he believed, if left alone with the officers of the 99th, Taggart-Blane might very well let the Royal Strathspeys down by giving way to his fears. "No other reason, sir."

"Well, he's attached to E Company, certainly. Very well then, take him—take him! Now, Captain Ogilvie, Major Gilmour will be conveying a report of our discussion, and His Highness Jarar Mahommed's agreement to the terms suggested, to General Fettleworth. It is vital that he reaches Peshawar—vital for the peace and stability of the Frontier, and vital to the rest of us who will remain here as hostages. Do your best!"

"I shall do that, sir, of course. When do you wish me to leave?"

Rigby-Smith said, "That's a matter that must first be settled with Jarar Mahommed." He looked towards the Ghilzai leader, who was smiling slightly. "Well? When shall he leave?"

Jarar waved a hand. "He may leave at once, and I shall give the orders for his men to be re-armed by my palace guards, also the orders for his safety on the march. This is a matter of urgency to me as well as to you, Rigby Sahib! I wish the soldiers well, in their long march."

Ogilvie addressed Rigby-Smith. "Then, sir, I had better start making my preparations. Have you any special orders, sir?"

"None—other than to reach Peshawar with all possible

despatch, Captain Ogilvie! And to take good care of the ladies *en route*. The good wishes and the hopes of us all go with you. Look well to your commissariat, Captain Ogilvie. Jarar Mahommed has given his approval for a due percentage of the camp followers to accompany you—a mixed blessing, of course! There is just one other thing."

"Sir?"

"It must be obvious to you that I could have chosen another of my officers for this mission. The fact that I have not done so, that I have preferred to entrust Major Gilmour and his family to you ... I would like to say that this was done with my fullest intent and deliberation." Rigby-Smith gave an embarrassed cough, moved his long neck about within his uniform collar, and glanced briefly at the stony face of Major Fry; but then met Ogilvie's eye squarely. "I have been impressed with your bearing on the march, Ogilvie—"

"Thank you, sir—"

"—and I know that you will do well. That is all. Good-bye and, once again, good luck."

"And to you, sir. Major Gilmour, are you to come with me now?"

"No, I have a few words to exchange with Jarar Mahommed," the Resident said. "I'll have my wife and daughter prepare for the march, and then I'll meet you in the courtyard. I'll not take long, I assure you."

Ogilvie turned away and walked from the chamber with Subedar Gundar Singh behind him. He found himself wondering about Colonel Rigby-Smith: that officer, so stiff-necked, so formal and previously so unfriendly, had very greatly surprised him by being so forthcoming in his praise. Making his way back to the room where he had been imprisoned, he reported formally to the adjutant, telling him of his orders. After giving the officers such information as he could, he left again with Taggart-Blane, who looked most remarkably relieved not to be left behind. They went out into the enclosed courtyard where, beneath a high moon that shed silver over the towering walls of the palace, the sepoys were clustered with the camp followers, shivering in the cold night air and huddled together for comfort.

Ogilvie called for the havildar-major, who rose from the shadows in a corner of the courtyard and saluted.

"Sahib!"

"Havildar-Major, rouse out E Company if you please. They'll be re-armed by the palace guard and they're to prepare to march at once, with a proportion of the camp followers and the commissariat train, no more than sufficient to take us through the Khyber to Peshawar, you understand?"

"Yes, Sahib."

"We'll be escorting Major Gilmour and his family, with terms for discussion. I want you to impress on the sepoys that E Company has been chosen by the Colonel Sahib for a very special and important mission."

"Yes, Sahib." Eager eyes looked directly into Ogilvie's. "I am to accompany this mission, Ogilvie Sahib?"

Ogilvie shook his head. "I'm sorry, Havildar-Major. You'll be needed here—to keep the sepoys in good heart. I shall be taking Subedar Gundar Singh."

"Yes, Sahib. And also...."

"What is it, Havildar-Major?"

There was a very obvious embarrassment in the native N.C.O.'s voice and bearing as he said, "Sahib, I beg a word privately, a word for your ear alone."

Ogilvie frowned, glancing sideways at the subedar and Taggart-Blane, who were talking together and, apparently, not listening. "Very well, Havildar-Major," he said, feeling a strong sense of trouble on the way. He moved some paces clear of the other two, followed by the havildar-major. "Now, what's troubling you, Ram Singh?"

"You will take also Taggart-Blane Sahib to Peshawar, with E Company, Sahib?"

"Yes, I shall. Why do you ask?"

There was a silence, then the other man said heavily, "Sahib, it is not fitting for me to talk, yet..."

"Well, come on," Ogilvie said with sudden impatience. "Say what you have to say, for God's sake, man!" He stared hard at the havildar-major, whose bearded face was working with some strange emotion. "You have said—so much. Now you must finish. Come!"

84

"It is an order, Ogilvie Sahib?"

"It is an order, Havildar-Major."

"Then I must obey." There was still the terrible hesitancy, the obvious effort to break through a close inhibition. "Sahib, my life has been dedicated to my duty, my military duty to the Raj. I have a great respect for the regiment, for the officers, Sahib. I—"

"Yes, yes! I would never presume to doubt your loyalty, Havildar-Major. Please hurry. I wish to be on the march as soon as possible."

"Yes, Sahib. Because I love the regiment and the Raj, I do not like to see things that could affect the discipline of the sepoys, Sahib. Favouritism, over-friendliness ... this is not good, and can be misunderstood by the sepoys, the younger ones, and can be used against the officer who indulges in it."

"You refer to Taggart Sahib?"

The havildar-major inclined his head. "Even so, Sahib. Taggart Sahib is young and inexperienced in Indian ways."

Ogilvie felt a shiver of real apprehension run through his body, but knew he had a duty to perform now. He said harshly, "You must speak, Havildar-Major. Have you anything precise to say?"

"There is a young sepoy, Sahib—Mulata Din, fresh from his father's fields. There is too great a degree of friendliness from Taggart Sahib, and it is not good. I have observed many things, Sahib, in cantonments at Peshawar and whilst on the march through the Khyber, at bivouacs in the dark hours. Mulata Din—"

"You speak of friendliness, Ram Singh. What friendliness? What things have you observed? You must say. It is important that I know."

"Sahib, there have been things that would be grievous hearing for a British officer. It is not seemly for me to speak of detail. There have been occasions when the familiarity has been too great, and too great the bodily proximity. I can report no more than that."

"But there has not been ... Taggart Sahib has not—"

"No, Sahib. This thing has not progressed to such an extreme as that of which you hesitate to speak. I will say

85

only this: Sahib, amongst my people there is a saying...
*there is a boy across the river with a bottom like a peach,
but alas, I cannot swim.* What I am saying, Sahib, is this.
When the river is no longer there, the proximity may become greater with the removal of the hindrance." The
havildar-major paused, his face grave and sad. "Sahib, I am
the Havildar-Major of the 99th Light Infantry, and I must
do my duty."

"How do you see that duty now, Ram Singh?"

"Sahib, I have made my report. That is all I have to do."

"You feel no need to report further—to the Colonel
Sahib, for instance?"

"I do not, Sahib."

Ogilvie nodded; his mind was racing. What had been
suggested was extremely distasteful and serious. Possibly it
had been a mistake for Taggart-Blane to be seconded to a
native regiment; to some extent it had made things easy
for him, the opportunity for sin had been handed to him on
a plate—out here in the sub-continent, the natives took a
different view from a Briton's of such deviations. From now
on, a constant vigilance would be necessary. Ogilvie
wondered if he should take this man Mulata Din out of
the line, leave him behind in Kunarja, but after only a
moment's reflection decided against this; such action would
lend too much point to the affair, which could in Ram
Singh's mind have become greater than it was in fact. No,
the vigilance must be his own ... he let out a long breath
and said crisply, "Thank you, Havildar-Major. I shall do
what is necessary now. You have done your duty, as was only
proper. Now, let us not waste time. Have my company
fallen in and mustered. We move out the moment the Major
Sahib is ready."

7

"CAPTAIN OGILVIE OF the 114th Highlanders ... my wife."

"How d'you do, ma'am—"

"And my daughter Katharine."

Katharine Gilmour offered her hand; Ogilvie took it, found it warm and soft. The girl was young and fresh, no more than eighteen years of age he guessed, and she seemed unafraid though she must surely have an awareness of the rigours of a winter march through the Khyber Pass—a march that could prove extremely dangerous even with Jarar Mahommed's promise of a safe conduct. There was a smile on her lips, and a kind of mischief in her eyes—she had guts, Ogilvie saw, and saw with immense relief. He wasn't so sure about the mother, who was pale and weepy. He glanced round at his re-armed sepoys and said, "We'll not delay then, Major Gilmour, if you're all ready."

"Whenever you say, Ogilvie. We're in your hands now." His tone was easy and confident; Ogilvie had already taken a liking to this quiet and unassuming man who had been carrying out for so long a difficult and lonely task, isolated in the Afghan mountains from his own kind. Physically a small man, there was something in the steadfast eyes that increased his stature immeasurably. "I'll not interfere—I'd just like to make that plain from the start."

"Thank you, Major. I appreciate that—though I've no doubt at all I'll be much in need of your help and advice."

The British Resident laid a hand on Ogilvie's arm.

"When and if asked for, and only then, it'll be forthcoming. Ready, my dear?" he asked, turning to his wife.

Wordlessly, her face tight with strain, Mrs. Gilmour nodded. Gilmour gave her a hand to mount one of the horses provided from another company. Katharine Gilmour swung herself up easily enough, though both ladies looked incongruous riding astride with their long dresses rucked up around their waists; Mrs. Gilmour at least was very obviously embarrassed—this showed through even her apprehension for the future. Taggart-Blane came up to report E Company ready to march, and Ogilvie saw him run a lingering eye over Gilmour's daughter. There was something vaguely salacious in that look, and Ogilvie hoped there would be no trouble in that direction whilst on the march— though in all conscience it might be less unpalatable than what the havildar-major had seemed to suggest. Meanwhile, it was time to march out.

Ogilvie nodded at Taggart-Blane, who saluted, turned about smartly and ordered the sepoys to move out through the gates that now stood open. Moving his horse ahead to ride with Major Gilmour and a turbaned officer of Jarar Mahommed's staff, the Pathan who would when necessary show himself as the physical embodiment of his master's safe conduct, Ogilvie rode beneath the arch and out of the courtyard. With their ragged camp followers and the mule-train and the ammunition carts following on behind, the sepoys marched in silence through the narrow streets of the old town, streets that were still alive with natives, watching with glittering, moon-silvered eyes, and with brown hands itching at the hafts of the long knives. There was immense hostility in the very air of Kunarja, almost a physical smell of threat and menace. The British, even those known via the bush telegraph to be going back with their master's terms, were far from popular in Kunarja. Looking in fascination at the lean, hard faces, at the scanty clothing, the dirt, the stinking hovels spilling their refuse along the way, Ogilvie could scarcely wonder at the hatred, if the withdrawing of Fettleworth's 'subsidy' had added to this terrible oppressive poverty—which was on a scale that no-one at home in England could even begin to understand, to realise.

These poor ruffians made the slum-dwellers of the Gorbals, of the poorer quarters of Edinburgh, of Liverpool, of Cardiff and London look like princes of the blood!

"A penny for your thoughts, Ogilvie," Gilmour said by his side.

Ogilvie gave a hard laugh. "Pretty nasty ones, I'm afraid, Major! Life for these people ... why, it isn't life at all!"

"Yes ... I know. I've tried to do what I could, you know, to alleviate some of this. Not that that was really what I was sent here for, but a man can't just stand by ... I suppose you know the truth, don't you?"

"What truth?"

"Why, that the subsidy didn't reach this far—it seldom reached the streets of Kunarja. Like most native rulers, Jarar waxed nice and fat, but not these people!"

"Quite. The wonder is, Major, that it's *us* they seem to hate!"

Gilmour shrugged. "Oh, that's a simple case of loyalty to their own kind—also a full awareness of the fact that even if the subsidy wasn't largessed around the hovels and the open sewers, a damn sight less would have come their way when it was cut! Jarar's economies certainly wouldn't have begun in the palace, my dear fellow!"

Leaving the town behind, they marched on, in silence mainly, plodding along through the bitter cold for the entry to the Khyber, their breath steaming out into the hard moonlight like so many boiling kettles. They marched until the dawn, when Ogilvie ordered the column to halt for a make-shift breakfast. The sepoys fell out; some lay down on the hard ground, others remained standing, throwing their arms around their bodies. The havildars began shouting for the commissariat to come up, moving busily along the resting column. The camp followers, men and women and even children, mingled with the native soldiers. Fires were lit, and soon there was a welcome smell of cooking.

Taggart-Blane wandered off along the column, but was called back sharply by Ogilvie. "I'd like your help," he said. "Where were you off to, Alan?"

"Just to chase up the commissariat, James, that's all."

"Leave that to the N.C.O.s, it doesn't call for your

personal attention. I'd like you to see that the ladies are comfortable."

"Oh, all right, James. What the devil can *I* do for them, though?"

"Use your head," Ogilvie said with a touch of impatience. "Just some little attentiveness ... make them feel like *women*, even if it's only by guarding their privacy!"

"All right, whatever you say."

Taggart-Blane went off, looking uncertain of his duties. Gilmour was standing a little way apart, looking up at the sky, looking towards the towering mountains that enclosed the pass into British India, sniffing the keen bite of the wind off Himalaya. He looked round as Ogilvie approached. "I think we're in for it," he said.

"Snow?"

Gilmour nodded. "Plenty of it, too. You've been through the Khyber in snow?"

"Not while it's been actually snowing."

"I have—once. It wasn't easy, Ogilvie. God, the freezing cold, I can feel it still! You can scarcely make out the tracks at times, and there's those bloody great long drops." He caught himself up. "Still—there it is, and no use crossing our bridges!"

"It'll be hard on the ladies, Major."

"Don't I know it!" Gilmour gave a short, humourless laugh, like a bark. "I had a tussle with myself, whether or not to ask to bring 'em out with us, you know. I fancied Jarar was the greater risk, however. If things go wrong..."

"If things *do* go wrong, what happens to the regiment?"

Gilmour looked at him quizzically. "Do I need to put it into words?"

Slowly, Ogilvie shook his head. "No, you don't really, Major."

"Jarar's on the primitive side, you know. All these people are the same—basic barbarians. Talk about Genghis Khan! I've seen minor princelings out here do the most diabolical things—at least, diabolical in *our* terms. Flaying alive, boiling alive in oil, staking men out for the ploughs to over-run. Nothing I could do, but God! It used to make

90

my blood run cold. I'd sooner my womenfolk faced the snows than that!"

"I don't wonder."

"Mind you, Jarar's not so bad as some. I said as much to your Colonel, and I say it again, but if the terms aren't met almost anything could happen. This is a hard country, with a hard history, a history of the most abominable violence and cruelty. I won't dwell on that, though—with God's help and a touch of luck, *we*'ll soon be out of it!"

"Will you be coming back, Major?"

Again Glimour laughed, and shielded his eyes against the sunrise—a blood-red orb appearing over a declivity in the mountain range. "Well, that depends on many things, Ogilvie! Talking of which, I think we need a second line as it were. I mean, you should know what the terms are— just in case I don't get through myself, you know—"

"It's my job to see you do, Major."

"I know. But other people may have other ideas. Jarar Mahommed's edict doesn't run one hundred per cent along the Frontier, Ogilvie. There are other interests, conflicting ones. Some of the tribal leaders would be glad enough to see Jarar take a tumble—"

"Which is why I'm here with my company?"

Gilmour nodded. "Yes, exactly. Well now, here briefly are the terms as discussed with Jarar, and agreed subject to Calcutta's concurrence. They're perfectly simple and straightforward: the subsidy to be maintained to the extent of seventy-five per cent; a British regiment to be stationed in Kunarja for the protection of the Residency when rebuilt, and to keep an eye on British interests including the free passage—so far as the Ghilzais are concerned, that is—of the Khyber. Jarar to give active assistance as and when required for the movement of any British troops in and out of his sector of Afghanistan. Broadly, that's the lot. Have you got that?"

"Yes. Is there anything in writing, Major?"

"There is. I have the document—it's all set out in detail and signed by Jarar Mahommed, in the presence of Rigby-Smith and Jarar's own major-domo, as witnesses. Jarar has the duplicate, signed by myself as the representative of

General Fettleworth. I have that document on my person, in my wallet. You'll have to take that if necessary, of course." He smiled. "You have my full permission to rob the dead or wounded! When you read it, if you do, you'll see that Jarar enters into a number of ancillary promises, to keep the Pax Britannica intact, and never, never again to destroy the Residency or incarcerate the Resident in his blasted palace!"

"Think he'll keep them?"

"Oh, yes," Gilmour answered with confidence. "So long as he has that subsidy, he'll toe the line. It should never have been withdrawn! It's such a pity we have to be subservient to the dictates of that set of bloody fools in Calcutta ...only, for God's sake, Ogilvie, don't quote me on that!"

Ogilvie grinned. "I won't, don't worry!"

They walked together to where Gilmour's family were sitting on some ground spread with thin blankets in the lee of a rock. The women were well wrapped against the cold, but were shivering nevertheless, and Mrs. Gilmour was tending to weep at intervals, though in general she was doing her best to give the impression of stoicism in the face of misfortune and danger. Ogilvie was nevertheless convinced she would crack before long. He had a word with the ladies, then went off to walk down the resting column for some words of encouragement to the sepoys. As soon as the frugal meal was finished, he passed the order for the march to be resumed; and shortly after this they were all on their feet or on horseback again, stumbling along over the hard, ice-cold ground and the rocky jags for the Khyber. Within minutes Gilmour's prediction was fulfilled and the snow, the blinding, blizzard-like snow, started driving down.

*   *   *

The snow was hurled into their faces by a tearing, biting wind, a wind that froze men to the bone and sent great white flurries whipping around them like whirligigs. Gilmour advised that they should press on so long as any movement was at all possible and so long as they could still make out the track. To stop now, Gilmour said, though the time might well come when they would be forced to, would be to invite burial in the drifting white danger, and a creeping paralysis of cold that would end in the snow-sleep of death.

"There's one thing," Gilmour shouted above the howl of the blizzard, his lips close to Ogilvie's muffled-up ears, "we'll be reasonably safe from any bandits while this lasts! Poor buggers'll all be safe at home like sensible men ... not that I wouldn't a damn sight sooner take my chance with them than with this!"

"Me too," Ogilvie shouted back. They rode on, their faces stiff and blue. Already the snow was lying a good six inches deep all along the track, and drifting in places to a depth of two or three feet into which the horses plunged almost to their bellies. The sepoys, on foot, were having a truly wicked time of it; but, when Ogilvie had ridden down the column, he had heard few complaints. The same could not be said of the miserable-looking camp followers: they were already wailing and whimpering at the harshness of the conditions, and making very heavy going of it all.

"Where's young Taggart-Blane got to?" Gilmour asked suddenly.

"What was that?"

"*Where's Taggart-Blane?*"

"Rearguard. With my subedar. Watching out that no stragglers get left behind."

"They'll not do that," Gilmour shouted. "The sepoys won't leave their own kind behind in Afghanistan, Ogilvie, any more than we would."

Ogilvie nodded; that was true, but he had wanted to take every precaution. Men could fall into a drift and perhaps not be noticed unless there was a rider behind them. As for deliberately leaving stragglers, wounded men particularly ... this would never be done in Afghan territory. Terrible things were customarily inflicted on captives, and indeed a regiment never left its dead unburied if it could possibly be avoided—even the dead could be defiled. This was partly why the camp followers were such a drag upon an army; they couldn't be left behind either. Ogilvie peered ahead through the blinding drive of snowflakes; he could see, in

93

fact, little more than half a dozen yards and the speed of the advance had slowed to no more than a crawl now. At any moment they might come off the track, finish in a maze of rocky jags and buried stunted trees, or at the bottom of a precipice: this latter would become more than a possibility once they entered the Khyber. Had it not been for Gilmour's guiding presence, Ogilvie knew he would have been hopelessly lost already. But Gilmour knew this terrain well, under all kinds of weather conditions, and he could read the lie of the almost invisible land and navigate by the individual rocks as though possessed of magical powers. Even he, however, would be bested when darkness fell, so to press on now was the thing to do, and then rest the column, and hope that frost-bite would not strike, through the night.

* * *

"And this is where we'd better call a halt, Ogilvie, if you want my advice. It's as good as we'll find. All right with you?"

"If you say so, Major." Ogilvie lifted his right hand; the snow had slackened now and the daylight had not yet gone; the nearer files could see his signal. Ogilvie pulled up his horse; behind him Mrs. Gilmour and Katharine also stopped. The column came to a halt, and Ogilvie turned in his saddle, looking for Taggart-Blane. A few moments later he saw the subaltern, riding forward from the rear with Subedar Gundar Singh.

"How are the sepoys?" he asked as he dismounted.

"In a pretty poor way, I think."

"So are we all! Anyone dropping out?"

"A few." Taggart-Blane looked ill, on the point of dropping out himself but managing to keep going. He was not without guts. "I had them put into the commissariat wagons, and the camp followers are looking after them. Are we halting for the night now, or what?" His eyes strayed to the women, concentrating, as before, on Katharine Gilmour's legs.

"Yes," Ogilvie said, "we're making camp—"

94

"*Camp?* Without any damn tents?"

"Call it what you like! Bivouacs would be a better term —and even at that, they'll not be up to much! Alan, see that the sepoys all find adequate cover against any more snow, if you please, and pay particular attention to the men who dropped out. You can tell the camp followers, the women included, I'll have their bloody hides if any man's not fit to march tomorrow! I beg your pardon, ma'am," he added to Mrs. Gilmour, apologising for his sudden coarse language. "Under stress, one is apt to swear—I'm sorry!"

There was no response from Mrs. Gilmour, whose face was pinched and frozen-looking; but Katharine smiled and said, "Oh, please, you really shouldn't worry, Captain Ogilvie. Such a very little word! I'm sure my mother doesn't mind."

"And you, Miss Gilmour?" He returned her smile.

She glanced at Gilmour, who had gone to his wife's side. "I've heard worse," she said, bending towards Ogilvie and speaking in a lower voice, and still smiling. "Would you mind helping me down from my horse, Captain Ogilvie?"

"Why, of course!" He reached up and she swung herself down into his arms, so that for a moment he held her bodily. He felt a curious thump in his heartbeats; she was soft and yielding, and her skin smelled of fresh, expensive soap and an elusive perfume—which was quite a feat considering she had lately been in Jarar Mahommed's palace where fresh water and washing would scarcely have been a frequent occurrence in the usual run of events.

He set her down in the deep snow. "Well, there we are," he said, sounding foolish.

"Thank you, Captain Ogilvie." She looked into his eyes for a moment, then turned away and stared about her. "Did Father choose this place?"

"Yes."

"I hope he knows what he's doing. Where do we sleep?"

"In what cover we can find, Miss Gilmour. I shall see to it that you and your mother have as comfortable a bivouac as possible, you may be sure of that, and you'll have every privacy."

"And a sentry?" She dimpled at him.

95

It was her look, as much as anything, that caught him aback and he gaped a little and repeated, "A sentry? For your protection against bandits? Certainly—"

"Against *men*, Captain Ogilvie, bandits or not!" She dimpled again. "Do I shock you?"

"Er ... no, of course not, I—"

"Oh, yes I do, and I apologise humbly." She reached out and took his hand, very briefly. Then she had turned away to her mother and her back was towards him. It was, he noted, a very attractive silhouette against the dead white of the virgin snow beyond the track. His heart still beating rather more noticeably than usual, he moved away down the column. Taggart-Blane had already gone off in execution of his orders and already, too, the sepoys were beginning to settle into their sorry bivouacs behind the rocks and boulders, dragging their inadequate clothing over heads and faces to keep out the snow. They would have to be aroused at intervals throughout the night, made to get up and move so as to keep their circulation going. In point of fact the snowfall had eased still more now; with any luck at all, they might pass not too terrible a night, though the cold would be with them still, would indeed be with them all the way into India. So too would be the snow already fallen ... Ogilvie shrugged and moved on down the line. They would have to put up with it, that was all! One couldn't expect to fight all one's campaigns under blue skies—and come to that, the heat and dust and the parched throats of summer were, in their way, every bit as bad! Or were they? Great heat was not a physical hurt like great cold. Katharine Gilmour was probably a summer person; Ogilvie could imagine her in a summer dress, beneath a parasol, beside an English tennis lawn at some country house-party in the Shires, or the Dukeries, or cool and fresh in the secluded garden of some great London house ... he swore suddenly as he plunged into a deep patch of the wretched snow and almost fetched up against a nasty-looking jag of rock protruding only partially from the snow's mantle. As he recovered Taggart-Blane came from the rear of the line, towards him. "I think it's snowed itself out," he said. "And about time too."

Ogilvie nodded. "Let's hope so. How're the men now?"

"Making the best of it. They're a good crew, James. Some of the younger ones are taking it hard, though—not that they're complaining. I'll keep an eye on them. Like a mother!"

"I might sound out the women."

Taggart-Blane raised an eyebrow. "What for?"

"In case any motherly comfort is required—if there's any actual illness. I'm sure the daughter would help, though I don't know about Mrs. Gilmour. As a matter of fact, if she would, it could be the best thing for her—to have something to do."

"Oh, I think we'll manage, James. Now, what are the orders for the night?"

Ogilvie said, "I'll want a guard of four sepoys and an N.C.O. to patrol the bivouacs continuously, and keep damn well alert for any trouble—bandits and so on, though I don't really expect any attacks while we're still in Jarar's own territory. The really dangerous part will be after we've entered the Khyber. I want you to arrange a rota for the guard—one hour shifts throughout the night—and all the men are to be roused once in every two hours, and made to move around a bit, otherwise there could be danger of frost-bite."

"Right, James. And us?"

"One of us, you and I and Gundar Singh, will have to remain awake. Let me know when you've organised the guards, then I'll take over for the first watch."

"What about Gilmour?"

"I'd sooner leave him to look after his womenfolk, then we'll have one less worry to cope with!"

"Well, yes, that's a point, I suppose." Taggart-Blane threw his arms around his body, trying to beat some warmth into his veins. The day was darkening now and soon the last of the light would be gone; but the snow had almost stopped. Just a handful of flakes hovered, dithering groundwards in air that was now still and quiet. Taggart-Blane turned away to his duties, making towards the huddled line of sepoys, black humps in the whiteness, beginning to lose their outlines in the gathering night. They were all dog-

97

tired now, wearied almost to the point of exhaustion by the
long struggle through the snow.

*   *   *

Major Gilmour had insisted on standing a share of the
guard duty. His wife and daughter, he said, would be perfectly all right without him constantly in attendance, and
he himself was a soldier of experience. Ogilvie accepted his
offer gratefully enough when he realised that Gilmour was
determined not to be a passenger on the march; and it was
in fact during Gilmour's watch that the trouble, the
agonising trouble, struck.

Ogilvie, sunk in a deep sleep, felt the hand shaking him
urgently awake. He came up from the depths quickly, to
hear Gilmour's voice, sharp but kept low and with some
curious undercurrent in it. As he sat up he saw that although
it was still not snowing, the night was overcast and moon-
less, with a heavy sky holding further snowfall to come. He
could make out Gilmour only as a vague blur bending over
him, a blur that was shivering with the intense cold.

"What is it?" he asked urgently. "Bandits, Major?"

"No, no. Something that could be worse than bandits,
Ogilvie. I think you'd better come and see for yourself. It's
your subaltern, young Taggart-Blane."

"What—?"

"I'm afraid it looks remarkably like buggery, if you'll
pardon the word. He doesn't realise I saw ... I did think of
making a noise and passing on my way, then I thought that
was perhaps not quite fair on you. You may want to deal
with this once and for all. After all, he's one of yours. I hope
I did right, Ogilvie." There was the suspicion of a chuckle.
"D'you know something?"

"What, Major?"

"I know this is far from funny, but really! Within range
of the Khyber! Feller must be in the direst need. You'd
think the sheer cold would make the whole thing impossible!"

8

SOUNDLESSLY THROUGH THE snow, Ogilvie had approached. Furiously angry and sickened, he had seen the two men, close together. There had been some movement. He could not be entirely sure that he had witnessed the act of buggery; the light was not enough, but he believed Gilmour's estimate had been correct. Deeply embarrassed, he had withdrawn to a distance and had then called out for Taggart-Blane. There had been an exclamation, a sound of fear; and within the minute Taggart-Blane had come up, shivering violently.

"What have you been doing, what was going on with that man?"

"Nothing...."

"Nothing! Oh, come now! I know what I saw, I have eyes! You'd better tell me the truth, and quickly." Ogilvie glanced around; tactfully, Gilmour had left them alone.

Taggart-Blane said stonily, "The man had frost-bite. His feet were frost-bitten. I had to do what I could. I ... massaged his feet. That's all. You'd expect no less, surely?"

"I'd have expected you to rouse out Miss Gilmour. Frost-bite is nurse's work—not an officer's."

"Officers be damned. When a man's—"

"Keep your voice down, damn you! You bloody fool! We don't want this to spread—"

"I tell you, James—"

"I know what you told me, yes. What I saw didn't look

99

to me like frost-bite. Have you no regard for your position at all, none? Don't you realise the implications, of a British officer and a sepoy being found in such circumstances? If there should be any complaint from the man—"

"There won't be."

"How sure are you of that?"

"Very sure. I repeat ... oh, for heaven's sake, James, are you going to go on doubting me? I tell you again, *he had frost-bite!*"

"Which can be checked on, of course. If he really has been frost-bitten, no doubt the time will come when it'll be obvious enough even to a layman—and in any case there's doctors in plenty in Peshawar! How bad is this—this frost-bite?"

After a pause Taggart-Blane said, "Not so very bad, I'll admit. It was the beginnings of it, though—or anyway, that's what I diagnosed. I acted on that diagnosis, James."

"So you could be wrong?"

"Doctors themselves are wrong at times, aren't they?"

Even the biting cold had sunk into the background of Ogilvie's awareness now; for possibly the first time in his military career, he was understanding how much more was involved in command than the mere exercise of authority and the successful conduct of an action. He said, "For your sake, Alan, I hope *you're* not wrong this time!"

Taggart-Blane said surlily, "I don't see why this should go any further."

"Then you think you might have been wrong?"

"I don't know! I don't believe so. But surely that's not really the point, is it, James? Isn't the point the fact that I *thought* he had frost-bite, and that I did something about it?" There was pleading in the voice now, and a growing fear. "Don't you see? Can't you understand that?"

"I don't know what I see. You'll have to give me time to think about this." Ogilvie hesitated. "Suppose the man does make a complaint, officially, when we reach Peshawar? I know you said he won't—but just suppose he does? What then?"

"You mean you'll be hauled over the coals for not having made a report to the Colonel?"

"I wasn't thinking of myself, but yes, that would be the case. I'm not asking you to consider that, though. I'm asking you to consider your own position."

"Even if he did complain ... and he won't, because there was nothing to complain about, unless he has it in for me for some reason ... it'd be his word against mine, wouldn't it? A sepoy's word against that of a British officer?"

Ogilvie felt the angry flush spreading over his face. "That is unofficer-like, ungentlemanly—and unmanly too, which is even worse! You'll take your medicine if it comes to that. Remember, I'm a pretty material witness myself, and—"

"You seem very certain of what you saw—what you think you saw!"

"I saw an act—"

"In the dark?" Taggart-Blane was sneering now. "It was dark, James, very dark!"

"Not so dark that I couldn't see what was taking place. If you want me to be precise, then I'll be precise. I saw an act of what I took to be buggery—"

"What you took to be! What experience have you, dear James, how often have you seen that act taking place? Oh, it happens in the Army, of course it does, but I'll wager you haven't seen it every day of your damn service, James! You can't swear to what you saw. You must admit to an element of doubt if you're as honest as I think you are, basically. For my part, I swear no such act took place at all." Taggart-Blane hesitated, his eyes searching Ogilvie's face through the gloom. "But ... if you're so sure ... you'd testify?"

"I would have no option, and you know that very well."

"Oh, I see." Another sneer came into the subaltern's voice. "And—the regiment, James? The dear old regiment? What would the rest of the Division say about the Queen's Own Royal Strathspeys? Have you thought about that?"

Ogilvie flinched. Curtly, angrily, he said, "That's enough. You'll leave the regiment out of this—"

"Oh, my dear old James!" Taggart-Blane gave a high, sardonic laugh. "You can't very well do that, can you?"

For one moment of red-hazed fury, Ogilvie almost struck Taggart-Blane with his fist, but controlled himself just in time. He said, "You'll go to your bivouac and stay there till we move out, and I need hardly say, you'll talk to no-one at all about this. Is that understood?"

"Oh ... yes." Taggart-Blane, his moment's defiance past, now seemed utterly dejected and downcast. "What are you doing—relieving me of my duties?"

"No, because you can't be spared on the march. Also because, as I've said, I need to think about this. You'll carry on as usual, except that you won't go near the native lines alone until further orders. You'll make quite sure you stick very rigidly by that order. That's all. Get out of my sight."

"You're prejudging this, aren't you? You've already made your own mind up!"

"No, that's not true. I'm taking sensible precautions, that's all. Now do as you're told, and get out."

Taggart-Blane hesitated, then turned slowly away and stumbled off through the lying snow. Ogilvie called him back before he had gone more than a few yards, and asked, "The man's name, the sepoy. Who was it?"

He could almost have answered the question himself. Taggart-Blane said, "Mulata Din."

*   *   *

Mulata Din, the old havildar-major had said, was a young boy, fresh from his father's fields, and Taggart Sahib had been, for an officer, too friendly with him, to the detriment of good order and military discipline—or possibly so. Ogilvie, as he turned away from that interview, felt sickened. Of course, in a sense he had asked for it, in asking for Taggart-Blane to accompany the march in the first place; and now he could not duck his responsibilities, however great the burden. To some extent he now held the honour of the regiment, his own regiment, in his hands. If there was to be a complaint, if as a result of that complaint there was to be a Court Martial, a lot of mud must stick to the good name of the 114th and even he, for the rest of his career, would be known, in the comparatively small, closed world that was the British Army, as the officer who had become involved in one of the most abominable and hateful crimes in the military book of rules...

Ogilvie was unaware that Gilmour had come up behind him until he felt the friendly hand on his shoulder. Gilmour asked, "Well, what's the result of your talk with him?"

"He says the man was suffering from frost-bite."

"Frost-bite, hey? That's a new one! I'm sorry, Ogilvie, I know this is deadly serious, but if it wasn't, well, there'd be a funny side after all. Frost-bite! Do you know, when I first came out to India in a trooper, the men used to lie with their wives under rugs on the open deck, since their accommodation was separate. Charitable persons used to say it was the wind that was shaking the rugs." Gilmour gave a quiet laugh. "I repeat my apology, Ogilvie. I know this is different, and I know it's horrible too, but I'd hate to see you go to pieces over it!"

"Oh, I'll not do that, Major, but I do admit I'm most terribly worried."

"Which is not a good thing for the safety of us all on the march. You must clear your mind of this, until we reach Peshawar. I think you'd better tell me all the details so far as you know them. It'll do your soul good!"

Ogilvie repeated his conversation with Taggart-Blane; when he had finished, Gilmour said, "Well, you'll just have to wait and see—there's nothing else to be done at this stage. There either will or will not be a complaint from the sepoy. I would rather think he won't say anything—in fact, I'd be a very astonished man indeed if he *did*. Sepoys don't complain against their officers, and there's all sorts of not very flattering reasons for that abstinence, believe me! In addition, if there's any guilt around at all, half of it could very well lie with the sepoy himself. As another addition, this business isn't so horrid to the Indians as it is to us."

"So I've been told, but—"

"There was some Indian prince, not long ago, who paid a state visit to London, and the Queen put on a magnificent banquet in his honour. She was intrigued, so I heard, about a young boy in the prince's retinue ... I forget what they told her his function was, but it certainly wasn't the truth. However, to be serious again, Ogilvie ... I feel sure there

103

will be no complaint, and if I'm right, there will be no scandal."

"But what then, Major? Do I just sit tight and say nothing?"

"Well, that's rather up to you, isn't it? I wouldn't presume to interfere, naturally, but if you want my advice, then I'd say this: if what you think you saw—what I think I saw also—did in fact take place, then a man of that sort should be eradicated from the army." Gilmour's voice had hardened now. "What's happened once can happen again. And the eradication can take place—so long as there's no official complaint—without any scandal attaching to anyone. You must know the ways of the army, Ogilvie. Colonels can require an officer to send in their papers ... and it would be most foolish for the officer concerned to refuse his co-operation!"

"That's equivalent to being found guilty without trial, though."

Gilmour said, "Yes, I know. It has to depend on how *certain* one is in one's own mind. When you are, you act for the good of the regiment and the service, and make a good clean cut. It's primitive, but it works." He paused, with his hand once again on Ogilvie's shoulder, then added, "I think you'd better clear your mind on one point: the frost-bite, true or false?"

"Yes, but how, without a doctor?"

"My daughter's done a little nursing in the Residency. She's interested in it, and she's read a number of books— I don't know how much she *really* knows, but I can always ask her to have a look at the man's feet and pass a lay opinion. She won't mind."

"It's awfully good of you, Major."

"Thank Katharine, not me, Ogilvie. Would you like me to wake her now, strike while the iron's hot—or frozen?"

Ogilvie gave a tight smile. Gilmour's wit failed, at such a time, to appeal. "If you wouldn't mind," he said. While he waited in the lee of a large rock, Gilmour went off to wake his daughter, having first assured Ogilvie that there was no need for her to be given any other explanation than that the man had been observed to be in distress. Gilmour was back with the girl and a storm lantern inside five minutes, and together they went down the line of men, found a naik and told him to take them to Mulata Din. In the flickering light from the lantern, they saw that the young man was awake and was staring at them with fearful eyes, black pools of reflected light. He was little more than a child in spite of his military status and his weapons of war close at hand: young and small and fresh-skinned, *virginal* ... if a man had such proclivities, this youth would be an obvious victim of his desires.

"Mulata Din," Ogilvie said, "we believe you are in distress about your feet. Is this so?"

Mulata Din stared past him at the waiting naik, seeming not to understand. Ogilvie's command of the sepoy's dialect was not good, as it happened. The naik translated. Mulata Din's eyes, still fearful, widened and he answered, "This is so, Ogilvie Sahib."

"Then the mem-sahib will look, and try to help. Show us your feet, Mulata Din."

The young native moved the pitifully thin blanket that was over his body, and displayed his naked feet, which, though pale and almost bloodless, didn't look to Ogilvie's admittedly inexperienced eye to be showing signs of frost-bite. The toes were wriggling, at any rate, and there was no apparent sign of the waxiness that he believed to be attendant upon frost-bite. Katharine Gilmour bent close, going down on one knee in the snow while her father held the lantern. She felt the feet with what seemed to be expert precision, and a very gentle touch, and asked a few questions in dialect, which Mulata Din answered volubly; he seemed comforted by the touch and presence of a woman. Katharine said a few words to him, smiled kindly, and got up. Mulata Din once again pulled the blanket over his slim legs.

"Well, Miss Gilmour?" Ogilvie asked.

"Oh, I doubt if it's frost-bite," she answered. "Indeed, I'm sure it is not, though it could become so. He's desperately cold, poor fellow, though I dare say no worse than anyone else."

"You said it could become so. Could you be more explicit, Miss Gilmour?"

105

She gave a light laugh, and looked at her father quizzically, then back at Ogilvie. "I don't really think so, Captain Ogilvie, not being a doctor! Why is this man so special, may one ask that?"

"Just answer Captain Ogilvie's question, my dear," Gilmour said. "It's rather important, but we can't say more than that."

"Oh, very well, then." She shrugged. "I think it could become frost-bite if he doesn't keep on rubbing those feet, or anyway keep them in motion—"

"*Has* he been rubbing them, Miss Gilmour?"

"Yes, so he says. If he hadn't, it's quite likely they'd be in a much worse condition. Rubbing with snow is said to help."

"He rubbed them himself? He didn't ... get anyone else to do that for him?"

"He said he rubbed them himself, yes. He spoke of no-one else." She sounded puzzled, glancing again at her father's solemn face.

"Then the rubbing has in fact helped him? If it had not taken place, he could have frost-bite already?"

"I think it might be reasonable to say that, Captain Ogilvie." She smiled at him, dimpling as she had done earlier. "Are you satisfied now? You have my recommendation that it would be beneficial if you were to set all the men to rubbing legs and arms!"

"I'll keep it in mind," he said, smiling back at her. "Thank you for your help, Miss Gilmour. It's much appreciated, I assure you." He accompanied the Gilmours back to their bivouac. It would soon be morning, and they would be on the march again; with luck they should reach the Khyber in the next two days unless there was more snow. As he went back to his own bivouac and tried to find sleep, Ogilvie reflected that Katharine Gilmour's report had not really helped his peace of mind; nor, in fact, could it lead him to any definite conclusion. Taggart-Blane *could* have been speaking the truth, he himself *could* have been misled by the darkness; on the other hand there was no reason to suppose that Mulata Din was in any different state from any of the others—indeed, Gilmour's daughter had suggested as much. Why, then, had Taggart-Blane picked on Mulata Din? *Why?* Possibly there was some innocent explanation; at all events, everything that was in Ogilvie urged him to believe so. To believe anything else of a brother officer was to diminish, in a sense, his whole belief in the integrity and honour of the British Army, in the concept of comradeship in arms.

* * *

The snow held off, and shortly after dawn the urgent march for the Khyber was resumed across a deep, crisp blanket of white but under clear skies and a thin, but very welcome, sun that sparkled along the wintry trees and mountain-tops rearing ahead, and turned the lying snow to a sea tinted with gold and pink and green. That sun brought men's spirits back to life a little, and in the keen snow-free air they marched better, and made good time. Once again, Taggart-Blane and Subedar Gundar Singh brought up the rear of the line, keeping watchful eyes on any stragglers. Ogilvie himself rode frequently to the rear, keeping an eye on Taggart-Blane as much as upon the marching column of sepoys. From time to time he rode with the womenfolk, trying to draw them out, to take Mrs. Gilmour's mind off the rigours of the journey by talking of happier things, of Peshawar and Simla, of England which neither of the women had seen for many years. But Mrs. Gilmour, clearly sick, was too preoccupied with her fears and her current discomfort, simply answering his tentative questions as briefly as possible, and offering no conversational openings in return. Ogilvie was relieved when Gilmour came up alongside his wife, and he was able, without offence or rudeness, to give his attention to Katharine.

"When do you think you'll see England again, Miss Gilmour?" he asked.

"That depends on my father, Captain Ogilvie. He loves India—he'd never settle at home again. Besides, his work is here."

"But he'll get leave?"

"Oh yes," she said. "He'll get a home leave next year, but

that doesn't mean to say he'll go home to England! My grandmother lives in South Africa, in Cape Town, and that's where we'll go, I expect."

"You sound as though you'd like to see England again?"

"Oh yes," she said, and seemed to catch her breath a little. "I'd love to, Captain Ogilvie. Just to see an English field again, and a quiet stream. A little Cotswold village... or Yorkshire... Wensleydale in summer, and Aysgarth Falls. The sound of—of *happy* water. It's so different out here." She gave a sudden violent shiver, one that had no connection with the terrible cold of Afghanistan. "So very different! The water sounds are—cruel, I think, is roughly the word. Harsh and discordant. Do you know what I mean?"

Slowly, frowning, he nodded. "Rushing rivers of war and death. Yes, I do know. I've seen so many men lost—" He checked himself; this was not the time to remind a young girl of what could lie ahead in the Khyber Pass. He kept to himself his memories of actions along high tracks with boiling tumults of water far below, of blood running with the water across the fords, of men and horses falling to the impact of the guns, of snipers' bullets, of bodies whirling away on the river's flood. He kept it to himself, yet knew that this girl had something similar in her mind. She had started to say something when she broke off, and looked up into the hills to their right. Ogilvie followed her glance and saw, as he had seen from time to time earlier, the wild-looking tribesmen watching distantly, with their rifles slung across their chests, brooding men in an eternal silence. Katharine shivered. "They never leave us alone, do they?"

"So long as they don't molest us, Miss Gilmour, we've no need to worry. They'll be reporting our progress back to Jarar Mahommed in Kunarja—that's all." He paused, seeing the girl lift a hand to her eyes to shade them. "Miss Gilmour, is the snow affecting your eyes?"

"Yes, it is—the glare—"

"I know. It's something we'll all be troubled with. Close your eyes from time to time, to rest them ... but otherwise, don't worry." He refrained from mentioning the possibility of snow blindness. "You were about to say something, weren't you? When you saw the Pathans on the crest?"

"Oh—yes! Simply that at the moment I'm so much more interested in England than in the Indians! Tell me about your leave, Captain Ogilvie, and let me enjoy a good old bout of homesickness!"

"All right, if that's what you want," he said, and he did so. He told her about London, about the music-halls, the summer-dusty green of the trees along the Mall, the hooves of the horses clopping along the wooden blocks of Piccadilly, of the Thames seen from Tower Bridge and from Westminster Bridge, half a world away. He spoke of Kensington Gardens and the gracious houses along the Bayswater Road, of parties at the great residences of Park Lane and Mayfair, of Her Majesty's Foot Guards beating out the solemn ceremony of Retreat on Horse Guards Parade, the rolling thunder of the brass and the drums echoing off the time-worn buildings of the Admiralty, the Foreign Office, the India Office itself, the bastions and symbols of England's might standing rock-fast in the heat of a London summer evening. He told her, as they rode on along the snow-covered Afghan track, of Scotland, and Corriecraig, of his uncle's splendid monster, the Panhard-Levassor, and of the chauffeur whom his uncle insisted on calling the 'engineer'. He told all this and more, but of one aspect of his leave he never spoke at all: Mary Archdale. He wasn't certain of his reasons for this omission; but after Major Gilmour had ridden up between them, and separated them in order to discuss the future of the march with Ogilvie, he realised in retrospect that Katharine Gilmour's eyes had held an unspoken query, as though she had suspected a reservation in his discourse, and was intrigued because of it...

When that night the column was fallen out, and bivouacs made, Ogilvie, with Taggart-Blane in mind, used their closer proximity to the Khyber as an excuse for doubling the watch. After consulting with Gilmour, he announced that Gundar Singh and the Major would take one turn of duty together, alternating with himself and Taggart-Blane. Taggart-Blane hunched his shoulders and looked the picture of misery, but said quietly, "Oh, all right, James, I know why this is, but I understand how you're placed considering what you believe. You're wrong, but there it is, you have to do what you think best."

"As commander of the column, I've many things to take into account."

"Yes, I know, I'm not really complaining." Taggart-Blane hesitated, then almost blurted out from lips that were blue with the penetrating cold, "James, I'd like to talk to you about—about something. Just a general talk, I mean. Would you mind?"

"Of course I wouldn't mind, but not just now." Ogilvie looked along the line of men waiting for the food to be brought up by the camp followers. With the going down of the day's sun their spirits had noticeably sunk again. "I want to see the sepoys settled down first. I only hope to God we don't get fresh snow during the night."

"Looks overcast and heavy again, doesn't it? God ... I feel I can't take any more of this bloody cold, it eats right into a man."

Ogilvie nodded. "It's the same for all of us, Alan. We'll have that talk by-and-by," he added, "if you think it'll help."

"Thank you, James."

"Come along with me, and we'll try and keep the sepoys' peckers up with a few words of hope!"

They went down the line of half-frozen, suffering men, and just before the last of the light went Ogilvie, glancing up, just happened to see the silhouette of two more tribesmen on the heights, tall, bearded men clutching those old-fashioned, long barrelled rifles with snaking bayonets affixed. Most probably they were more of Jarar Mahommed's retainers, indeed almost for a certainty they would be; but they were a grim reminder of the less amenable elements who might lie in wait ahead, inside the Khyber, when they moved into the areas where, as Gilmour had said, Jarar's edict did not necessarily run. There was much on James Ogilvie's mind as he walked with Taggart-Blane along the primitive bivouacs and chatted, so far as his command of the dialect allowed him, with the half-frozen sepoys. That night one of his fears was realised and the snow came down again, not this time with the wind to drive it, for the air was relatively quiet; but it drifted down solidly, silently, suffocatingly.

Ogilvie, whose watch it was when the snow set in, roused Gilmour. "Do we march or stay?" he asked.

Gilmour sat up, shivering, and studied the falling snow for a moment. "We'll not march," he said. "Not at night, in this. We don't want to lose ourselves, Ogilvie—but staying put has its dangers too. My advice would be, rouse the men and keep' em on the move. You know—doubling on the spot, as it were! Keep 'em well together, too—no dispersing."

"The general idea being to keep them on top of the snow—"

"Rather than under it, yes, that's it, Ogilvie. If necessary we'll have to hang on to the hillsides like goats ... anywhere where the damn stuff won't lie too deep. It'll be hell, but we'll come through, never fear!"

That night they lost eight sepoys and nineteen of the camp followers, all from exposure; and there was no opportunity for the talk with Taggart-Blane, a fact that Ogilvie was later bitterly to regret.

*   *   *

They managed, next morning when the snow had stopped falling, under the most appalling difficulties, to clear enough ground to bury the dead in shallow hacked-out graves which they covered with stones and boulders and fragments of rock, knowing that soon the graves would once again be deep beneath a covering of snow. The sick—those who had not quite died from the rigours of that terrible night of clinging, like Gilmour's hypothetical goats, to the hillsides—were placed in the commissariat carts or carried in makeshift litters by the camp followers, and the march was resumed under Gilmour's navigational guidance. Progress was a good deal slower now, the going much more laborious. Both Gilmour and Ogilvie were worried about the time factor. Again at intervals they could see the watchful tribesmen, the Ghilzais, on the crags and peaks, the still-silent rifles pointing down towards them as if to remind them of what would happen should they make a wrong move. They went along now without much conversation, no more indeed than was strictly necessary for the passing of orders, for everyone was too tired, too bone-weary to waste precious breath. They merely stumbled on, plodding one half-frozen foot before another and dragging their bodies painfully after it. Taggart-Blane was red-eyed and drawn, with a dead-white stubbly face, a face, Ogilvie thought, too young for its sprouting beard. He was riding as though in a trance. Ogilvie himself was keeping going by sheer will-power and doggedness, forcing himself not to give way to his almost overpowering urge to go to sleep in the saddle, steeled by the knowledge that his was the responsibility and he must not fail in his duty. Gilmour seemed almost untouched by the hardships, the hunger—for they were conserving all supplies by a strict rationing—and the lack of rest. The man seemed almost invigorated by hardship, in fact, glad to meet a challenge. His wife, on the other hand, was in a bad way now. She had been placed in a commissariat cart, drawn by mules and positioned at the head of the line of march, where Gilmour could keep a personal eye on her. The sick woman lay in the cart as though already dead, unmoving but with her eyes open, open and staring blankly at the sky through the gaps in the wind-flapped canvas hood. It was clear now that they would be lucky to bring her alive through the Khyber; and as they rode Gilmour, who had just remounted after trying to encourage his wife by his presence at her side, brought the matter up obliquely.

"It's God's will, Ogilvie. That's the one way to look at it."

Ogilvie knew what he meant. He said, "I'm most dreadfully sorry, Major. But you're looking on the worst side, aren't you?"

"Perhaps. I pray to God I am, Ogilvie. But we've so far only touched the fringes. I blame myself now. I should never have brought the women, in spite of Jarar ... but there, it's no good thinking along those lines, is it? What's done is done."

"We must always look for hope, Major. It's bad to—to even think of the worst."

"I agree with you, but certain matters must be discussed and must be planned for. Not to plan may well leave us in a greater difficulty at a moment when we are least able to cope with it." Gilmour hesitated, then went on in a voice harsh with his own emotion, "Ogilvie, if my wife should die whilst we are in the Khyber ... I should like to take her body through into India. What do you say to that?"

"It shall be whatever you wish, sir, you have my word on that."

"Thank you, Ogilvie, thank you with all my heart. But I must remind you there will be difficulties. The sepoys do not readily accept the carriage of the dead—they're such a superstitious bunch. Also, they know we'd not allow them to carry their own dead on the march even if they wanted to. It could appear invidious."

"I shall accept that if necessary."

"But you are in command, Ogilvie. Can I ask you to jeopardise our mission?" He lifted a hand and rubbed at his snow-affected eyes. "I *have* asked you—and I know I'm wrong to do so!"

"It's all right, Major."

"Wait. There are other aspects. Sometime or other we're going to be attacked. If this happens after my wife's death, then her body will need the same protection as if she were still alive. The Pathans ... their vile revenges, even against the dead. I think you understand me?"

"Yes, I do. In the circumstances, Major, is it wise to ask for this? If the protection is not fully effective—" He stopped, unable to put the rest into words, and not needing to.

Gilmour said, "For my part, yes, I'm being unwise. I hope the cold hasn't affected my judgment—I don't believe it has, though it is becoming extremely trying to us all already. But, you see, my wife has always expressed a horror of dying in Afghanistan and of perhaps having to be buried on Afghan soil. She has not been happy in Kunarja, Ogilvie. She detests Afghanistan. But she was happy among the English community in Peshawar. I shall feel it no less than my duty to see, to the fullest extent of my ability, that her

113

last wish is carried out. I think I failed her in life, Ogilvie. I must not fail her in death."

"Of course, I—"

"She has not liked being exiled from England. She was very fond of home, you know, very fond ... naturally, she realised I had a duty and that my life was out here, on the Frontier. I have never felt that I have sacrificed myself. But I may well have sacrificed her."

And now you must make amends, Ogilvie thought. He looked sideways at Gilmour, saw the reflection of the man's bitter thoughts, the thoughts that were taking charge of his face. It was late now to make amends; and amends could prove cumbersome, dangerous and foolish. But Gilmour's mind was made up and it clearly meant everything to him that he should do this thing, and Ogilvie had not the heart to put forward further objections. He said no more; they must concentrate on keeping Mrs. Gilmour alive, though from what he had seen of her as she lay so inertly in the commissariat wagon he felt this to be a hope unlikely of fulfilment. They rode on in silence, each occupied with his own thoughts and fears for the future.

Two days later, a depleted company who had left more dead behind them on the march, they entered the Khyber.

9

THEY HAD MOVED past Torkham, the fortress at the Khyber's
western end, entering the pass without incident. Shadowed
by the high peaks of the Safed Koh they had made agon-
izingly slow progress along the icy, snow-covered track that
sometimes ran through the floor of the pass and sometimes
ran loftily above the gorges, above the terrible drops down
sheer rock sides on to jagged boulders and the rushing river,
the waters that Katharine Gilmour had, with so much truth,
called cruel. Again and again—more and more often now—
they had seen themselves to be under observation from the
hawk-faced men on the heights. Word of their coming
would be passed ahead; this they knew. What they did not
know, what they could not be certain of despite the assurance of Jarar Mahommed's personal representative who still
accompanied them, was whether or not the wild Pathans on
the peaks belonged to tribes friendly, or tribes opposed, to
the Ghilzai leader in Kunarja.

"It's almost too friendly," Gilmour said after a whole day's
march had brought not even a stray sniper's bullet. "It could
be a good sign, of course—a sign that Jarar's in full control
and we'll get through intact. But it could be the precise
opposite—it's possible we're being drawn into a trap, nice
and deep!"

"And you think that's it, Major?"

Gilmour hesitated. "I do, yes. With my knowledge of the
tribes ... yes, I'm afraid so. It's just a feeling, perhaps,

Ogilvie—but it's a strong one. I sense danger—more with every mile. As I've told you, Jarar has many enemies."

"Well, we just have to go forward, Major."

"Right—we have!" Gilmour, his face and hands blue with cold, stared around the crests, frowning. Once again they were passing through a snow-free period and the skies were relatively clear though far from bright; the peaks stood out well, sentinels over the brooding silence of the pass. Vultures, apart from themselves, were currently the only signs of life. Vultures were the inevitable accompaniments of any march of men along the passes or in the plains, the horrible predators that waited for the next meal, veritable symbols of death-in-life. For the moment, even the watchful tribesmen were absent, though it could be presumed that the straggling sepoys were under covert observation from somewhere in the fastnesses of the mountain-tops. Suddenly Gilmour said, "Ogilvie, my wife is sinking. It's not good. If only she could be more protected from this terrible cold.

"I'm very sorry, Major."

"It'll come hard on Katharine."

"Yes. Does she realise?"

Gilmour nodded. "I believe so. I've said nothing, and she is putting on a good face for her mother's benefit—but yes, I think she knows it can't be long now." He said no more after that, and seemed sunk in his own thoughts as they moved on. Ogilvie was in a fever of impatience now as gradually the distance to safety lessened but left so far still to go, so far in which so much could happen. He was concerned still about Taggart-Blane; the exigencies of the march had not yet allowed him to have that talk the subaltern had wanted, and now in any case Taggart-Blane seemed to be avoiding his company, remaining surlily aloof during the halts for rest and meals, carrying out his duties and then going off alone to sit by himself. He was looking more and more pinched, more and more dog-weary like the rest of them; but there was something else in his eyes—a deep-seated gnawing anxiety that showed only too clearly where his real anxiety lay. Such preoccupation was bad for the conduct of the march, and as they rode along that day, Ogilvie determined that he would have that heart-to-heart talk with Taggart-Blane during the forthcoming night's bivouac, though in all conscience he felt he could offer little relief to the man's mind.

As it happened his good intention was once again frustrated. The column had only just been halted for the night's camp and the sentries posted, when Gilmour, who had spent the last hours stumbling along on foot, grey-faced now, by his wife's side, came up to Ogilvie and said, "She's gone. My wife's dead."

"Oh ... I'm sorry. How's Miss Gilmour taking it?"

"I don't know. She's very pent-up. Well now, Ogilvie, we have to face the future—the immediate future." Gilmour swayed, and Ogilvie reached out a hand to steady him. "Your promise. That stands?"

Ogilvie nodded. "Of course. I gave you my word."

"I'm offering you the opportunity to withdraw. It's night, and we're resting anyway. The digging of a grave will cause no delay. Naturally, it can only be a very shallow one ... but we have an abundance of rocks and boulders to build a cairn."

"I'll not withdraw, Major. We'll take Mrs. Gilmour through to British India, to Peshawar, and proper burial where she wished it."

There were tears in Gilmour's eyes now. "You realise the risks, Ogilvie, the difficulties?"

"Yes."

"And you still ... ?"

"Yes, Major."

"Damn it all, it's totally inadequate to say thank you, Ogilvie. I must ... go to my daughter. Meanwhile, none of the sepoys knows. We must try to keep them in ignorance."

Gilmour turned on his heel and walked away through the deep snow towards the wagon where his wife's body lay. Looking after him, Ogilvie saw Katharine, faintly in the gathering dark, move from behind the wagon to meet him, and saw father and daughter embrace, and then, feeling like an eavesdropper on grief, he turned away and walked down the line, as he had for so many nights now, to see the meagre food distributed under guard, and the men settled into their refuge behind the jags of rock.

Sending for Taggart-Blane, he told the subaltern of Mrs. Gilmour's death.

"I'm sorry to hear that, James, very sorry."

"I've promised the Major we'll take her on to Peshawar for burial, Alan. That means a strong guard on the commissariat cart, in case of any sudden attack. But I'd prefer it if the news didn't spread that she's actually died. The sepoys—"

"You'll never keep that dark!"

"We can try at all events. So far, no-one knows except you and I. The Gilmours'll put the best face on it that they can, and if the girl's seen to weep, or break down, it can be attributed to her mother's *likely* death, but not to her actual death. Understand?"

"Yes, I suppose so. What about Gundar Singh? Is he to know?"

"Yes, I think he'll have to—I'll talk to him myself, soon. All you have to do is to keep your mouth shut."

"That's all you trust me to do, isn't it!"

"No, it's not, and you know it. For God's sake, man, stop this brooding! You've got the makings of a good officer—you've stood the march splendidly—"

"I feel bloody awful, as though I can't march another step, the cold's right in my guts, and if you call that splendid—"

"We all feel the same, and the fact that you're keeping going is what's splendid. Don't denigrate your own capabilities, Alan. The world doesn't like a boaster, true, but it never rewards self-abnegation!" He paused, and laid a hand on Taggart-Blane's shoulder. "You know very well what the trouble is, and so do I, of course. I told you once before, you have to put that behind you for now, you simply *have* to, for all our sakes."

"Do you expect me," Taggart-Blane asked bitterly, "to forget the whole thing as easily as all that?"

"No. But I do expect you to make an effort. When the thought comes into your mind, push it out again before it gets a grip! It can be done, you know—"

"Really? Do you really think so? When you're faced with utter ruin, the complete collapse of a career, the disgrace of

118

your family, being bloody well drummed out of your regiment, all because somebody's made a bloody great mistake—like *you* have?"

"If it's a mistake, nothing will be—"

"*If* it's a mistake! You see, James, you *don't* believe me, you simply don't trust me any more. Do you imagine the knowledge of *that* gives me any confidence—or any incentive to forget and look bloody happy? Do you? Or are you a complete bloody idiot?"

Ogilvie hesitated; he knew he had in a sense been preconditioned towards a disbelief in Taggart-Blane's protestations of innocence, preconditioned by those remarks from his uncle, from Lord Dornoch, from the officers of the sepoy battalion and from the sepoys' havildar-major. With these remarks going through his mind again, he said, "Of course I realise how rotten it is for you, but never make the mistake of thinking yourself already judged. That's not the case at all, and of course I trust you. Now, what about that talk you wanted with me?"

"I don't want it now."

"Don't be such an obstinate ass. I'm perfectly willing to talk—'

"No, thanks. I can cope with my own problems, James, without help from you or anyone else. It might have helped to talk earlier, but not now. The time for that is past—it's too late."

Ogilvie looked at him sharply. "How d'you mean, too late?"

"I don't need it any more. Now, for God's sake, leave me alone, can't you?"

'If that's really what you want—"

"It is! Just tell me the night's orders, that's all. Are the watches to be the same as usual?"

Ogilvie shook his head. "I'm leaving Gilmour out tonight. The man's swaying on his feet, and though he may feel he'd rather do a duty turn to keep his mind occupied, I want him to sleep—or if he doesn't sleep, at least to be handy by his daughter. But as the only other British officer, I'll want you to be in charge of a watch, so you won't be standing it with me."

"Is this a sop?"

"No, it isn't, but it's proof that I trust you. I'll take my watch with Gundar Singh, and you'll take yours with your havildar, whatsisname—"

"Bandra Negi."

"Right. Now, if you'd like that talk after all—"

"No, thanks. I appreciate what you're doing, all the same. God, I'm bloody well frozen." Taggart-Blane turned away, then halted and looked back. "Who'll take the first guard duty, James?"

"I will. I'll have you and Bandra Negi roused out at midnight."

Taggart-Blane nodded and went off along the trodden snow and was soon lost to sight. Ogilvie stood, throwing his arms about his body and thinking, wondering whether he had in fact made a foolish decision after all. On the whole, he fancied not. Taggart-Blane would surely not repeat his indiscretion! He was a desperately worried young man already; the last thing he would do would be to make matters so much worse that he would stand condemned for certain.

* * *

Before settling down into their sorry bivouacs, Gilmour and his daughter spoke to Ogilvie. Katharine Gilmour was stiff-faced, keeping what seemed to be an iron grip on her emotions, but her eyes, haunted and shadowed eyes, were a more faithful indication of her feelings. Ogilvie felt desperately sorry for her and her father; this dreadful winter march through the Khyber snows was bad enough without a very personal loss to turn it into more of a nightmare; and the very taking of the body, in its undignified bier, through difficult and probably hostile territory must be a heart-wrenching business for them both.

Inadequately, he felt, he expressed his sympathy to Katharine Gilmour, and she nodded without replying. Gilmour said, "With regard to the secrecy, Ogilvie ... we'll keep it up as long as we can, which in fact is not likely to be very long. I've spoken already to the mule-driver—we must trust in him."

"I'd forgotten about him," Ogilvie said. "Do you think we *can* trust him?"

Gilmour shrugged. "If we can't, it's too bad. There's no more we can do." He glanced at his daughter's face, then gestured meaningly at Ogilvie: he seemed only now to realise that this was a painful matter to discuss in her presence.

"Is there anything I can do, Miss Gilmour?" Ogilvie asked. "If there are any extra comforts you need, I'll see what can be provided, though—"

"You've been very kind all along, Captain Ogilvie," she said, her voice flat, quite toneless. "I'm sure there's nothing else you can do now, and I shall not ask for anything that's not available to anyone else in any case. My mother would have said the same thing. She had a very strong sense of duty. If she had not had that, she would not be dead." There was a lash in her voice now, and Ogilvie saw her father flinch from it. "She would not have been in Afghanistan at all. But now that she *has* died ... even if the Khyber is territory largely run by Afghans, I think she would rather have been buried here, than be a cumbrance to a military campaign!"

"My dear, such a word—"

"But I say it again, Father, a *cumbrance*. She would have hated that! You are wrong, wrong to do this—"

"But her one wish always, Katharine—"

"Was to do her duty! And how, Father, do *you* know what her wishes ever were? How often did you pay the smallest attention to them, if they conflicted with what *you* had made up your mind to do?"

"I, too, had my duty, Katherine. Now it is my duty to carry out what I know to have been her very dearest wish."

"I think—"

"There is no more to be said. No more, I tell you, Katharine." Gilmour turned from his daughter's passionate face, his own stony and closed. "Ogilvie, there is no change, no change at all. If you will excuse us now—"

"Of course, sir. Good night, Miss Gilmour." Ogilvie turned away, feeling distressed. The girl had spoken cruelly enough, which he would have guessed was totally out of character and the result of immense pressures of grief and physical hardship, but there could have been truth behind her words. The British Raj did not always exact its sacrifice in terms of death in battle, nor did it confine its demands to the menfolk alone. For a fleeting moment Ogilvie reflected, as he moved with difficulty along the track, where the snow was being blown into flurries by a rising, dismal-sounding wind, that the Queen-Empress, sitting alone but powerfully, so well cushioned inside the thick, battlemented walls of Windsor Castle, must surely have ice in her veins and gunpowder in her head if she could remain so aloof and confident when her position and her regality were maintained on a scaffold of so much suffering.

*   *   *

Ogilvie awoke abruptly, very suddenly, fancying he had heard rifle-shots coming through the now snow-filled wind. He scrambled to his feet, shaking off a blanket covered with snowflakes, and came out from behind his large boulder to meet the wind full force as it funnelled along the pass. It was totally dark still, a curtain of black with no glimmer anywhere. Faintly, he heard shouts, then more rifle- or revolver-shots, again distantly.

He could see no-one.

Feeling ahead of himself, moving by touch and memory, he found the Gilmours' bivouac and found both of them wide awake, with Gilmour coming out with his revolver in his hand. "What's the trouble?" Gilmour shouted in his ear. "Bandits?"

"I don't know yet. I wanted to make sure Miss Gilmour was all right first. I'm going to find out now."

"I'll come with you—"

"No, Major. I'd much rather you stayed with your daughter. It'll relieve me of one anxiety. Please."

"Very well, but let me know ..."

Ogilvie didn't hear the rest; he was already moving towards the sound of the last rifle-fire, though this had stopped now. All along the line, the sepoys were struggling to their feet, shouted awake by the havildars and naiks. Towards the rear, where the camp followers were milling around in the beginnings of panic, he found Havildar Bandra Negi.

"What is it?" he shouted above the wind, almost falling over the man.

"Sahib, it is bandits on the hillside, but nothing of importance, and we have driven them off already—"

"They'll be back! Have we any casualties?"

"I cannot say yet, Sahib—"

"Where is Taggart Sahib?"

"Here, James." Ogilvie swung round; Taggart-Blane had come up behind him. "It's all right, we've coped. I'd have called you, of course, if it had gone on any longer—but it didn't!" He sounded highly excited, almost feverishly so.

Ogilvie said, "Well done, Alan. We'll stay on the alert now, till we move out. They could try again, you know. In the meantime, we'll see to any wounded. Bandra Negi?"

"Sahib!"

"Check if we have any casualties, and report to me. Also, send along the personal representative of Jarar Mahommed."

The havildar went off. To Taggart-Blane Ogilvie said, "From now on, we're going to be in the thick of it. We've probably reached the end of Jarar Mahommed's area of jurisdiction now. It's been bad already. Now it's going to be worse." He looked all around, trying to pierce the thick darkness of the night, but he could make out nothing, though he fancied there was just a touch of lightening in the heavy sky. With Taggart-Blane he moved down the line of bivouacs as the men were dispersed by the N.C.O.s along the track, ready now and waiting for anything that might happen. It would, in Ogilvie's experience, be rare if the attack was not resumed before the approaching dawn.

Nothing happened, however; there was silence from the hillside, silence from the sepoy line too, apart from the occasional snick of rifle-bolts, and metallic sounds as equipment shifted on the watchful bodies.

Bandra Negi was taking his time; there was a definite lightening by the time he came stumbling up, and Ogilvie, with some surprise, noted a staring anxiety and fear in the havildar's eyes as the man approached and saluted. "Well, Bandra Negi?" he asked.

"Sahib, there is one casualty. A man dead. There are no wounded."

"Then we've been lucky, Bandra Negi! Who is the dead man?"

"Sahib, it is Mulata Din."

"*Mulata Din!*" Involuntarily, Ogilvie glanced at Taggart-Blane, standing by his side. He saw fear reflected in the subaltern's face: a terrible fear, an almost crazed fear that, however, quickly vanished as Taggart-Blane got control of himself. But it was a naked, self-revelatory exposure of inner feelings that increased Ogilvie's own concern. He turned to the havildar, keeping his voice as level, as dispassionate, as he could. He said, "I'm sorry, Bandra Negi. He must be buried, and quickly—" He broke off, having noted something odd in the man's bearing. "Yes, Bandra Negi, what else have you to say?"

"Mulata Din was shot in the head, Sahib."

"Yes?"

"Sahib, the bullet passed through, to embed in the ground beneath him." Bandra Negi extended an open palm. "This is the bullet, Sahib."

Touched now by a hideous fear of his own, Ogilvie took the bullet and examined it. The light was poor still, but he needed no light. The feel, the outline, was enough: Ogilvie had handled too many such bullets not to know it immediately and for certain. The bullet had been fired from a British Army revolver. A moment's thought told Ogilvie that the attacking bandits, though they might well be in possession of stolen or captured British arms, would be highly unlikely to use a close-range weapon such as a revolver in anything other than hand-to-hand fighting. Unless there had been any incursions into the sepoys' bivouacs by the attackers, the only revolvers that could have fired that bullet were few enough: Major Gilmour, himself, Taggart-Blane, Gundar Singh and the four havildars were armed with revolvers. *No-one else.*

Ogilvie asked, "Did the tribesmen enter our lines, Bandra Negi?"

"No, Sahib."

"Not to your knowledge?"

"Sahib, I am certain no bandits came near the bivouacs. Not one was seen by me or by any man I have spoken to."

"Then how do you account for this killing, Bandra Negi?"

The havildar hesitated, then said, "Sahib, it is ill to make accusations, but..."

"Yes, Bandra Negi?"

"I have no more than my thoughts, Sahib."

"Then you will tell me your thoughts, Bandra Negi. That is my order."

"But Sahib, I cannot—"

"You will find me a hard man to deal with, if you do not obey at once, Bandra Negi."

"Yes, Sahib." The havildar's voice was low and full of distress, and he seemed shrivelled by more than the biting cold. He glanced briefly towards Taggart-Blane, and Ogilvie, following that sudden shift of the eyes, saw the horror written deep into the subaltern's working face. Then Bandra Negi went on, his very breath crackling and freezing as he spoke, "Sahib ... there is a havildar—Lal Binodinand—I saw him coming from the direction of the bivouac of Mulata Din, just before I joined Taggart Sahib, when the attack had started. Taggart Sahib will support this. He also was there, and must have seen Lal Binodinand."

Ogilvie looked at the subaltern, saw the chattering teeth. "Is this right, Mr. Taggart-Blane?"

White-faced, Taggart-Blane nodded. "Quite right."

Withholding comment on Taggart-Blane's own proximity to the dead man at the relevant time, Ogilvie turned again to the havildar. "What are you suggesting, Bandra Negi?" he asked.

"Sahib ... that Mulata Din was murdered, deliberately shot through the head. It could have happened no other way than at close quarters. The bullet must have come from immediately above the head, it was not fired at an angle, from the hillsides."

"And you suggest further, that it was Havildar Lal Binodinand who fired this bullet? Is this what you are saying?"

Bandra Negi hung his head. "Yes, Sahib. You asked, and so I answered, and I did my duty."

"Yes, it was your duty." Ogilvie took a deep breath, and asked the next question, one he was bound to ask: "Bandra Negi, on what do you base your accusation, other than the apparent proximity of Lal Binodinand to Mulata Din? Where lies the motive? Was there, perhaps, bad blood ... a quarrel?"

"Yes, Sahib. There was much bad blood."

"On what count, Bandra Negi? What was the reason for this bad blood?"

After just one more fleeting glance at Taggart-Blane, the havildar's face closed up tight. "Sahib, I cannot say—I do not know."

"Think, Bandra Negi. Think well!"

The havildar shook his head. "I do not know, Sahib."

"Are you sure?" Ogilvie studied the man's face closely. "This is the truth?"

"It is the truth, Sahib. I can say only this—that it may have been the terrible cold of this march, and the snow that affects men's minds."

Bandra Negi was shaking a little, but the face was set obstinately. Further probing at this stage would obviously be a waste of time. "Very well, Bandra Negi," Ogilvie said. "Now go, and bring Lal Binodinand to me here. Say nothing to him of why I want him. While I am talking to him, go again, and bring the other two havildars to me, to wait at a distance until I make a sign for them. Bring also the sepoys who were bivouacked next to Mulata Din."

"Sahib!" Bandra Negi saluted and turned about. When he had gone Ogilvie said, "Well, Alan?"

"Well, what, James?" Taggart-Blane's eyes flickered from left to right; the subaltern was extremely ill-at-ease.

"So Mulata Din's frost-bite has been laid to rest."

"It would seem so."

"I was wondering..."

"What were you wondering?"

Ogilvie shrugged. "If you had any comment to make, that's all."

"I? No—I have no comment. I'm sorry—as I would be at the death of any man, especially by murder. It's pretty horrible, isn't it?"

"Yes, it is."

There was a silence between them, as they stood there in that grey, cold dawn. Taggart-Blane's cheeks were as grey as the dawn itself, as haggard now as the bare Afghan hills. After a moment he said roughly, "Now, look here, James, what are you suggesting?"

"At this stage, nothing. Nevertheless, there is one thing I must ask of you."

"Well, ask, then! Hurry, before I bloody well freeze!"

Stiffly, reluctantly, Ogilvie said, "Hand me your revolver, if you please."

"If I please? And if I *don't* please?"

"Then I shall take it from you."

Taggart-Blane gave a high-sounding laugh. "By God, you'll need assistance to do that, I can tell you!"

"Don't let us make a scene of this, Alan." Ogilvie was sweating in spite of the intense cold. "Give me your revolver —don't be more of a bloody fool just now than you can help—for God's sake, man, don't you see I *have* to do this, and don't you see it's better if it's done privately, between the two of us?"

"I see that you're a bastard—that's all I see!"

"There are times when one has to be. Now—your revolver." He reached out a hand. Taggart-Blane backed away, gave another high, almost hysterical laugh and reached for the revolver at his belt. He spun the weapon and caught the barrel as if to hand the butt to Ogilvie, but instead, with a swift and sudden movement, he flung the revolver in to the air, away to his left, in the direction opposite the hillside from where the recent attack had come. It went up spinning, in a wide, flat arc, then dropped, There was no sound of its landing, and Ogilvie knew very well why: the bivouacs had been made that night on the track where they had fallen out—almost literally— and a matter of a score of yards to one side was a precipice descending sheer to a rocky gorge and a fast, tumbling river.

"Now get it if you can, you bastard!" Taggart-Blane cried,

shouting the words into Ogilvie's face with a kind of triumph. Blood dripped into the snow at his feet, but he seemed not to notice, not even to be aware of the strips of flesh torn from the insides of his fingers where his ungloved hand had touched the bare, freezing metal of the revolver.

10

NOTHING WAS SAID to Gilmour, other than that an apparent bandit attack had been repulsed with only one casualty; Ogilvie didn't want to bring more worry to Gilmour at the time of his own loss. At full light the hillside was scoured for casualties amongst the attackers, but nothing whatsoever was found. Ogilvie was left with another anxiety: had Mulata Din's killer staged an alarm simply as cover for his own misdeed? It was not unknown along the Frontier lands for men to fire at shadows, and such would not have appeared unduly remarkable this time. No-one among the sepoys, it was discovered, had actually seen any bandits, nor had they seen any answering gun-flashes from the hillside after the British rifles had opened; and the Pathan from Kunarja, the representative officer from Jarar Mahommed's bodyguard, had been as baffled as Ogilvie and had been unable to help.

Another worry, also, accompanied Ogilvie as the march was resumed: Lal Binodinand, under close questioning, had confessed his enmity towards Mulata Din, and had given a reason for it, a reason that had brought no comfort whatever to James Ogilvie: the havildar, who, it seemed, had regarded the young sepoy as his own personal protégé, had become jealous of the British officer, Taggart Sahib. Whatever might happen now, the good name of the Royal Strathspeys was going to be dragged through some very filthy mud. Lal Binodinand had protested his complete innocence of the killing, but, after an agonizing half-hour of indecision, Ogilvie had felt obliged to hold the havildar in arrest pending a report to the military authorities in Peshawar; and Lal Binodinand was now marching under the not-too-obvious escort of one of the naiks and two sepoys. Ogilvie had taken the decision with great distaste; it went against the grain to make any man march in arrest through the Khyber in such terrible conditions of weather and possible danger. He was well aware that he was perhaps going too closely by the book; but felt that on balance, and in all the circumstances, this was not a matter upon which he could properly exercise an officer's discretion, however indecisive his investigation had proved. The men who had been bivouacked nearest to Mulata Din had been of no help, repeating again and again that they had seen no-one. As to the revolvers, both Bandra Negi and Lal Binodinand had produced empty chambers for inspection; so had the other two havildars. All the bullets, they said, had been fired into the darkness, which could have been perfectly true and could scarcely be questioned. There had been no need to check Gilmour's revolver; thus, only Taggart-Blane's remained unaccounted for, but this was possibly unimportant for he, also, whatever the facts, could have claimed six shots at the enemy as well. The fact of his throwing the weapon into the chasm could have been no more than an act of childish temper at being regarded as suspect: on the other hand...

Ogilvie hardly dared dwell on the implications. He knew very well that Taggart-Blane had had a motive for the killing, and, now that Lal Binodinand had spoken of his jealousy, the sepoys might very well know too. There could be trouble over Ogilvie's action, or lack of it, in not also putting the officer in arrest.

Meanwhile, with two corpses on its hands now, the march continued.

*   *   *

"You think I did it, don't you, James?"

The question was abruptly put, without warning:

Taggart-Blane had ridden up the line from the rear, leaving his post without orders to do so. It was on the end of Ogilvie's tongue to send him back with a flea in his ear; but he saw that the subaltern needed to have it out with him. Taggart-Blane looked really ill now, ill with worry and fear and the rigours of the long haul from Kunarja as they began to make the approach to the area which led below the frowning fortress of Landi Khotal, high-perched on its lofty peak to guard the passage of the Khyber.

Ogilvie shrugged and said: "It's not for me to think anything."

"Oh, don't be quite so bloody military! Don't always go by Queen's Regulations, dear James. I told you once what Cunningham said. Too serious, too stiff. Too bloody *rigid*, I'd call you. You have a mind—or I suppose you had once. Has the army turned you into a machine like all the others?"

"I hope it hasn't." Ogilvie gave a short laugh, felt his iced-up lips crack. "I don't think it has. What do you want me to tell you?"

"That you believe me. That you don't think I shot that sepoy."

"That hasn't arisen. I've never asked you that question."

"No, but it's what you may be thinking. That's what I want to get straight." Taggart-Blane paused. "Do you think I *will* be asked that question, in Peshawar?"

"Why should you be?"

"Oh," the subaltern said with a touch of passion, "for God's sake, don't let's fence with words now! You know very well you've had those other suspicions—I tell you again, they're groundless, but you must surely have them in mind!"

"It's pointless to talk about all that, Alan. I'm only the company commander. This is a long way above my head, and anything I say, when the time comes, will only be opinion. It won't be evidence."

"You have no evidence."

"I have nothing to say about that and in any case my thoughts don't matter ... but in so far as they do—to you, that is—you have the evidence of them in what I've done in putting Lal Binodinand in arrest. Isn't that good enough?"

"Well, perhaps. I don't know. I wish I could feel you really believed me, James." He hesitated. "I'm sorry about that damn stupid business over the revolver. I apologise for my rudeness, my utter boorishness."

"It was stupid from your own point of view. Damn stupid. Don't worry about my feelings! They don't matter."

"I hadn't fired any rounds anyway. I didn't see any point in blazing away into the dark with a revolver, like those havildars."

"Then it's a pity you chucked it away, isn't it?"

Taggart-Blane shrugged. "Oh, not really, I could have reloaded, couldn't I?"

"I'd have known that, if I'd felt the barrel. It'd still have been warm—I was pretty quickly on the scene, you remember."

"Oh, come, James! By the time you asked me for it, it'd have been stone cold."

"Being precipitate's never a good thing, anyway. Bear that in mind for the future!"

"If there is one! It's obvious Lal Binodinand's going to involve me to some extent."

Ogilvie nodded. "That seems likely enough. On the other hand ..." He paused, not wishing to put his thoughts into words, to be too precise. He had some knowledge of the British in India by now. They had a habit of looking after their own. It could well be that Lal Binodinand would be seen as a handy scapegoat, a native who could be called a liar if and when he made any reference to a British officer. Yes, even possibly in a case of murder! Had this business remained at the level of indecency, Ogilvie now realised, it could have been treated on a domestic basis with no dirty linen being washed in public at all. But murder ... perhaps not, after all. And even if it were ...

"Well, go on," Taggart-Blane prompted. "You were saying, *on the other hand* ...?"

"Just thoughts. Now listen. I've put Lal Binodinand in arrest as you know, but ... Alan, if you have anything to hide—*if*—then I doubt you'll find any peace of mind in the future, if you allow Lal Binodinand to be your whipping boy."

"I've nothing to hide—I told you!"

"Then in that case—"

"But they wouldn't hang Lal Binodinand without proof, and when they have that, then I'm in the clear."

"Yes. I doubt if they'll hang the man without such proof as can be called adequate, certainly. But in army terms, in the circumstances of the Frontier, adequate is an arguable quantity. I think you'd do well to ponder on that."

"So you don't believe me."

"I've never said that."

"No. Now I'll say something instead. I've said it before. You're a rotten bastard, Captain bloody Ogilvie!" Taggart-Blane wheeled his horse suddenly, causing it to rear with dangerously flailing hooves, and went back towards the end of the column, his cheeks flaming, his mouth compressed into a hard, bitter line. Ogilvie rode on with a set face. He was in no two minds about what he would say when questioned. Whatever might be his feelings for his regiment, he would never be able to stand by and see a man hanged until he was beyond all doubt proven guilty; and would be in honour bound to substantiate Lal Binodinand's statement that there had been more than a proper friendliness existing between Mulata Din and a British officer.

*   *   *

In a sense, the fact of Mulata Din's death had been a help. A sepoy's body was being carried onward and not left in Afghan-dominated territory; thus, when the news spread, as in fact it did quickly, that Mrs. Gilmour had died and was being taken on with the march, the murmurs of there being one law for the British and another for the sepoys themselves were stillborn. Death was still not a happy accompaniment to a march, but at least the sahibs were playing fair. The line of men stumbled on, their senses dulled into a state of almost total passivity by the cruel hand of winter. The track was an abomination now, covered with a layer of snow and ice, while far below in the gorge the water lay solid, overcome at last by the bitter cold. In this gorge they lost some of the mule-train, and with the animals

133

went too much of the food and ammunition; the food in particular could ill be spared. Sadly enough, the occasional sepoy who went over could be better spared than the commisariat: in a march that appeared, so far at any rate, to be protected from attack by the fiat of Jarar Mahommed, loss of personnel meant only less mouths to feed. Losses among the camp followers were even easier to sustain. That nondescript band of low-grade humanity had long since ceased its monkey-like chattering, and was plodding on in silent misery, even the tears of the women and children freezing upon their cheeks as they were caught by the bitter wind, the wind that penetrated any covering that man could devise for his protection.

They passed below Landi Khotal, backed to the north by the great mountain of Tor Tsappar. Here they moved with greater security, for the fortress was currently held by the Khyber Rifles, an irregular regiment of militia serving under British Political Officers, and an attack by tribesmen was unlikely in the vicinity. As they came under the fort, Ogilvie made an attempt to communicate by heliograph; but there was too little sun, and the sentries, it appeared, were not as alert as they might have been. There was no answer from the fort, and the weary column of men saw no sign of life at all as they struggled along the track.

It was after another night, and another day's march, when they had left Landi Khotal well behind them and yet one more night was approaching, that the attack came. They were on the lookout for a suitable place to make camp; the sepoys were moving like automatons, numbed into complete insensitivity, stumbling along with nothing more than their own instinct for survival to keep them going, with nearly half their number now sick and lying in the commissariat carts or tied to the backs of the plodding, weary mules. Gilmour was riding with Ogilvie, ahead of his wife's body. The horses were having almost a worse time of it than the men, with their hooves sliding and slithering on ice where the snow was not half-way to their hocks. Katharine, whose sick horse had had to be shot soon after passing Landi Khotal, was riding in a cart behind her dead mother.

Gilmour, as they moved into a narrow sector of the pass,

had remarked that the march was almost over. "A little under ten miles to Jamrud now, Ogilvie, that's all."

"All!"

"Oh, I'm far from making light of it, I'm as wearied by the conditions as anyone else, but the worst should be over now. With Jamrud virtually in range, we're coming into—" He broke off, then said sharply, "Ahead there! D'you see anything, Ogilvie?"

"No . . ." Ogilvie, screwing up his eyes against the snow's painful whiteness, stared ahead. Then, a moment later, he saw it: the movement of a rifle against the white. "Yes, by God I do! Strewth, the hillsides are coming alive with men!" He turned in his saddle, stood in the stirrups as his horse came round, and shouted down the line: *"Scatter, get off the track . . . take what cover you can find behind the rocks!"* Before he had finished passing the order, the firing had started from ahead, while more bullets swept down from snipers concealed on the heights above them. There was utter confusion along the track; as the ranks broke men and animals milled about, carts were overturned, there were screams and oaths as the bullets struck. Alongside Ogilvie the naik in charge of the sepoys escorting Mrs. Gilmour's body died with blood gushing from his throat. Ogilvie saw the Major wheel his horse to bring it and himself between the tribesmen ahead and the body in the cart. From the rear, Taggart-Blane rode up, pushing his horse expertly through the panic-stricken sepoys.

"It's a bloody mob back there!" he said.

Ogilvie nodded. "Get the men clear of the track at once, and see that every man who can hold a rifle, sick or not, is ready to fire back from cover—"

"Can't we mount a charge, James?"

"Not yet—we're a rabble, not an army! Besides, the terrain's not right for a charge—these bastards know how to choose their own ground!" Ogilvie stared around him. "Where's that man of Jarar's, his personal representative—"

"Dead, James. He got one of the first bullets."

"Damn! Well, come on, get the men in cover, and when we've done that, we'll think about re-forming when the time's right. Get a move on!"

Taggart-Blane nodded, turned and rode back coolly enough, shouting the native troops into some kind of military awareness, urging them with oaths off the track, riding them off with his horse; they were too weary, too close to exhaustion, even to think for themselves now, to see where comparative safety lay. Very many died before the track was clear of men. Ogilvie, with a bullet through the flesh of his upper right arm, stayed on the littered track until all the sepoys were clear and the two carts containing the bodies of Mrs. Gilmour and Mulata Din had been drawn into shelter behind a large jut of rock that gave overhead cover as well. Then he took cover himself behind the same rock, with Gilmour and his daughter. There was no sign now of Taggart-Blane; but a few moments after Ogilvie had moved behind the rock, Subedar Gundar Singh appeared, with blood running down his face from a glancing bullet, and reported that Taggart Sahib was rounding up the camp followers with the assistance of Havildar Bandra Negi.

"I have come for orders, Ogilvie Sahib," he said.

Ogilvie nodded, and peered over the top of the rock. "Right, Gundar Singh. I want you to pass the word to all the men, that they're to remain in cover until further orders. They're to return the fire whenever they sight a good target, but there's to be no indiscriminate firing. We may be held here a long time for all I know, and we must not waste ammunition. That's vital. See to that, if you please, Gundar Singh."

"There is the question of the commissariat—"

"Yes, we can't risk losing our supplies. You'll have to organise a party to get the carts into cover—or if that can't be done, see that the carts are well covered by the rifles. You understand?"

"I understand, Sahib, yes."

"Then off you go, Gundar Singh."

The subedar moved away; in the last of the day's light Ogilvie saw him drop to the ground and wriggle cautiously away on his stomach, across the snow, dangerously slowly because of that deep white carpet, making for the next piece of cover. When Gundar Singh was out of sight, with the enemy bullets snicking into the snow behind him, Ogilvie turned to Gilmour. "How long d'you think it'll take for word of this to reach Landi Khotal?" he asked.

Gilmour gave a humourless laugh. "Not this side of Christmas, I'm afraid! You don't imagine those tribesmen will let anyone get away? We're bound to be cut off to the rear."

"You don't think the ambush is likely to be seen or heard by any friendly tribes? Tribes friendly either to the British or to Jarar Mahommed?"

"Well, that's always possible, but we can't bank on it. I—"

"I could send a man through with a message."

Gilmour shook his head. "No good, Ogilvie. He *might* get away under cover of the darkness, but I doubt it. In any case, we're well past Landi Khotal, and if anybody goes anywhere, it must be to the mouth of the Khyber itself—to Jamrud, and the field telegraph to Peshawar. That's a damn sight nearer now."

"Yes, I suppose so. It might be worth trying, at that." Ogilvie paused. "So near safety, Major, as you said not so long ago! It seems curious, doesn't it?"

"How do you mean, curious?"

"I mean that they should wait till we're nearly through the pass"

"Nothing odd about it at all," Gilmour said. "It's simply that we've now passed beyond Jarar Mahommed's limit of rule and sway—that's all!"

"D'you think these people know about the terms, and mean to stop them getting through?"

"I've no idea. They may indeed. On the other hand, they may be just engaging in the good old tribal pastime of attacking anything that moves in the area. It's a thundering pity Jarar's man died." Gilmour ducked suddenly as a bullet snicked the rock above his head. "The bastards! In any case, Ogilvie, it's no good theorising about who they are. They're shooting and they mean to wipe us out. They could do it, too, by a process of attrition. Have you any idea what the casualties are to date?"

"I haven't had time to think about that yet. I'll get a report when I can." Ogilvie listened to the bullets whining overhead or striking off rock fragments. In this cover they were safe, at least until the enemy decided to move round and mount a flank attack. Almost despairingly he wondered what the next move should be. From the sound of the rifle fire, he judged that his force was well outnumbered; there would be little hope of mounting a successful counter-attack—as things were, he would hardly have the time to re-form the sepoys. The moment they all emerged from cover, they would be dead men; and they had not the strength, in either a numerical or physical sense, to shed their cannon-fodder as it were and emerge from the fire as still a fighting unit. The darkness would be a help, of course; but it was still too great a risk to take with the enemy in his commanding position. The only possible source of action would be, in Ogilvie's opinion, the passive and undramatic one of sitting it out and hoping to reduce the enemy faster than they themselves were reduced. The cover was good on both sides, whilst to attack, the enemy must, like themselves, come out into the open.

He said as much to Gilmour.

"It's a good point," Gilmour agreed. "We'll just see who can last the longest—who can stand the suspense better!" He laughed again. "That honour could well go to the enemy. They're more used to it—and to this infernal cold! In the meantime, there's going to be a delay in getting Jarar's terms through, Ogilvie, if ever they get through at all."

"How serious is a delay going to be, Major?"

"That depends on the length of the delay. It could be serious for Rigby-Smith and the rest of his regiment in Kunarja. If nothing is forthcoming after what he considers a reasonable period, Jarar may well become vindictive."

"Surely he'll get word of this attack?"

"He may—or he may not. Oh, I know all about the bush telegraph, Ogilvie! It depends how long it takes to operate, and on the extent of Jarar's impatience to boot! When it's a question of a set-back, he's not the most resigned of men."

"If the regiment is massacred—in Kunarja, I mean—"

"If the regiment is massacred, my dear Ogilvie, it means a full-scale frontier war, with the result that all the tribes will unite behind Jarar's standard!"

"Which could suit him very well, perhaps ... don't you think, Major?"

There was a pause; then Gilmour said, "You mean, you think Jarar could be behind this attack, Jarar himself, trying to stir things up so that he extends his sway in Afghanistan? Yes, that could be! I have had it in mind myself, to be truthful. That makes it even more vital that the terms should go through, and go through quickly. I doubt if even Jarar would commit an overt act of war, such as massacring Rigby-Smith and his men, whilst terms virtually of his own choosing are under discussion."

"What are you suggesting now, Major?" Ogilvie winced with the pain in his arm; he fancied his uniform was stiff with blood, but it was too dark to see. "I've already said, it might be possible to send a man through—"

"Yes. I think I should try to get through myself, Ogilvie. I know the Khyber well, better than anyone else present I would venture to say. I can get a relieving force sent through to you here, and deliver the terms personally to General Fettleworth. Yes, that is what I must do."

"It's a desperate risk. What about Miss Gilmour?"

Gilmour turned his head and looked towards his daughter, who was crouched, a just visible bundle in the darkness against the background of snow, beside the cart containing her mother's body. "She knows what duty is, Ogilvie. She knows that *too* well, perhaps! I shall leave her in your hands, to bring her safely through to Peshawar."

"It's a big responsibility, Major."

"But one that I believe you know how to take. I shall have every confidence in you, Ogilvie."

"Thank you for that, Major." Ogilvie paused. "You've already said, you don't think a man could get through, so how—"

"A man couldn't get through *at this moment*, no! Those Pathans are far too alert—but the alertness will fade a little, as you'll see. When the time's right, and I rather fancy that'll be when we get some more snow, then I'll make a break for it. Remember, there's not a lot of distance to cover now, as far as Jamrud at all events. And now I think I'll get some sleep, Ogilvie."

Ogilvie nodded. "Is there anything you want, any help I can give?"

"You can prepare me a picnic basket if you will, my dear fellow, and a good supply of ammunition!" Wrapping himself tightly in his greatcoat after scraping a hollow in the drifted snow, Gilmour lay down. Ogilvie maintained his watch as best he could, dozing from time to time as sleep overcame him. The firing continued, more or less spasmodically, from both sides; a good deal of ammunition was in fact wasted. There was no actual attack. Working under cover of the total dark, and as silently as possible, the sepoys under Gundar Singh brought in the commissariat carts. At each attempt there was renewed firing, and the force suffered a number of casualties, but the operation was successful and the food was saved. Ogilvie saw to it that basic provisions were made ready for Gilmour's use on his solitary trek for safety. Meanwhile Gilmour slept soundly in the hollowed-out snow bed. At midnight Taggart-Blane crawled up on his stomach to report the casualties: thirty-two sepoys dead, including two N.C.O.s, and another twenty wounded. As for the camp followers, it was impossible to be sure of the situation, but it seemed that they had suffered very heavy losses and, owing to their propensity to panic, would certainly lose many more.

"I was wondering about increasing the guard on them," Taggart-Blane said.

"No. We can't take the risk of losing more soldiers. It's hard, but they'll simply have to take their chance. How's the general morale?"

"Bad, James, very bad indeed. I doubt if we're going to come through this. We're all in a fair way to freezing to death!"

"Don't *you* lose heart! I'm going to need you more than ever now. Gilmour's going through with the terms, on his own."

"Is he, by God!" Taggart-Blane seemed about to say something else, but instead Ogilvie felt his arm suddenly seized and then felt Taggart-Blane's breath fan his face and the subaltern's mouth brush his ear. "Something's moving, behind you. On the right of the rock. I can't see what it is."

Ogilvie, feeling his very flesh crawl, turned his head and lifted his revolver. He could see nothing, hear nothing. There was no firing anywhere just at that moment; the night was peaceful, as peaceful as any in his own highland passes far away in Scotland. Then, suddenly, there was an excruciating pain in his side and he let out a cry. He felt something heavy come down on him and something strike his head, saw vaguely the sudden twist of Taggart-Blane's body close by, and before he passed out he heard the stutter of gunfire and the bullets from what sounded like a Maxim gun snicking into the rock, and the long scream of agony, a sound of death, coming from the direction in which Mrs. Gilmour's body lay in its primitive bier.

11

THE BRITISH REGIMENTS in garrison at Peshawar and Nowshera were in a festive mood, making advance preparations
for Christmas, not now far off. The Officers' Mess of the 114th
Highlanders, lacking James Ogilvie absent on active service,
and having had no news of him since he had marched out
with the Rawalpindis, were perhaps less celebratory than
the other regiments; but on the whole were no more inclined
than were other British officers to wear their hearts on their
sleeves during the Christmas season. At Division, amid a
metaphorical jingle of sleigh bells, Lieutenant-General
Francis Fettleworth, who always enjoyed any occasion when
he could make speeches about the Queen and the Raj, was
busily engaged in discussions with his aide-de-camp on the
subject of the organisation of a dinner he was proposing to
hold for the benefit of some visiting Civilians from Calcutta,
a dinner to be held on Christmas Eve.

He was laying down the law on the seating plan when his
Chief of Staff interrupted him.

"What is it, Lakenham?" Fettleworth asked with a
touch of irritation. "I'm really rather busy—"

"Yes, sir, so I see." Brigadier-General Lakenham's sardonic and sweeping glance took in the scribbles and dia-
grams and crossings-out that constituted the all-important
seating plan, and took in the dandified, simpering figure of
the aide-de-camp, Captain Grassbrook, latest in a lengthy
line of A.D.C.s worn out by Bloody Francis. "Something of

greater urgency has turned up, I'm sorry to say."

"What? What's turned up?"

"This, sir." The Chief of Staff laid a document before the General, on the top of the seating plan.

"Can't I ever be left in peace, blast it all?" He prodded at the document. "What's this, then?"

"A report from one of our Political Officers, sir. Major Blaise-Willoughby—"

"Feller with the monkey? I thought he'd left us."

"He has, sir. He's at Army Headquarters in Murree ... on Sir Iain Ogilvie's staff. He—"

"What's he sending reports to *me* for, then?"

"He *isn't*. Not directly, that is." Lakenham bent and tapped the document. "This report was made to the Army Commander in Murree, who has sent it to you, sir—for necessary action."

"Oh." Fettleworth seemed taken aback. "Why the devil does he bother *me* with it?" He nodded at the A.D.C. "All right, Grassbrook, that's all for now." As Captain Grassbrook left the room, Fettleworth looked up at his Chief of Staff from beneath beetling white eyebrows. "It's so damned important to give these beastly Civilians a good impression, y'know. *Damned* important! That's why I'm taking such pains with this dinner."

"Yes, sir."

"They do appreciate good organisation ... and they're a bunch of blasted gluttons, too. Filling their bellies always keeps 'em happy! Don't forget that, when you succeed to high command, Lakenham."

"No, sir."

"Now, the report, where is it? Ah, yes." The General started to read and, after a moment, looked up. "Who's this from—originally, I mean? Who's the feller in the field?"

"I don't know that, I'm afraid. I don't think it's important anyway. The facts are plain enough." Lakenham summarised them for his General's benefit. "A Political Officer unknown, returning from detached service in the Khyber has observed and reported a small British force under attack from tribesmen between Landi Khotal and Jamrud—nearer to Jamrud than to Landi Khotal—"

143

"He'd have been dressed as a native, would he not, this Political Officer?"

Lakenham fumed at the non-sequitur. "Yes!"

"No indication as to the identity of the force?"

"No, sir, except that they are sepoys."

Fettleworth studied the report again, at closer quarters this time, through a large magnifying glass with a brass handle. "Damned odd. I've no knowledge of any force moving in the Khyber—have you? Which way are they moving?"

"They're not, sir—"

"Oh, don't be—"

"They're *stationary*, sir. Or were, when last seen."

"Oh. Yes, yes! An ambush, no doubt. Where are they *from*, then?"

"We don't know, sir. As you suggest, we have no official intimation. Nevertheless, I think we can make a few good guesses."

The Divisional Commander looked up. "Intelligent appraisals, Lakenham."

"As you say, sir."

"Well?"

"Rigby-Smith's regiment, sir, was sent through to Kunarja—"

"By God, Lakenham, d'you know, you're right! So it was, so it was!" Fettleworth sat back at arms' length, his scarlet tunic-sleeves outthrust vigorously against his desk. "There's been no word from there, has there?"

"Not a thing, no."

"And you think this is the Rawalpindi Light Infantry, do you, hey?"

"It's possible it's a detachment of theirs. If you'll read the report again, you'll see that it refers—"

"Ah yes, yes, a force of approximately company strength, yes, I see." Fettleworth drummed his fingers on the desk-top. "Well?"

"Well, what, sir?"

Fettleworth snapped, "What's your opinion, for God's sake?"

144

"I repeat, sir, I think it likely this force has been detached and despatched by Rigby-Smith—"

"For what purpose, though?"

Lakenham shrugged. "I suppose it's just possible he's sending terms for a settlement with Jarar Mahommed. After all, he was sent in for that purpose—"

"No, he wasn't. He was sent in to restore order and ensure the safety of the British Resident. Do let us get our facts correct, Lakenham."

"Very well, sir, then perhaps he's sending the British Resident out for his own safety."

"And remaining behind himself, with the main body of his regiment?"

"For all we know, sir, he may be accompanying this force. On the other hand, if he is remaining behind, it may well be to discuss terms of a settlement with the Ghilzais, mayn't it?"

"Well, possibly, possibly. I wish I knew! How the devil are we going to find out?"

Lakenham said, "By making contact with the force, sir."

"What?"

"I think you are missing the point of this despatch, sir." The Chief of Staff breathed heavily down his nose, feeling frustrated and annoyed; his General could be exceedingly obtuse at times, though he had an underlying and often useful craftiness that helped the command quite considerably in their dealings with the natives. "The force has been under attack—I repeat, *under attack*—and will undoubtedly, in my opinion, now be liable to attack all the way through the Khyber to Jamrud. The report speaks of many sick or wounded, in litters and commissariat wagons. The weather there is diabolical, as we all know. I—"

"You're suggesting I send a relief force?"

"It might well be wise, General Fettleworth, it might well be wise."

"But the—the damn G.O.C. makes no such suggestion! I suppose he's landing me with a decision." Fettleworth pulled at his drooping, yellowish moustache. "By God, Lakenham, that son of his—Ogilvie! He's with the sepoy battalion." He looked up. "D'you think *he's* marching with this force that's under attack? Do you?"

"I have no idea in all the world, sir, but it's a possibility."

"H'm, yes, it is." Fettleworth ruminated for a while, then went on sagely, "Yes, you may be damn right, Lakenham! It may be necessary to send someone in to meet 'em, I suppose. Who've we got that's any good?"

"Our only experienced battalion is the one brigaded with the sepoys, sir—the 114th Highlanders. Young Ogilvie's own regiment."

"But they're our only Scots!"

"True, sir, but—"

"I wanted their pipers for my dinner on Christmas Eve."

"Quite, sir, quite. But the demands of—"

"Yes, yes, yes, I'm not a bloody fool, Lakenham." Fettleworth frowned, then said energetically, "By God, I tell you what! Why shouldn't we use the blasted Khyber Rifles, sitting on their arses in whatsit, Landi Khotal—hey, Lakenham?"

Lakenham shook his head. "No, sir. With great respect, that would take far too long—and in any case, in order to contact Landi Khotal, a patrol would have to pass the point of ambush—"

"Yes, yes, that's true." Fettleworth drummed on his desk. "Oh, very well. You'd better tell Lord Dornoch to prepare his regiment to march. Those Highlanders are rough and ready and uncouth enough, God knows, but they should be well used to snow!"

*   *   *

Two weeks before Christmas Eve, the Queen's Own Royal Strathspeys proceeded from cantonments for the mouth of the Khyber, accoutred for war and dressed for a foul winter and accompanied by their pipes and drums. Bloody Francis had managed to make their departure into an occasion, and had insisted on the pipes and drums playing them out in full splendour, for some of the Calcutta Civilians had arrived already in Peshawar. He himself took the salute, standing on a dais in a cold wind out of Afghanistan that spoke of the northern and western snows. The 114th High-landers marched out, in better heart now than for months past, to succour a brother regiment of the British Raj, marched as the upholders of the Pax Britannica that had for so long, through so many generations, held the Frontier more or less in check with a curious but mostly effective mixture of benevolence and violence that had begun with the days of the East India Company's army. They marched out as soldiers of the Queen, past Bloody Francis and his staff and the highly-placed Civilians, with their colours streaming along that cold wind, with the kilts of the files a-flap around their knees, with the pipes and drums beating out the throat-catching strains of 'The Heroes of Vittoria', 'The Old 93rd' and the 'High Road to Gairloch'. As Lord Dornoch rode past he gave the Divisional Commander a punctilious salute, equally punctiliously returned. General Fettleworth, an emotional man whenever he thought of Queen and Empire, had tears in his eyes as the haunting notes of the pipers faded away into the distance, towards the barren Afghan hills.

He descended from the dais, blinking.

"Stout fellows," he said to one of the men from Calcutta, dressed in sombre black, and up and about remarkably early. "Stout fellows all!"

"Yes, indeed, General. A necessary evil in a sense."

"Evil? What the devil d'you mean?"

There was a shrug. "Oh, a mere figure of speech, General. A pity they're so essential—that's what I meant, don't you know. Long term solutions are seldom brought about by soldiers."

"I consider that a rather unnecessary remark, Mr. Peabody."

"Then I apologise." Mr. Peabody smiled placatingly, but there was a touch of malice behind the smile.

"I should think so! I suppose you know why I've had to send them in, don't you?"

"Of course I do, General."

"No, no! I don't mean the relief of this force under attack. I mean the original *basic* reason, Mr. Peabody. It was because of the damn meanness of you people in Calcutta—stopping me paying that subsidy. Meanness and crass *stupidity*, I call it, Mr. Peabody!"

Peabody's head went back in angry disapproval, but Fettleworth didn't give a damn. His breath rasping down his nostrils like that of a war-horse, he made for his headquarters. He was much out of temper; nobody had ever dared call his soldiers *evil* before and, by God, if ever they did so again, then they had better watch out. Bloody Francis had a nagging suspicion that some of his officers regarded him as something of a dug-out, an anachronism; but he would never have it said that he had ever failed to stand like a rock between his combatant troops and the damn clerks from Whitehall and Calcutta!

12

THE ATTACK, THE outflanking attack on the rock where
Ogilvie had been taking cover, was of short enough dura-
tion, a counter-attack by a number of the sepoys under
Gundar Singh had overborne the tribesman who had used
the Maxim, but not before he had killed the late British Resident in Kunarja. Gilmour's body was lying in an attitude
of protection across the body of his wife; and his own body
was riddled with bullets. Katharine Gilmour, who was untouched, was hysterical. Taggart-Blane, also unharmed, was
forced to seize her and hold her arms to her sides. Ogilvie,
coming painfully back to consciousness, heard the subaltern's shaking voice pleading with her to be quiet.

There was an agonising pain in Ogilvie's back, to the right
of centre and below his ribs. When gingerly he felt beneath
his clothing, his fingers contacted a nasty stickiness. He had
fairly obviously been knifed; and had it not been for his
thick clothing, he guessed he would most probably be dead.

He called out to Taggart-Blane.

"Oh—James, thank God you're alive!" Taggart-Blane's
voice was high, betraying his nerves. "I can't leave Miss
Gilmour, she's like a wild-cat."

"You can talk, anyway. What happened? What's the state
of things?"

Taggart-Blane told him that Gilmour was dead and so
were the two tribesmen who had mounted the sudden foray.

"One of them came right down on top of you, James, and knocked you out, I think."

"Who got him off me?"

"I did." There was a short pause. "I shot him. I shot him dead."

Ogilvie said, "Thank you, Alan. Are you all right?"

"Yes. How about you?"

"I've been knifed and I appear to be losing rather a lot of blood. Otherwise I'm all right." He tried to get to his feet, but was overcome by a wave of pain that caused him to sink back dizzily on the lying snow. "Damn! I'll need to lie low for a while, I'm afraid."

"I'll see to you when I can. I can't do anything just now. I daren't let Miss Gilmour go."

Ogilvie said, "Give her a hard slap."

"All right." There was a muffled yell from Katharine Gilmour, a sudden oath from Taggart-Blane, and then the sharp sound of two hard slaps across the face. Ogilvie heard the girl cry out: "Oh!" and then she started weeping bitterly and he saw her, a vague blur against the snow, move away from Taggart-Blane and sink to the ground.

Taggart-Blane came over to Ogilvie, and bent close. He asked, "Are you going to be fit to continue the march, James?"

"I'll have to be. Bring me Gilmour's wallet, will you?"

"His wallet?"

"That's what I said. He has Jarar Mahommed's terms written down and signed. Get it off him and bring it to me."

"Right!" Taggart-Blane moved off; he came back quickly with the wallet. Opening it, Ogilvie felt for the thick fold of paper, then slid the wallet into his own pocket, feeling the blood welling through his uniform as he did so.

He said, "Gilmour had hoped to make a break-out when the snow started again, and take the terms through to Peshawar. There's an urgent need of speed now."

"You told me what he meant to do." Taggart-Blane drew in his breath sharply. "Does this mean—"

"I'll have to go, and leave you in command here. Can you cope?"

"I'll cope, but you'll never make it, you know. You need

rest and medical attention. This bloody snow's murder—"

Ogilvie shook his head. "It's absolutely vital—"

"First things first! I'll get some of the medical supplies sent up." Taggart-Blane crawled away out of sight before Ogilvie could stop him. Remembering that Katharine Gilmour had some nursing experience, Ogilvie called out to her; a job to do would be the best thing for her now. As he called, she roused herself, and moved across towards him. She would perhaps massage some warmth into his half-frozen legs while he was immobilised.

"Taggart-Blane's gone to get some medical stuff. I'd be no end grateful if you'd dress my wound when he gets back, Miss Gilmour."

"Of course," she said. Shivering violently, she knelt down by his side. Her very presence, he found, the presence of any woman really in this outlandish Afghan pass, brought comfort and a touch of happier times. There was even a faint scent still clinging to her, a delicate but pervasive perfume that very nearly brought tears to his eyes; on all previous occasions in his experience the smells of the Khyber had been very, very different. The customary odours along the Khyber were of guns and powder, hot metal, men's sweat, animals' dung and the stench of death under hot summer suns when action had meant too long a delay in burial.

*   *   *

Sporadic firing was kept up throughout the night, a night during which there was no further snow. Ogilvie felt that the firing was designed principally to let the British know the Pathans were still there, and to keep the soldiers in their places. An actual attack might come with the daybreak, or the Pathans might prefer to carry on the process of attrition. When at last dawn came, Ogilvie was able to take stock of their situation. The casualty reports indicated another ten men and some more mules lost to the snipers during the night, and there were more wounded in varying degrees of severity. The dead included Subedar Gundar Singh, a sad loss that reduced the leadership to two officers, one of them— Ogilvie himself—far from fit. Katharine Gilmour had attended to the knife-wound, washing the flesh with snow and applying a little of one of the new antiseptic ointments. After this she had placed a lint pad over the wound and then securely bandaged it. In the absence of a medical man, this was the best that could be done and Ogilvie, with the wound cleaned up, felt a good deal easier in his mind if not in his body. All movement of his torso was extremely painful, and tended to start the bleeding going. In consequence he was forced to lie still so far as possible. As the day lightened Taggart-Blane came and squatted beside him.

"It looks as though there's more snow on the way, James," he said, looking up at the overcast sky. The snow-heavy clouds had settled right down on the peaks, half-way to the valleys, giving the whole area a pressed-down feel, a sense of claustrophobic confinement. "You said you'd hit the trail, didn't you, with Gilmour's despatch, when the snow came." He shook his head in doubt. "It's no good, you know. You'll have to face up to it. You're on the sick list."

"I've still got to do what I can as soon as I can."

Taggart-Blane smiled. "Said like a man! No-one doubts your guts, James. But what about the expediency? You'd die from loss of blood on the way. What'd be the point of those terms ending up in a gorge, or under the snowfall somewhere along the track—or in enemy hands? Don't you see that?"

"Yes, of course I do—" Ogilvie broke off as another shaft of pain ran through his side. "In war, risks have to be taken. At best the whole thing's a chance, isn't it?"

"It needn't be. It really needn't be."

Frowning, Ogilvie looked hard at Taggart-Blane. "What d'you mean, Alan? What are you suggesting?"

"Well, you're not the only pebble on the beach! I could go, couldn't I?"

"You?"

"I don't see why the hell not! I'm assuming it has to be an officer, and British—"

"Yes, that's true."

"I'm the only one left to fill *that* bill. You're out, you really are." Taggart-Blane's face was anxious; he was trembling, like a pointer waiting for a bird to fall to the guns.

"You'll have to accept your own limitations. Besides, I want to go."

"Why?"

There was a pause. "I thought you'd realise why."

"Remember the objective—the sole objective: to get the terms through to Peshawar, safely and quickly. That's vital. Nothing else matters—nothing!"

"Yes, I know that. But ... I want to prove to myself that I can be a soldier, don't you see?"

"You've done that. You saved my life last night. Isn't that enough?"

"No. That was a sort of automatic reaction, no more than anybody would do. If I hadn't killed that native he'd have killed me as well as you. James, I want to go. That's all!"

Ogilvie looked at him hard; then, after a moment, he said with a sudden smile, "Not quite all."

"How d'you mean?"

"The desire to go is important, I'll agree. But the ability is even more important. Are you sure you can make it?"

The subaltern's eyes were shining now. "Does that mean you'll send me?"

Ogilvie temporised. "You don't know the Khyber as well as I do, and even I don't know it as well as Gilmour, and—"

"Gilmour's dead, you're *hors de combat*, James! I may be bloody awful, but I'm all that's available as a substitute— and I did come through the Khyber quite recently. I'll find my bearings all right, don't worry!" He paused. "Well, James? Is it on?"

Ogilvie pursed his lips, still basically in doubt; there was truth in all Taggart-Blane had said, but he was so inexperienced, so callow! On the other hand, delay now could be as fatal as total non-delivery of the terms. Really, that had to be the deciding factor. Ogilvie looked up at the sky once again. "The snow won't be long now," he said drily. "That'll be your cover. I'll send a sepoy with you as guide—there'll be at least one man who knows the Khyber well."

*   *   *

When that evening the snow came, it was a blinding

153

blizzard that left men gasping with its viciousness. The likely depth of snow ahead now, between their current position and Jamrud, would be too much for any horse; Taggart-Blane, with the terms thrust into an inner pocket of his uniform beneath greatcoat and layers of blankets, left on foot with the sepoy guide, thrusting manfully into the tearing snow-storm, two whitened figures that were out of sight before they had moved a dozen feet away. Invisible to the British, they would, Ogilvie prayed, also be invisible to the watchful Pathans—who would probably not be at all watchful just in the moment that they were struck by the first lashings of the blizzard.

At all events, there was no gunfire; the only sound was that of the roaring, funnelling wind.

Ogilvie lay behind his rock, alone now with Katharine Gilmour and Bandra Negi, and the bodies of Katharine's parents and of Mulata Din. He found he was avoiding looking at the Gilmours' commissariat cart with its pathetic burden; he wished, for the girl's sake, that it could be moved away, but he felt a personal responsibility now for the bodies. For her part, Katharine had insisted on remaining with him, partly, as she said, to keep an eye on his wound and partly because she was finding she could not bear the proximity of natives and had nothing but revulsion for the thought of sharing any other rock alone with them. So there they remained, in the overshadowing presence of the dead.

After Taggart-Blane had vanished Ogilvie, with his mind on Mulata Din, asked the havildar about the N.C.O. who was still held in arrest—Lal Binodinand.

"He is among the wounded, Sahib."

"No!" Ogilvie was filled with horror and self-reproach at the thought of a man, held prisoner at his own order, being wounded whilst unable to fight back. "I am sorry to hear this, Bandra Negi! How bad is the wound?"

"Very bad, I think, Sahib. A bullet penetrated, close to the lung." Bandra Negi paused. "He prays for death to come to him, Sahib."

"Yes, it would be the better thing, perhaps," Ogilvie murmured, half to himself. "From now on, there must be no question of an escort. Lal Binodinand must not have that anguish."

"Sahib, I have already so commanded, knowing it would be your wish, but being then unable to contact you."

"Good. You did right, Bandra Negi, and I am pleased."

There was a silence after this, a silence of men, only shattered by nature, by the appalling racket of the wind. Then the havildar, fingering a beard that was stiff with ice, asked, "Sahib, how long are we to remain in this place?"

"Who knows? Until the tribes leave us, which is not likely, or until we can break out with a hope of success. I can say no more than that."

"The men are suffering, Sahib. The cold is eating their bodies and their hearts. In the daytime, some say they have terrible images dancing before their eyes, brought about by looking always into the snow and the wind ... some say their very eyes are frozen into balls of ice. Even to touch their equipment means the loss of flesh—even though they wear their mittens. Soon many more men will die, Sahib."

"I know this, Bandra Negi."

"Yes, Sahib. But the sepoys ... they would much prefer to die fighting."

"So would I, Bandra Negi, so would I!"

"Then perhaps we can fight, Sahib? Like Taggart Sahib, if we were to attack under the cover of the snow—"

Ogilvie broke in firmly. "No, Bandra Negi. We would never see the enemy. The reason Taggart Sahib was able to get through, was because he could not be seen. That works both ways."

"Yes, Sahib, I know that you are right, of course. But could we not *all* do as Taggart Sahib did, and pass through the lines of the tribesmen?"

"I doubt it very strongly, Bandra Negi. We are still too many, and some would blunder into their lines, and then there would be slaughter. Also we are burdened with too many wounded. Say no more now. The responsibility is mine, and I must weigh many things."

"One of them being the dead, Sahib?"

"Yes."

"And the memsahib?"

155

Ogilvie nodded. "And the memsahib, Bandra Negi."

The havildar shook his head and looked sad. Ogilvie knew only too well that what Bandra Negi had said about the likelihood of more men dying from the general conditions was perfectly true. Ogilvie himself felt at times unable to think, to make the best use of his powers of judgment: his very brain seemed frozen, his blood to run sluggishly in his veins. To move after being still was a nightmare, as frozen clothing met the flesh of neck and wrists. They could scarcely expect to survive much longer. Ogilvie's thoughts turned towards Taggart-Blane, unhopefully. The subaltern's sepoy guide, provided on the recommendation of Bandra Negi, might know the Khyber well enough; but it was still a tough assignment for a grass-green subaltern virtually fresh out of Sandhurst! Certainly Taggart-Blane had conducted himself well in such action as he had already seen, and Ogilvie admitted to himself now that in fact this had surprised him; but currently Taggart-Blane was potentially facing a very different sort of action—action in which he would be alone and unsupported, thrown utterly upon his own resources of initiative and courage and decision. If he should fail to get through, if he should give way to the appalling weather conditions, let alone bandits, then the consequences of the non-delivery of Jarar Mahommed's terms would be to bring the long darkness of massacre and battle to the North-West Frontier.

*　　*　　*

Ogilvie still found any movement painful, though the bleeding from the knife-thrust, Katharine told him when she re-dressed his two wounds, had stopped.

"It's going to heal quite nicely, Captain Ogilvie," she said. "We shall continue with the massage until you're able to move about. Has it helped?"

He nodded. "I'd have frozen without it! But I wish you'd let Bandra Negi take a turn, or one of the sepoys."

"No. Nursing you is *my* job, Captain Ogilvie. It's the one thing I can do to help."

He smiled at her, gratefully. "Your father would be

proud of you, Miss Gilmour—and the men will bless you for a saint!"

"Oh, nonsense," she said. Of her own free will she had crawled out from cover, escorted by Bandra Negi, risking the bullets of the Pathans and her own repulsion for the natives, to do what she could for the other wounded behind their various rocks and boulders. As with the dawn the snow had eased, some of the fire had come dangerously close to her; but she had been well covered by the sepoys' rifles, and by the captured Maxim, and some half-dozen of the ambushing tribesmen had been picked off without further loss to the remnant of the British force.

"How's Lal Binodinand?" Ogilvie asked.

"He's terribly sick, I'm afraid. He feels the slur, the dishonour, very keenly, I can tell you. He rambles on about his innocence."

"Have any *facts* emerged?" He paused, then risked the question: "Any names, perhaps—of who else might be guilty?"

She shook her head. "No, nothing like that. He's not fully conscious, Captain Ogilvie, he's in delirium most of the time. There's a good deal of fever, and the wound is septic at the point of entry, though I've done what I could."

"I'm sure you have, Miss Gilmour." He hesitated, then reached out a hand to her, impulsively. "We've come to know one another pretty well the last few days. We're going to have to go on living fairly intimately for God knows how long, too! Would you think it cheek if I called you Katharine?"

She laughed, for the first time since her mother had died. It brought life back to her face. "Why, that's very nice of you," she said.

*   *   *

There had been no more snow; above them the sky was blue, and a pale sun shone, not enough of it to bring warmth to near-frozen bodies, but enough at least to bring a more cheerful spirit and a reminder that there were sunnier lands beyond the Khyber Pass. Enough, too, to

157

force Ogilvie to consider a distasteful task, for even the vaguest hint of less icy conditions to come meant that their cargo of dead must be protected against any decomposition. While Katharine went once again about her self-imposed task of attending the sick and wounded with the dwindling medical supplies, the faithful Bandra Negi scooped up handfuls of the lying snow and packed it tightly about the bodies of Major and Mrs. Gilmour and Mulata Din, pressing it down hard so that it became virtually a block of enshrouding ice.

Coming back safely through a renewed spurt of rifle fire, Katharine saw what had been done but didn't comment. She said, "James, there are so many cases of frost-bite, it's really terrible. There's not much I can do, beyond setting the men to chafe each other's limbs as often as possible."

"Well, you've done your best."

"I hope so." She ran a critical eye over him. "You seem much better. Please don't overdo it, though."

"I won't," he promised her, recognising a note of anxiety in her voice. "How's Lal Binodinand now?"

"Still much the same, a little worse perhaps."

"How long d'you think he'll last, Katharine?"

She shook her head. There was a curious look in her eyes, he noticed. "I don't know. Perhaps—long enough to be hanged."

"That's a hard way to put it."

"Put it how you like, it could be that way. And if so, then it's hateful, utterly hateful and abominable, to keep a man alive and in pain only to hang him in the end!"

"But Katharine," he said, taking her hand, which was chapped and raw and blotched with frozen blood. "He'll hang only if he's found guilty, don't you see? He has to live, in order to answer the charge, and—and perhaps prove his innocence! Surely you can see that?"

"Oh yes," she said dully. "Yes, of course I see it. But ... oh, never mind!" She looked around her, at the rock, at the jagged peaks above; her face held a high colour, almost feverish, and her eyes were bright and hard. "Do you know, there are times—yes, many times—when I hate, hate, *hate* the British Raj and all it stands for!"

Her fists were clenched and shaking; she had thrown off Ogilvie's hand when she had been racked by the torrent of emotion waiting to come out. He said, "Katharine—"

"How long have we been here? *How long?*"

He shook his head; he didn't answer. He was filled with an immense weariness. All count of time seemed to have deserted him and his feeling was that they had been in the Khyber since time immemorial, day succeeding day to bring more cold, more snow and danger, more strain to himself and his sepoys and to this girl—more strain and a terrible tightening of the rations and of the drinking water, long since eked out with melted snow which at least kept throats moist. He said, "It's been a long, long hell, Katharine, I know that, but—"

"Then can you not do something about it? Can you not order an attack? Are you not a British officer?" Wildly now, she gestured at the commissariat cart. Her eyes were bright, more so now, though the lids showed fatigue and hunger. "My father would have mounted a counter-attack by this time, you may be sure! Why, why, *why* do you not do so?"

"There are many things to be considered," he said lamely, feeling himself flush. "Among them you yourself."

"You should not use me as your excuse!"

"Please, Katharine. Don't make things more difficult."

He reached his hand out to her again; but she turned away, tears streaming down her cheeks.

* * *

Around the perimeter there was a stir of movement, of what seemed to be sudden alarm. There was a renewal of the firing from the crests, but, oddly, no bullets came down upon them. They stared in puzzlement; the Pathans were showing themselves now, and moving—moving away, firing ahead along the pass. Ogilvie felt the thump of his heart, and a surge of crazy hope, a hope that surely must prove false!

Then they heard it, and it was unmistakable.

Very distantly yet, a mere suspicion of a sound beating out thinly into the freezing air, but coming almost imperceptibly closer as they listened and waited ... the heart-stirring sound of drums, the wailing of bagpipes moving towards them along the track out of India. Not a word was spoken, but everywhere men came out from cover to stand and watch the sudden turn of events and then to cheer the Highland soldiers in.

Distantly still, they saw the splash of colour against the everlasting snows. To Ogilvie it seemed almost as though it must be a mirage, a cruel trick of eyes affected by the white glare from the snow that had been with them for so long. Then his attuned ears picked out Pipe-Major Ross's own composition, 'Farewell to Invermore', just before the pipers shifted into 'Cock o' the North' and, with yells and wild cries the Highland line opened with their rifles and Maxims, bringing complete confusion to the ambushing tribesmen; fighting, now that fighting had come to them, as they had always fought before. There was, Ogilvie saw with a full heart, nothing basically wrong with the Royal Strathspeys.

He laid a hand on Katharine Gilmour's arm and this time there was no turning away. "It's all right now," he told her gently. "It's my regiment. It's the 114th!"

13

RE-FORMING AFTER A brief action, the kilted Scots marched in behind the skirl of the pipes and halted on the Colonel's order. To hear the parade-ground voice of Bosom Cunningham, the Regimental Sergeant-Major, was music as good as the pipes themselves in Ogilvie's ears. As the wind died in the pipes and the beat of the drums ceased, Lord Dornoch recognised Ogilvie.

"By God, James, it's you! I had the feeling it might be." Dornoch, heavily wrapped in thick clothing and wearing a Russian-style fur hat, took Ogilvie's hand in a hard grip. "What the devil have you been up to? You look in poor shape, and so do your sepoys."

"We're not too bad to march, Colonel—"

"Bravely said, but untrue. No—I'll not stand and argue that point! Tell me your news ... and who's the lady?"

"Major Gilmour's daughter—Miss Katharine—"

"Good heavens! My poor young lady, I'm doubly glad to have been of some assistance! James, what's happened—where's Gilmour?"

Briefly, Ogilvie told Dornoch of the march and of Gilmour's death, and of that of Gilmour's wife. The Colonel was gravely concerned and troubled as he studied Katharine Gilmour's tired, drained face. "A tragedy," he said quietly. "A real tragedy. Your father's whole life was given to his natives—I know his reputation well. I'm deeply sorry, Miss

161

Gilmour—deeply sorry. He was a brave man, one of the best the Raj could have produced. And your mother—"

"Thank you, Lord Dornoch," she broke in, looking down at the trodden snow. "It is a great loss to me."

"Of course." Dornoch turned away towards the hills, shaking his head. "Now we must look to the future. James, what's this you said about Taggart-Blane?"

"He volunteered to go through to Jamrud, Colonel, with the terms that Major Gilmour had been carrying to General Fettleworth."

"An officer of his lack of experience—and you let him go?"

Ogilvie pointed out, "Colonel, there was no-one else—and he had a native guide, a man who knows the Khyber well."

Dornoch shook his head. "I take your point, but I fear he'll have been lost. *We* saw no sign of him on the march, that's certain! If he had come through before we entered the pass, we'd have been informed by Jamrud, I feel sure."

"He—or his guide, Colonel—they may have felt it safer to leave the track and take some other route."

"There is no other route known to us."

"To *us*, Colonel, perhaps not. But to the guide? These men have ways that are unknown to—"

"Yes, yes, that's perfectly true, but I can't afford to use such an assumption as any basis for decision. It's too vague, too unlikely. And by now time's running short, and affairs will not be happy for Colonel Rigby-Smith and his regiment in Kunarja." Lord Dornoch stared around the pass, at the cruel jags of rock, at the hillsides now apparently clear of Pathans. The rifles of the Royal Strathspeys had accounted for a large number of the former ambushers, and the rest had made themselves scarce for the time being. "By God, this place gives me the shivers, James!"

"There are similarities to Scotland, Colonel."

"True—but give me the Pass of Drumochter before this any day! Now: I must make the assumption that the terms will *not* in fact have reached General Fettleworth in Peshawar. I'll not rule out entirely the possibility that Taggart-Blane may yet get through—he may have met some temporary set-back, some hold-up, or he may be wounded—

but it's a very faint possibility in my opinion. That leaves us with the likelihood that Rigby-Smith will be in danger and must be relieved. We'll not delay, James. I'll resume the march as soon as possible." He paused, scanning Ogilvie's face. "I need hardly say, you'll not be coming with us."

"But, Colonel—"

"No argument, if you please. You and Miss Gilmour will continue for Peshawar under escort—I'll detach a half-company for your protection. You'll take all your sepoys with you—both the sick and the fit. They've had enough, poor fellows, more already than any man should be expected to stand. I shall manage very well in Kunarja with the main body of the regiment. You will also take—" He broke off. "A word in your ear, James."

"Yes, Colonel."

They moved away a little, out of earshot of Katharine Gilmour. "That poor girl," Dornoch said in a low voice. "You must take the bodies of the Gilmours through with you, of course. I note there's a third body packed in snow in one of the carts. What's the story of *that*?"

Ogilvie, hating his task, took a deep breath and told Dornoch the facts, such as they were known, of the murder and what had gone before it. Dornoch was shocked to the core. "A murder—and this terrible business, this sordid involvement of one of my own officers! Are you sure of your facts?"

"As sure as I can be, Colonel, though I couldn't swear to what I saw. But you did once mention—in regard to Taggart-Blane, you said—"

"Yes, yes." Dornoch tugged at his moustache. "I never really visualised a—a manifestation, though! By God, it's damned appalling! A British officer and a sepoy! I doubt if we'll ever keep this within the regiment, James, even if this havildar should hang—and who's really to say he's guilty? My God, I'm half inclined to hope Taggart-Blane doesn't come through the Khyber!" He blew his nose, hard.

"I think we should not cross our bridges, Colonel. As you have said, it's likely enough that Taggart-Blane *is* dead, and the havildar, Lal Binodinand, is undoubtedly dying."

"Dying?"

"I believe so, Colonel."

163

"I'll have the Surgeon-Major look at him."

"I think he's already attending to the sick and wounded, Colonel."

Dornoch said, "I suppose you know one thing."

"Colonel?"

"Lal Binodinand must be kept alive. He will go back with the rest of the sick, of course—with you. I'll send the Surgeon-Major also—you have so many sick and wounded, and there is Miss Gilmour. Dr. Corton will be better used if he accompanies your column."

"We haven't so far to go as you have, Colonel."

Dornoch nodded. "I know that. But you yourself are far from fit, and I consider it vital that you should get through —since you have the outline in your head, the outline of Jarar Mahommed's terms. You shall report them personally to General Fettleworth—and I can only hope you'll reach him in time. But as to Lal Binodinand: he must be kept alive in so far as medical knowledge can ensure his fitness—"

"Simply to hang, Colonel?" Ogilvie felt a horror similar to Katharine Gilmour's, now he heard the matter expressed in words by another man. "Is this not ... sheer cruelty?"

"Cruelty or not, I have given you what you are to regard as an order. I shall give the same order to Surgeon-Major Corton—an order which he can, of course, obey only to the best of his skill and ability as a medical officer. Lal Binodinand cannot be allowed to die, and I think you must know very well why!"

"I do not, Colonel. I—"

"Then think, man, think!" Lord Dornoch said harshly as he turned away to make back towards the others. "Here is a clue: do you wish it said throughout British India, in the messes and the clubs, in the courts and the Government offices in Calcutta, that the 114th Highlanders have a very neat and conclusive way of looking after their own?"

*　　*　　*

It was true, Ogilvie thought with a heavy heart as half an hour later he stood and watched the regiment move out. Lal Binodinand had in his dying agonies become a kind of

164

symbol—a symbol of justice! He shuddered; what form of justice was it, that could make a man of honour like Lord Dornoch issue such an order? Dornoch had spoken under the pressure of his feeling for the regiment and had possibly been too forthright, expressing himself too baldly; for Ogilvie knew instinctively that genuine justice had also been in the Colonel's mind when he had made that statement: Ogilvie's own words to Katharine Gilmour came back to him—Lal Binodinand had to be accorded the opportunity of proving his innocence if he could. Regiment or no regiment, Dornoch would countenance no interfering with that basic human right.

The main Scots column moved off from that place of ambush, that arena of the dead, with their colours fluttering out along a cold wind but beneath a sky that was still clear, with the pipes and drums beating out bravely into the grim surround of the hills, and the regimental tartan blown around the blue-tinged knees of close upon a thousand men. Ogilvie stood at the salute as the Colonel went by behind the pipes and drums, stood motionless until the long column had all gone past and the pipes at the head had faded into the vast distance of the Khyber. Singing came back to him, the song of men keeping up their spirits as they marched and slid and stumbled away to war:

> You trusted in your Hielan' men,
> They trusted you, dear Charlie,
> They kent you were hidin' in the glen,
> Death or exile bravin'.
> Will ye no come back again...

The sounds faded; and soon the rear of the column had marched away out of sight. Turning, Ogilvie became aware of Katherine Gilmour standing by his side. She said brittly, "You've a very deep feeling for your regiment, James, haven't you?"

He nodded. "Deep enough—yes, I have. We've had a long history. I don't suppose you happened to notice the colour?"

"The battle honours? Yes, as a matter of fact, I did. Blenheim, Ramillies, Malplaquet, Plassey, Minden, the

165

Siege of Gibraltar, Salamanca, Vittoria, Waterloo . . . the Mutiny. Yes, James, it's a long record. I can understand your pride, but don't ... don't ever give your life to the army, to *India*. Please!"

He lifted his eyebrows. "That's a strange thing to say, Katharine."

"Is it so strange?" He saw she was crying now. "Perhaps it is ... I don't know. I'm barely able to think for this terrible cold and the everlasting snow, James. But this India, this British Raj ... it's not worth it, not worth the deaths and the sacrifice and the sheer heart-break. They *need* us here more than they realise, of course, but they don't *want* us. They hate us! Why don't we let them see what it's like without us? Why don't we pull out and leave them to it, leave them to the bloodshed and the horror and the cruelty of their revolting land? *Why don't we?*"

*   *   *

With the escort of the half-company under Second-Lieutenant Renshaw, one of the Sandhurst-fresh subalterns who had joined the regiment with Taggart-Blane, the going seemed much easier. It was a friendlier feeling, to be marching—or in his case riding in a commissariat cart on Corton's orders—with his own regiment, his own kind about him. The sick and wounded were now in good hands, which was another comfort; and Katharine Gilmour, who had collapsed from sheer exhaustion soon after the main body of the regiment had left, was also being properly cared for.

During a rest halt, Surgeon-Major Corton reassured Ogilvie about the girl. "I'm not worried, James," he said, puffing at a pipe. "She's tough physically—she'll be as right as rain once she's properly fed and rested, never fear!"

"Is there any fever?"

"A little—just a touch. Nothing to worry about, I promise you." He tapped out his pipe against his boot. Soon after this the column was once again on the move. When they fell out that night to make their bivouacs, Ogilvie estimated that they had little more than twenty-four hours' march ahead of them to Jamrud and British India, always provided there was not a further heavy fall of snow. Once again as they halted Corton came to him, this time with more gravity in his demeanour. "I want to talk to you about Lal Binodinand, James," the doctor said. "He's not good. The prognosis is poor, decidedly so, unless, that is, I take certain measures. Unless I do take those measures, if I may drive the point home, James, the man's going to die—and you're not to tell me that would be the best thing, which I think is what you *were* going to say?"

"Yes. Why can't he be allowed to die in peace, Doctor?"

"Because the Colonel says he cannot—and it's not just the fact of the Colonel's order that I have in my mind. He happens to be entirely right from all points of view—I needn't go into them all now, I'm sure. Besides which, James, I'm a medical man. It's my job to save life."

"For the hangman."

Corton shook his head. "That's a stupid thing to say, and I'll not argue it now. Let me tell you about the measures I'll need to take." He paused. "Are you listening, James, or are you still sunk in some treacly pool of obstinate melodramatic thoughts?"

"I'm listening."

"Good! Well now, there's a bullet lodged in the man just below the left lobe of the lung. The wound's a mess, full of suppuration, and the poison's spreading too fast—and that's in spite of all Miss Gilmour did so splendidly, and I mean splendidly. If she hadn't done what she could to keep the wound clean, the man'd be dead by this time. But I have to get that bullet out, James, and that's a fact."

"You mean you'll have to operate?"

"Operate's a rather grandiose term for what I have to do. I have to extract the bullet—and—"

"When?"

"I was just going to say, *now*. Tonight. Delay would be dangerous. I was hoping to avoid the necessity, but now I see there is no alternative."

"Why come to me, Doctor?"

Corton said deliberately, "Because I need the authorisation to perform what *could* be called an operation on the march. That is, I need the authorisation in this particular

case—which you'll agree isn't a routine case of wounding."
He paused. "I need something else, too."

"Well?"

"I need four men, four good strong Scots, James. He'll
have to be held down, you see. There'll be a lot of pain."

"But you have anaesthetics!"

"No, James, that's where you're wrong. I haven't any at
all. The mule-cart containing them has become a casualty of
the march. It fell into a gorge during the afternoon."

"Rum, then, or brandy?"

Corton shook his head. "I'm afraid not. There's a little
brandy, but by no means sufficient to be of any help. I've
had to use most of it already, on the other sick and wounded.
You must remember, you brought me a very large sick
parade, James, larger really than emergency medical comforts on a march can be stretched to cover. No, this must be
done without any such aids at all. I'm sorry; but there it is.
I'm asking you to detail four reliable men—men who won't
be squeamish when they have to listen to screaming, or
when they see blood produced not by battle but by the
surgeon's knife. There's a difference, believe me!"

Ogilvie sat up straight, staring at the doctor. "For God's
sake," he said, "why not let him die?"

"I can't possibly, and you know that very well. What I
can do, that I must do. I have a duty to my own ethic, my
own training, as well as to my Colonel. You speak of God's
sake. If I also may be allowed to invoke Him—I have a duty
to God as well! James, I am going to extract that bullet,
whether you like it or not, and you are going to give me
your authorisation—you know in your heart you have no
choice. Now, please let me have that detail: four strong
men, and as soon as possible!"

"You can't do it now, Doctor: there's no light! Why
didn't you bring this up earlier—while there was daylight?"

Corton shrugged and said, "There's an element of danger
in the excision, so close to the lung. I hoped we'd get away
with not having to do it until we reached Peshawar. Now
I see that we can't. As to light ... we have storm lanterns—"

168

"Which will make it very easy for any tribesmen to pick us off, Doctor!"

"Now, James, I'm not inexperienced in the ways of the Khyber. I've practised medicine, aye, and surgery too, in these parts long before you joined the regiment! When I was attached to the Seaforths I took off a man's leg in the Khyber, and by the light of storm lanterns at that. All we need to do is to bring two of the commissariat carts together, and rig blankets over to form a tent of sorts. That'll be fine. So now, James, I'd be obliged if you'd give the orders to prepare me an operating theatre. Will you do that?"

Slowly, reluctantly, Ogilvie gave a nod. "Very well, if you're really convinced we'll be doing the right thing."

"Of course I'm convinced, though I see you're not. But think, man, think—and use a little sense! Would you like to feel you'd let a man die when medical effort could have saved him? Would *you* like to be made the man's executioner?"

"Is that really how you would see me?"

Corton gave a short laugh. "I make no moral judgments, James. No, I doubt if I would see you like that ... I understand the way you're thinking. But I believe that's how you would come to see yourself, and I believe you would not march easy through the Khyber again, and past this spot! Come now, do your part, James, and I'll do mine."

Surgeon-Major Corton turned away abruptly and strode off. Ogilvie watched him vanish into the darkness. Still reluctant to initiate the playing out of what he considered a farce, a farce that involved a man's life and suffering, he called for Bandra Negi.

The havildar was there in an instant. "Sahib?"

"Bandra Negi, Lal Binodinand's life, which apparently hangs on a thread, is to be saved by the Doctor Sahib. There will be much to do. Blankets, commissariat carts, lanterns, melted snow—perhaps many other things. See to this, and consult the Doctor Sahib as to all he needs."

"It shall be done, Sahib." Bandra Negi's right hand snapped to the salute.

"One more thing, ask my Colour-Sarn't to provide four privates, the biggest and most reliable men he has, to assist the Doctor Sahib. Also tell Renshaw Sahib that I wish all the other men to be constantly alert and watchful, to remain standing-to until the Doctor Sahib has finished." He made a dismissive gesture. "That is all, Bandra Negi."

"Sahib!" With another salute, the havildar turned away. Within the next few minutes Ogilvie heard the sounds of preparation, the subdued voices, the orders of Bandra Negi and Colour-Sergeant MacTrease, the creaking of the cart-wheels as they were drawn across the snow-covered ground of the pass. Dimly just before the last of the light went he saw the blankets being carried to the makeshift operating theatre, saw four of his Highlanders waiting to lay strong hands on the four corners of Lal Binodinand once the man was positioned on his blanket on the ground between the carts. It was to be a primitive business and a horrible one, for Lal Binodinand would surely know why he was being so conscientiously kept alive, and Ogilvie was certain that, were the man to be asked, he would choose to be allowed to die now. In any case it would be a miracle if he survived; Ogilvie wished he had put the point to Surgeon-Major Corton. There must be many poisons, here in the Khyber Pass, that could enter a man's body by way of the cutting and probing that Corton was about to do.

Within twenty minutes all was ready; Ogilvie heard the voice of Colour-Sergeant MacTrease, ordering the privates to duck under the tent of blankets. There was a glow from the lanterns as the men moved the covering, then once again total darkness. Knowing what he was going to hear, Ogilvie was still shaken to the core when he heard it: the terrible cries, the screams of a man in agony from the steely probings of Corton's instruments, the desperate callings upon his Gods, and then a nerve-wrenching sobbing that rose and fell, rose and fell, while Ogilvie's nails dug ferociously into his palms and he, in his turn, called loudly upon his own God to bring this fearful business to a speedy close.

*   *   *

It seemed hours later when he heard Colour-Sergeant

MacTrease giving an order to the four privates: "Get the blood off yersel's, quick—wash in the snow, lads. Hurry now!" There seemed to be an inference that native blood might be sullying.

Ogilvie called, "Colour-Sar'nt!"

"Sir!" MacTrease came up, halted and saluted.

"How's the ... the patient, Colour-Sar'nt?"

"It's for the doctor to say, sir, but to me he looks bad enough."

"But he's alive?" He spoke stiffly, through sore, cracked lips.

"Aye, sir, he's alive." MacTrease looked hard at Ogilvie. "You don't sound too good yersel', sir, if I may say so."

"Oh, I'm all right, Colour-Sar'nt." In truth, Ogilvie felt physically sick. "That's all, thank you. Carry on."

"Sir!" MacTrease saluted and turned about. As he marched away, Surgeon-Major Corton came up.

"How is he?" Ogilvie asked in a flat voice.

"Oh, he'll do! He came through it well."

"What if a fresh infection sets in?"

"Well, if it does, we should reach Peshawar in time to get him all the aids and comforts of the base hospital."

"I hope so," Ogilvie said shortly. It was true there was not far to go now, but Ogilvie was consumed with impatience to leave the Khyber's conditions behind him. Corton, he thought, sounded extremely pleased with himself. But for most of that night Ogilvie lay awake in his ice-cold bivouac and listened to the pitiful moans and cries of a man still in great pain.

14

Lieutenant-General Francis Fettleworth awoke with a start in the comfortable double bed in his residence at Peshawar. "What the devil!" he said. "Who is it?"

"Grassbrook, sir—"

"How dare you!"

"Sir?" Captain Grassbrook sounded surprised.

"Bursting into my bedroom—my wife's bedroom to boot! It's scarcely the duty of an aide-de-camp to—"

"Sir, the matter is most urgent, or so he says—"

"Says? Says?" Fettleworth sat up straight, red and rumpled in silk pyjamas. "Who says, for God's sake, Captain Grassbrook? Who says *what*?"

"An officer, sir, who has come through the Khyber with an urgent despatch, a *most* urgent despatch—"

"Come in person, Grassbrook—come *here*, do I understand you to mean?"

"Yes, sir. He—"

"What's his rank, and what's his name?"

"Sir, I—"

"Rank and name, damn you to hell."

"A Second Lieutenant Taggart-Blane, sir—"

"*Second Lieutenant?* A bloody *subaltern* having the damned effrontery to present himself here to me, in person? Good God, what's the service coming to, I should like to know? Hell and damnation. Tell him to go where he should have gone in the first place—to Brigade, if his own blasted Colonel isn't good enough—"

"Sir!" With considerable courage in the circumstances, the A.D.C. burst through the walls of his General's tirade. "Sir, I really must stress the importance of Taggart-Blane's despatch. His Colonel, sir, has marched through the Khyber on your orders—Colonel Lord Dornoch of the 114th. Taggart-Blane, however, comes from Kunarja and is representing Major Gilmour, killed in action in the Khyber. Taggart-Blane brings a document setting out terms of a settlement as tentatively agreed with the rebel, Jarar Mahommed."

Fettleworth's mouth had sagged a little open; now it shut with a snap. "Why the devil didn't you say so, then?" he barked. "I'll deal with this immediately, Grassbrook. Bring this young man to me in my study." Getting out of bed and feeling for his slippers, he glanced back at his wife. She was still fast asleep, which was what *he* should be, he thought with irritation. He pulled on his dressing-gown.

*   *   *

Taggart-Blane and his sepoy guide had come through a degree of hell, not from tribesmen—they had in fact seen none—but from the terrible weather in the early stages, at least, of their journey. Fearing attack along the route, Taggart-Blane's guide had suggested taking a different way to Jamrud, a way that led across the mountains through a narrow, dangerous, and little-used track, a track with constant perils of snow-filled declivities, gorges and chasms, and jagged rock. And cold—icy, terrible, wicked cold from the keen wind shouting all the way down from the mountains around Kabul.

But they had made it.

More dead than alive, Taggart-Blane felt, they had reached Jamrud. At Jamrud they had found no communication: the field telegraph line had been cut, apparently by marauding tribesmen. Taggart-Blane had set off again, to make the last few miles into Peshawar—snow-free miles now that they were eastward of Jamrud; and they had one slice of luck in so far as they made contact with a British patrol

173

a couple of miles to the east of Jamrud, after which they were literally carried into Peshawar. Taggart-Blane took time off for a meal and a quantity of hot drinks before reporting his urgent mission to the Divisional Commander: he felt he owed that much to himself. Bloody Francis, by all repute, was worse than the enemy to deal with, and he needed strength.

"Why, boy, you look quite done," Fettleworth said as the subaltern was ushered in by the A.D.C. Taggart-Blane blinked in surprise; he had not expected this, and was much relieved.

"I've come a long way, sir," he said, swaying.

"You must have a doctor look at you."

"I'll be all right, sir, until I've given you my report."

"H'rrmph." Fettleworth sounded dubious. "Sit down, then. What's your name again?"

"Taggart-Blane, sir, of the 114th Highlanders, attached 99th Rawalpindis who are currently held as hostages in Kunarja." He sat in a comfortable chair, feeling sick and dizzy now. Reaction, he felt, was setting in; but his mission was not complete yet. "Sir, I come with—"

"Yes, I know what you've come with, my boy." Fettleworth glanced at Captain Grassbrook. "Rouse out one of the blasted leeches," he said. "This young man needs attention, and quickly." When the A.D.C. had departed, he turned again to Taggart-Blane. "I understand you have the terms in writing?"

"I have, sir." Taggart-Blane unfastened his filthy clothing and produced Gilmour's envelope, handing it to Fettleworth with shaking fingers. The General opened it and brought out the document; he read it carefully and slowly, muttering to himself about the damned rebel and his impertinence. There was, however, a crafty and calculating look in his eye when he had finished.

"You've done well, Mr. Taggart-Blane," he said. "Very well indeed—splendidly! I shall not forget this, nor, I hope I may say, will the Raj, my dear boy. Have you anything further to report—of your own accord, I mean? In regard to your journey out, which must have been a terrible one?"

"It was terrible enough," Taggart-Blane said almost to

174

himself. "Terrible enough..." He pulled himself up. "Sir, Captain Ogilvie is attempting to march through the Khyber for Peshawar with one company of sepoys, but was under ambush at the time I left. Major Gilmour and his wife are dead. This was why I came with the terms ... Major Gilmour had intended bringing them through himself. I don't know who we were attacked by ... to me, they were simply Pathans." Again he felt dizzy and light-headed, and he began to laugh. "There were others killed, too," he said unsteadily. "I killed a man."

"Your first?"

"Certainly my first, sir—"

"You'll get used to it, my boy, you'll get used to it. Killing's never pleasant, of course, but it has to be done, and after a while it becomes *much* easier."

"General, you don't understand—"

"Nonsense, of course I understand," Fettleworth said briskly, "Why, I've killed plenty of men, damn it! Plenty! I know it affects different men in different ways, but don't let's have any stuff-and-nonsense about God. I think I may say, God also understands. I..." His voice tailed away in amazement. "May I ask, Mr. Taggart-Blane, what you're *laughing* at?"

"At your very wide knowledge, General."

"Hey? What? My wide knowledge about what?"

"About God. My apologies, sir. You really haven't understood at all, but honestly, I haven't the strength to go on. Have I your permission to sleep, sir?"

Fettleworth blew out his cheeks. The young man was in a bad way, certainly, and had done an immensely courageous thing, but that didn't excuse a subaltern going to sleep, which Taggart-Blane was all too clearly now doing, in his Divisional Commander's study. Fettleworth, however, was saved the unpleasantness of having to wake and eject a hero. There was a knock at the door and Captain Grassbrook brought in Fettleworth's Staff Surgeon.

Fettleworth gestured at the sleeping subaltern. "Poor boy's damn near dead," he said. "Wandering in the head a little, too, and I don't wonder. Come all the way from Kunarja with an urgent message—most brave! Do all you can for him, Doctor—all you can." He waved a hand towards Captain Grassbrook. "My compliments to Brigadier-General Lakenham. I wish to see him immediately."

When he was alone, Fettleworth sat drumming his fingers on his desk and staring across the study towards a photograph of Her Majesty sitting in an open carriage and being drawn along the Mall behind a Captain's Escort of her Household Cavalry. Fettleworth had obtained this photograph through the good offices of the *Illustrated London News*, whose photographer had taken the original. The Queen-Empress was in fact scarcely visible above the sides of the carriage, but the little black bonnet and the white hair were quite unmistakable enough to act as a spur and an inspiration to Bloody Francis Fettleworth. Gazing at the photograph now, the Divisional Commander pondered on Jarar Mahommed's terms and began to see in them a means of extending, even by a very little, the sway and rule of the little old lady in black. If he could do that, she would be delighted; and in the not too distant future he, Lieutenant-General Fettleworth, might receive the bestowal of her favour, expressed in terms of honours and promotion. For, impertinence though of course it was for a rebel even to think about terms, much less state them so categorically, those terms did indeed represent progress for the British Raj in so far as the rebel had offered positive safeguards for the British in Kunarja, peace in his area, and constant safe passage of the Khyber that would turn his roving levies into friends rather than enemies. If all this could be agreed during his, Fettleworth's, acting tenancy of the Commis-sionership in Peshawar—if thereby the 'forward policy' of the ever-expanding Raj could be advanced—fewer British lives need be lost and the way might be insidiously opened for Jarar Mahommed and his powerful sphere of influence to be welcomed much more positively beneath the genial, overall umbrella of the Raj. Much more positively...

But—first, the cash. And that, of course, meant the Civilians.

"Who," Fettleworth said some minutes later to his Chief of Staff, "are fortunately here in Peshawar—or enough of them are! Enough, that is, to make an appreciation of the

176

urgency, and inform Calcutta by telegraph accordingly. What?"

"You forget the question of time, sir—"

"Oh, no I don't!"

"Calcutta, sir, is not noted for its speed of decision. I—"

"I know that, Lakenham, my dear fellow. But *you* forget that Calcutta is not noted for its desire to do battle with the tribes when such can be avoided!"

"True." Brigadier-General Lakenham nodded, frowning, hunching his shoulders in an easy-chair. "True—oh, certainly. Yet they risked that very thing, sir, when they cut the subsidy in the first place. We mustn't forget that."

"But they didn't *appreciate* the risk then, Lakenham!" Fettleworth leaned across his desk with bulging stomach. "They took no notice of me at that time, blast 'em—but now it's different! There's a regiment held prisoner in Kunarja if young whatsisname's to be believed—and that's borne out by Gilmour's despatch. An entire regiment of the Indian Army! They're not going to find *that* so easy to sneeze at. Calcutta won't want a full scale frontier war to break out just on the brink of Christmas—and that, damn it, is precisely what I intend to threaten those blasted Civilians with! It'll be common knowledge that I've already marched the 114th Highlanders through the Khyber—and if Calcutta doesn't meet Jarar Mahommed's terms half way at least, then we'll undoubtedly have a war on our hands!" He sat back, puffing a little, his face a deep and dangerous red. "Don't you see, Lakenham?"

Lakenham said cautiously, "Yes, of course I see. But I presume you'll be consulting first with Sir Iain Ogilvie in Murree?"

"Then you presume wrong, Lakenham, for I intend doing no such thing. You yourself spoke of speed—and speed's to be the keynote. Think of poor Benson-Pope in Kunarja—"

"Benson-Pope? He's here in Peshawar. It's Rigby-Smith in Kunarja."

"What? Oh, confound you, Lakenham, I knew it was some double-barrelled name! Think of Rigby-Smith, then. We must hurry, Lakenham, we must hurry, and we must brook no delay. I shall handle this personally and at once!"

"I think, sir, you forget one important thing. Whatever the *speed*, Lord Dornoch must by now be well on his way to Kunarja with the 114th. Even assuming Calcutta's agreement by this very noon, sir—how does a despatch to Kunarja reach Jarar Mahommed before Lord Dornoch does?"

Fettleworth nodded: "I'd already thought of that! It's true enough, of course—but the point is, there's nothing we can do about it! It has to be accepted, has it not? We haven't wings to fly with. Lord Dornoch is a man of experience and discretion, and I trust him to act both promptly and properly to relieve Rigby-Smith if he finds it necessary. If he *does* find it necessary ... well, then, that's that, is it not?"

"In other words, sir, you're pinning your hopes on Jarar Mahommed not yet having taken any revenge on Rigby-Smith and his regiment?"

Fettleworth nodded again, vigorously. "That's it in a nutshell, my dear fellow. I've no doubt Jarar Mahommed has his Calcuttas just as I have—though for my part I would dearly love to have *his* way with them—cut off their blasted heads!" His face went an even deeper red. "My compliments to Mr. Peabody," he said, naming the most senior of the visiting Civilians. "Not now, but immediately he has breakfasted. I shall wish to speak to him privately."

*   *   *

By Christmas Eve the word, as ever on the sub-continent of India, had by some mysterious means spread throughout the cantonments at Peshawar, the word that a detachment of sepoys escorted by highlanders was marching in from the Khyber Pass after a gruelling experience, and was expected hourly. The result was that James Ogilvie and his half-company of the Royal Strathspeys, and all that were left of his suffering sepoys, were met by a wild acclaim from the whole garrison. Those of the column who were still marching immediately smartened the step when they heard the cheering. Colour-Sergeant MacTrease worked a miracle of recovery on the Scots, who were in any case nothing like so wearied as the sepoys. The sepoys were mostly being borne

178

along in the commissariat carts; so, still, was Ogilvie himself. Drawn almost unseeingly between the ranks of excited,
cheering men and women, he felt only sadness; there was
no elation. Too soon now, the other story must spread, the
story of beastliness and murder, and there must be a Court
Martial and then, perhaps, a hanging, for Lal Binodinand
lived yet, miraculously.

The Divisional Commander was there himself, in very
person, to meet his returned warriors, his face gravely concerned. "No ceremonial, Captain Ogilvie," he said, as
Ogilvie tried to get out of the commissariat cart's indignity.
"Fall out the men immediately—immediately! Poor fellows.
They're heroes to a man! They shall have a good Christmas
dinner, and the sick and wounded will have the best attention from my Medical Staff. How are you yourself, Ogilvie,
my dear fellow?"

"Not so bad as some, sir."

"Bravely said, bravely said! But you shall not stir until
you are better, Ogilvie, to be sure you shall not! I shall
come to you for your full report as soon as the doctors say
I may do so, but otherwise than that, you shall rest. You
have done splendidly—splendidly! I have had news of you,
you see, my dear fellow." Fettleworth beamed. "You will be
glad to hear that young Taggart-Blane got through safely,
and already I have acted to implement Major Gilmour's
despatch!" He paused, looking closely at Ogilvie's face.
"Why, what's the matter, my dear fellow?"

"Nothing, sir. I'm sorry, sir—just a twinge of pain, nothing more." Ogilvie's face was ashen. "I think I should give
you my report at once, sir. I'm quite fit enough for that."

"Where's your Medical Officer?" Fettleworth asked
abruptly.

"Here, sir." Surgeon-Major Corton had come up behind,
and Fettleworth swung round.

"*Is* Captain Ogilvie fit to make me a full verbal report
now, Doctor?"

Corton nodded. "Yes, sir, he is."

"Then, if you please, Doctor, see that he is taken to his
room and made comfortable, and I shall receive his report
there. And quickly, man, quickly, or we shall all catch our

death of cold!" Fettleworth's eye lit upon another of the commissariat carts. "God bless my soul, who's the woman?"

"Major Gilmour's daughter, sir—"

"The devil she is! Poor girl, poor girl. Is she sick?"

Corton said, "She has been, but all's well now. A good night's sleep in a decent bed, and some brandy first, and she'll be fine."

"Then I shall speak to her when she is fit. Ladies do not appreciate being fussed with ceremony when they are not feeling at their best. Clear your sick away now, Doctor."

Darkness was already approaching as the men cleared the parade-ground, the sick and wounded being taken over by the medical orderlies. Lieutenant-General Fettleworth remained until they had all gone, with his Chief of Staff and his aide-de-camp beside him. As the last of the returned soldiers moved out of sight, the garrison bugles sounded out for sunset. The notes rang loud and clear and melancholy across the parade now deserted but for Fettleworth's group and the colour-guard at the flagstaff. Fettleworth stayed motionless, as though cocooned in glory. The Queen's Colour came down, slowly, reverently, and as it began its gentle descent one bugle after another sounded out, lifting brassy voices from the various regimental flagstaffs in honour of the old lady in Windsor Castle. It was the end of one more day in India, one more chapter of Frontier service about to close if Fettleworth had his way ... his mind rioted, filled itself with extraordinary and conflicting thoughts and nightmares in which Her Imperial Majesty the Queen, Empress of India, was circumscribed and imprisoned by a handful of blasted Civilians in morning coats, hateful little men who were always doing their best to overrule the military power—but who didn't always succeed, rot 'em! As the bugles were stilled, Lieutenant-General Fettleworth gave a triumphant if inapposite snort. He had done king's work that day, damn it! Kings of old, who had really ruled in fact as well as in theory, could have done no better. He had virtually kicked the backsides of the Civilians from Calcutta, imposing his iron will and his splendour as Commander of Her Majesty's First Division in Nowshera and Peshawar, four grades removed from God, and he believed he had won the day. There would be much honour, and he would have struck that extra blow for Empire! Fettleworth, giving his nose a vigorous blowing, turned away and bounced into the building behind him, to receive Captain Ogilvie's report of the situation inside Kunarja.

15

"I DOUBT IF in fact, Ogilvie, you can add anything to Tag-gart-Blane's report, considering you both left Kunarja together," Fettleworth began, as he sat in a creaky wicker-work chair by Ogilvie's bed.

"No, sir."

"Not in terms of hard fact. But you are a more mature and experienced soldier, Ogilvie, and may have formed some impressions. Taking into account that you must have some acquaintance with the native mind, that is."

"Yes, sir. At least, I can report the opinion of a much more experienced officer than I—Major Gilmour."

"Quite. Now, how did he see the situation? Did he feel that the hostages were likely to be ill-treated—or should I say, *massacred* if the terms were not met?"

"He did, sir."

Fettleworth nodded. "As I thought—*just* as I thought! I'd like you to repeat that to the Civilians if necessary, and also tell 'em all about your experiences in Kunarja."

"Yes, sir."

"Now, did Gilmour feel action was urgent—really urgent —action, that is, on Jarar Mahommed's proposals—in order to prevent any such massacre? What I'm anxious to deter-mine, you'll understand, is how much *time* we have. Can you make an appreciation, Ogilvie?"

"Sir, Major Gilmour was, I think, of the opinion that Jarar Mahommed would probably not be precipitate ... that he would realise that more time would be needed, in view of conditions in the Khyber Pass."

"Yes." Fettleworth glanced up at the Chief of Staff, visible in the shadows behind the paraffin lamp on a table. "No need for the Civilians to be told about *that*, Lakenham."

"As you say, sir."

"I have to be in a position to force their hands. But in addition, Ogilvie, I must know if it is necessary to send yet more troops through to Kunarja, to back up your own regiment. What's your view? Come now—don't be afraid to express an opinion to your General, my dear fellow! No general can act without intelligence."

"No, sir." Ogilvie gave his opinion without further hesitation, for this was something he had thought about a good deal whilst being carried towards Peshawar. "I believe Lord Dornoch will have adequate strength to contain the situation, sir. Personally I believe Jarar Mahommed *will* allow more time for an answer to his terms ... and I also believe, and believe strongly, sir, that to send another regiment through now would act only to persuade him that we were about to reject his terms out-of-hand, and that we mean to try to subdue him by force."

"That sounds logical enough, indeed it does." Fettleworth paused. "Lakenham, what do you say to that?"

"I agree it's logical, sir. Whether or not we send more troops must, in my view, depend entirely upon how far you wish to extend this situation—"

"Damn it, you know very well I don't wish to extend it at all! I wish to preserve the peace! That's my one aim!"

Lakenham said, "Then I suggest we hold our hands—"

"Yes, and put some more blasted dynamite under the bums of the Civilians while we're holding 'em! It's *time* that's important now. Vital. Time, time, time! A quick reply from Calcutta on the telegraph—and *then* another expedition, with the confirmation of the agreement. And a hope in the meantime that Dornoch will be able to hold the balance between Jarar Mahommed and Rigby-Smith! Would you agree with that, Ogilvie, as the man who has so recently been on the spot as it were?"

Ogilvie nodded. "Yes, sir, I would. To be honest, I see no other course."

"Very well, then that is how the situation will be handled. Have you anything further to report, Ogilvie? Any recommendations for acts of courage, for instance, individual acts?"

"There will be some, sir, yes—"

"But all in good time, perhaps, all in good time." Fettleworth rose to his feet. "I should not overtire you now—"

"Sir, you already know of the deaths of Major and Mrs. Gilmour—"

"Yes, yes, indeed. A sad loss. They'll be buried with full military honours, here in Peshawar."

"There is also another death to report, sir."

"Obviously, there were many—"

"No, sir! There was ... there was a murder. A murder on the march."

*　　*　　*

"I could scarcely believe my ears, Lakenham! Murder's murder, and of course it's terrible—I'm not denying that. But this other thing, this damned buggery. Good God! A British officer, Lakenham, a British officer, getting himself involved in such a *disgraceful* affair. Lowering himself in the eyes of the damn sepoys—behaving like that with a bloody native! *In my command.* Just wait till those blasted Civilians get to hear about *this!*"

"I would hope they—"

"The whole bloody Division will become known as the Oscar Wildes!"

"We must not—"

"Frankly, I blame Dornoch—allowing such a cad to join his regiment! Bah!"

"Sir!" Lakenham, in the privacy of the General's study, almost shouted. "Sir, we must not lose our sense of proportion. The fact of the murder is, I agree, most serious. I don't condone the other thing, far from it, but I think we must both admit it's happened before—"

"When?"

Lakenham made a gesture of irritation. "I can't be precise, sir. What I'm saying is, buggery's never been unknown in the army. It may be distasteful—"

"Distasteful!" Fettleworth raised his arms in the air.

"But it happens, and we're not a bunch of old women, sir. We must not allow ourselves to react like a—a meeting of vicars' wives. Let us deal with facts and not concern ourselves with hysterical moralising. To this end I suggest we should not prejudge Taggart-Blane. I see no conclusive proof, *legal* proof—"

"But young Ogilvie said—"

"Young Ogilvie said too much in my opinion, sir. There's been too much hearsay and no—"

"On the contrary, Ogilvie acted perfectly properly, Lakenham. Perfectly properly. In the absence of his Colonel, it was his duty to acquaint me with every possible relevant detail. That happened to include the whole character of Taggart-Blane and the way in which he struck his equals. In—"

"I would not have considered it entirely proper, sir, to place a man in arrest whilst marching through the Khyber under war conditions. I consider that a somewhat over-rigid act, a case of going too much by the book."

Fettleworth shrugged. "Possibly, but it's hard to fault an officer for sticking to regulations in a case of murder. Remember Ogilvie was under considerable strain, both mentally and physically."

"True, but—"

"No, no, I'll hear of no blame attaching to him, Lakenham, none at all. Besides, no-one's suggested . . ." His voice tailed away, and he looked suddenly up at the Chief of Staff, his face, usually so red, almost green-looking now. "By God, Lakenham, it's just come back to me! God bless my soul! God give me strength!"

"I don't believe I understand, sir?"

Fettleworth thumped his desk. "That Taggart-Blane! God, and I treated him as a confounded hero!"

"He's still that, sir. He still came through the Khyber—"

"Yes, yes, yes. But listen. Taggart-Blane said to me, when I interviewed him that night, that he'd killed a man. *'I killed*

a man.' His very words! Naturally, I took them to mean he'd
shot a man in action and was being somewhat pansy about
it—but I see those words in a very different context now!
Why, the whole way it came out ... it was a kind of confession, Lakenham, don't you see? Ogilvie did admit the
evidence against that havildar was pretty thin in basis—
purely circumstantial. Good God, what a scandal!"

Lakenham stared back at the General, his own face
deeply troubled now. "By God, sir! A scandal indeed—if
true! But is there not a degree of—of pure *circumstance* in
this also?"

"No! *'I killed a man.'* Circumstantial my backside,
Lakenham! I was there—you were not. I heard the man! I
agree the hindsight, but repeat what is now my conviction.
Listen, Lakenham: a British officer, in a good regiment,
straight from Sandhurst, with his whole career before him,
monkeys about with a damn sepoy, a damn black native—
and then murders him before he can talk about it! Assuming the first crime, I can well imagine the second, damned
if I can't! Now—does that hang together, Lakenham, or
does it not?"

"I can't say, sir. This has taken me somewhat by surprise.
Er ... do you know whether the same sepoy was referred to
on both occasions—that is, by Taggart-Blane and by
Ogilvie?"

"No, Taggart-Blane simply said 'a man'. There was no
explicit reference to a sepoy as such—but damn it all,
Lakenham, it would be too much of a coincidence for me
to stomach, if it were *not* the same man, in the circumstances! Gad! The man's a rotter—a bloody cad! D'you
know something else?" Fettleworth thumped the desk
again. "He allowed another man to be put in arrest in his
place—and is continuing so to do! I've heard nothing of
another and more positive confession, at all events!"

"That is, if your suspicions are right, sir."

"Oh, of course—"

"And if I may remind you, I did make the point—"

"That Ogilvie acted wrongly in placing the havildar in
arrest—yes, yes. Well, perhaps you were right, Lakenham,
perhaps you were. Certainly that arrest complicates the
186

whole issue—now *this* has cropped up! Dear oh dear oh dear. This is a scandal that'll rock the whole British Army to its foundations!" Fettleworth got to his feet and stumped up and down his study waving his arms, his face back now to its customary dangerous red. "Buggery!" he said suddenly.

"Sir?"

"I said, buggery. To be sure, it's horrible enough—and I'm *not* a bloody maiden aunt, Lakenham—but I suppose it *could* have been dealt with internally—no damn fuss. But murder! Now, that's different. Isn't it?"

"Yes, indeed it is, sir."

Fettleworth blew out his breath through set teeth. He was thinking that in a personal sense all his efforts with the Civilians had been in vain. Even if he did bring off his aim of a peaceful solution to the current dispute, even if he did advance the 'forward policy' initiated by Lord Lytton in the seventies and eighties, it could prove an achievement all too easily overshadowed by such a scandal as he now envisaged. And the Civilians might retract anyway ... but reflection, just a moment's sane thought, told Fettleworth that this was going too far. They would not do that; but undoubtedly it would be far, far better if they were to hear nothing of this affair. Nothing at all!

"It's got to be kept quiet," Fettleworth said. "D'you hear me, Lakenham? *It's got to be kept quiet!*"

"That's easier said than done, sir."

"It's not impossible. Let us take stock: who knows of this so far? Taggart-Blane himself, Captain Ogilvie, the two natives—Lal Binodinand and Bandra Negi. The 114th's Medical Officer. Gilmour, no doubt, but he's dead—but possibly the daughter knows. You and I."

"A lengthy enough list, is it not?"

"I believe they can all be silenced. The havildar, Lal Binodinand, the man currently to be accused—he may die, though there's the doctor's report that indicates he's pulling through. An act of God may yet occur in that direction! I cannot help but pray that this may be so." Fettleworth, on the prowl around his study still, halted and stared bleakly at Lakenham. "I said they could all be silenced. Frankly, I'm not so sure in Ogilvie's case."

"Indeed?"

"There's something about that young man ... more than a trace of his father. Something else as well ... I don't know! Too damn serious, takes things too much to heart, I believe."

"A young man of, perhaps, little humour?"

"Possibly—though there's no damn humour in this situation, Lakenham! *Obstinacy*—that's it! Obstinacy, and a damned Scottish pride in—in seeing justice done, a kind of damn Bible-thumping Presbyterianism ... oh, the simile's not exact, I know, but you understand what I'm getting at, don't you?" Without waiting for an answer he went on, "Well, what do we do, Lakenham? How do we ensure silence from all concerned?"

"I suppose you could always give an order to that effect, but to do so would hold ... certain obvious dangers."

Fettleworth understood. He nodded. "I could scarcely do that, but there must be other ways."

"Yes, indeed, sir, but all equally dangerous in my opinion."

"Oh? I'll thank you to elaborate on that, Lakenham?"

"Surely it's obvious, sir? As you yourself said, this is a case of murder. It is not a case of ... let us say, some infringement of orders or of propriety, or of any simple act of misconduct. If we now indulge in any jiggery-pokery—"

"I have not suggested jiggery-pokery!"

"No, sir," Lakenham agreed diplomatically. "Not in so many words. But please allow me to continue. Any—er—improper handling of this, will be only too likely to bring us into conflict with the civil law and the civil power. Need I add the obvious—murder is not a *military* crime alone!"

"You sound like a damn barrack-room lawyer to me," Fettleworth said in an aggrieved tone.

"I'm sorry, but I'm simply putting the facts before you, sir, as it is my duty to do. There is another aspect which you must consider, too. In spite of all we've been saying, sir, we have as yet no evidence before us. Why, there has not yet even been a formal charge made! The plain fact is, and this is the *only* fact, a havildar is in arrest on a charge yet to be formulated, even though the nature the charge will take is plain enough. We must consider innocence, sir, as well as guilt." Lakenham lifted a hand and pointed a finger at the General, solemnly. "You and I, sir, must not act as a jury. To ensure a decent silence will not only be dangerous, but will also be unjust to whichever man is innocent of the deed—"

"Why? Why—if there is silence? If there is silence, who is to know what has happened?"

Lakenham shook his head. "The time for *total* silence is past, sir. Not even you can ensure it now! Much of this is bound to ... by God, *murder has been committed*! You must act fairly, sir."

Fettleworth threw up his hands. "Another damned Ogilvie!" he said with extreme bitterness. "God help us all! I've too much on my mind, Lakenham. It's too bad that this should happen whilst I'm in the middle of ensuring peace along the blasted Frontier!" He sat down at his desk with a thump. "I must have time—*time*, d'you hear? Can't you find a formula for procrastination?"

Lakenham said, "Very easily, sir."

"What?"

"It would be perfectly proper to await the return of the officer, whichever he may be, who would normally act as prosecutor in the first instance. I refer, of course, to the Colonels of the regiments concerned—Lord Dornoch, and Rigby-Smith."

"Good God, yes!"

"It would be very proper to delay matters until they are back in cantonments. In the meantime, I would advise that Division stays out of the whole matter. Hand this over to Brigade, sir, and suggest that for the time being Lal Binodinand remains formally in arrest whilst in hospital. I would also suggest, sir, that a reasonable discretion be permitted Captain Ogilvie, to talk in private with Taggart-Blane."

"To act as a spy, Lakenham?"

"No, sir. He could not be asked to do that, nor, I think, would he do it. In any case, I doubt if evidence obtained

189

that way would impress a Court Martial. My suggestion is that he simply talks generally to Taggart-Blane, and points out that an officer and a gentleman has a duty to protect the good name of his regiment. That is all." He paused, meaningly. "I think you understand, sir, do you not?"

Fettleworth stared back at him, a vein pumping away in his temple. "By God," he said slowly. "Yes, I do. A touch of genius, Lakenham! It could be the answer!"

*　　*　　*

Katharine Gilmour went to see Ogilvie in his sickroom, once he had emerged from an exhausted, almost paralytic sleep. She was looking pale and drawn but made light of her own condition, asking with obvious concern about himself.

"There's no need to worry about me," Ogilvie assured her. "I'm mending fast. What's going to happen to you, Katharine?"

"I'm going to friends in Murree," she said, taking a chair by his bedside at his bidding. "General Fettleworth's made the arrangements, and—and I suppose I'm grateful, for I've nowhere else to go." He saw the sparkle of tears in her eyes as she went on quietly, "Mother and Father were buried this morning, James. There was full ceremonial . . . I hated all that, I simply can't tell you, but of course it was the proper thing in Father's case."

"And your mother's. She was as much on duty as your father."

"Yes, that's true. And—I'm glad now it was in British territory. She *would* have been pleased to know . . . and it was all your doing, James. I—I came to say thank you, as well as good-bye."

He shook his head. "Never mind the thanks, I'm glad to have helped in any way I could, Katharine. And it won't be good-bye really . . . will it?"

She smiled. "Your parents are in Murree, aren't they? I expect we'll meet."

He said, "I'll make a point of that, just as soon as I get leave. Please don't be in a hurry to leave India, Katharine

—though I know you can't wait to see England again!"

"It pulls me, I'll admit, but..."

He looked into her eyes. "Go on, Katharine?"

"Oh ... it was nothing. No, I'll not be in too great a hurry." She got to her feet. "They told me I must not stay long. Good-bye, James, and ... thank you again." She held out a slim hand.

"Good-bye, Katharine." He held the hand rather longer than was strictly decorous. After she had gone, his room seemed twice as lonely as it had before. As he heard her feet tapping quickly along the corridor outside, his mind flicked, like a cinematograph, to Mary Archdale. He was unsure of his feelings, of the wisdom of his commitments. All that his uncle had said in Scotland came back to him. Of one thing at least he could be very sure: the Ogilvie family would warmly approve a friendship with the daughter of the late Resident in Kunarja, especially one so fresh, so virginal, so unspotted by gossip as Katharine Gilmour! But time alone could tell now which way his heart would take him; he believed he would meet with a response from Katharine, at all events. But there was still Mary; and he was in a turmoil as he lay in his bed, knowing that he must not allow himself to be swayed in any one direction, or against another, by such considerations as his uncle had propounded. Equally he must be sure that pride, and a feeling that he should not be subjected to family pressures, did not head him away from the quarter in which already he knew himself to be projecting.

Within the next couple of days he was up and about though under doctor's orders to take things easily. His first act was to visit Havildar Lal Binodinand in the military hospital. Curtly, he dismissed the armed sentry standing by the bed. The man retired, still watchful, to a discreet distance.

Ogilvie sat down.

"How are you, Lal Binodinand?" he asked.

"Sahib, in my body I am better. The Doctor Sahib says that I improve daily."

"And in your mind?"

A shadow passed across the man's dark brown eyes and

191

the lips trembled. "In my mind I am confused and sad, Sahib. I am a havildar of the 99th Rawalpindis, not a low caste criminal. I did not do this thing. I have never killed a sleeping man—nor any man save in war. I would not stoop to such a deed."

"Yet circumstances point to your guilt, Lal Binodinand."

"Sahib, I am not guilty, I swear it on my honour as a soldier of the Raj." Sweat, Ogilvie saw, was pouring down the man's forehead, running into the heavy beard. The eyes, liquid eyes, were beseeching. This looked very much like innocence to Ogilvie, who was already predisposed towards a disbelief in Taggart-Blane's protestations and who indeed felt in retrospect that the finger of circumstance had pointed more precisely at the British officer than at the native havildar. He was very deeply troubled; his own order had put this man in arrest—at the time he had seen this as a correct and inevitable action. It was also to some extent an irrevocable action, since to secure his release Lal Binodinand must now face charges and prove his innocence. In the absence of someone else to be put in arrest in his place, he could scarcely be set free now.

Ogilvie asked in a low voice, "Do you know of any other man who could have done this terrible thing, Lal Binodinand?"

"No, Sahib, I do not."

"If you did, if you had suspicions, you would tell me?"

"I would tell you, Sahib."

"You are not, perhaps, shielding anyone? You are under no duress?"

"No, Sahib."

Ogilvie got to his feet. "Do not worry, Lal Binodinand. You will receive justice from the British Raj."

"This I know, Sahib. It is my rock and my strength."

Ogilvie found a lump coming into his throat. He reached out and took the havildar's hand, giving it a firm and friendly clasp, and then, without further words, turned away and beckoned the sentry back to his post. He left the hospital, his face hard and his mind more than ever troubled. Arriving in the 114th's Mess, which by tacit agreement he and Taggart-Blane were using in preference to that of the sepoy regiment despite their continuing secondment, he was given a message by an orderly: his attendance was required forthwith at Brigade. He was to report personally to a Colonel Wilkinson, acting Brigade Commander in the absence in Calcutta of the Brigadier-General. He had some acquaintance with Wilkinson, a friendly enough officer who had himself lately commanded a native regiment of the Indian Army.

Colonel Wilkinson got to his feet when Ogilvie was shown into his office. He was a short man, and spare, with sharp, bright eyes in which lurked more than a trace of humour.

"Sit down, Ogilvie, I'll not keep you long."

"Thank you, sir." Ogilvie sat in a chair drawn up to face the desk. "I've all the time in the world just now."

"How're you shaping?"

"I'm fit now, sir."

"Good." Wilkinson rubbed his hands together briskly. "Ogilvie, I'll come straight to the point. It's about this unpleasant business in the Khyber, the report of which reached Division before it reached me."

"Yes, sir. I'm sorry about that, but the General—"

"Oh, forget it. Now, you'll understand that in a sense I'm acting in the room of your Colonel. Until he returns, the matter must largely rest, but there are certain details of procedure to be gone into." He paused. "You realise, of course, that none of this is to be talked about outside this office?"

"Yes, sir."

"Right. Well now, I've been contacted by Division. There's a little ambiguity in the air, I fear, but that's my worry, not yours. Also, I'm not too sure that correct procedures have been followed so far—by Division, that is— though I have to assume that Division, like God, is incapable of sin. Besides, there are many aspects of unorthodoxy about this whole affair. I don't think—indeed I *know*—I've never come up against anything quite of this nature in all my service. I refer to the apparent involvement of Mr. Taggart-Blane. Such a thing whilst on the march staggers the mind and makes the imagination boggle! What's your opinion of Taggart-Blane? As a man, I mean, not simply as an officer?"

Ogilvie hesitated. "Should I answer that, sir? I mean—"

"Yes, I know what you mean, and you have my assurance that this interview is entirely off the record. Please give me your answer. It will help us a great deal."

Ogilvie took a deep breath. "In my opinion, he's ... a little effeminate."

"But there was nothing effeminate about his getting through with that despatch."

"No, sir."

"Then ..." Wilkinson pushed things about on his desk. "Perhaps it isn't effeminate you mean, Ogilvie. Let me help you out. In broad terms, the word effeminate means womanly—woman*ish* I should say, rather—unmanly. Such a person would I think be unlikely to stand up to the rigours of your march from Kunarja and then proceed successfully, alone but for a guide, from the point of ambush to Peshawar. On the other hand, men of a certain propensity have often been known to act heroically, and to be excellent soldiers and officers." He looked straight into Ogilvie's eyes. "Now: would you have said Taggart-Blane was a homosexual? I mean, of course, before the alleged act of buggery?"

Ogilvie said, "Yes, I had that feeling, sir, though I detest saying this of a brother officer."

"Something in his manner—that sort of thing?"

"Yes, that's right. Nothing more precise than that."

"But if it were true, then you can see the implications? You can see a possible motive for murder, if his propensities suggest to a court that it was likely the act of buggery had indeed taken place?"

"Yes, sir, I can. I did in fact suggest as much to General Fettleworth, but he seemed not to take it in—"

"No indeed—at the time. Now I'll tell you something else I know, and which you don't, Ogilvie. Taggart-Blane has virtually told General Fettleworth that he killed a man."

Ogilvie started. "He said that? Taggart-Blane said that?"

Wilkinson told him the details, adding, "Of course, this

194

can scarcely in legal terms be held to constitute a confession, but nevertheless it's a pointer, don't you think?" He paused. "Tell me, Ogilvie: do you think Taggart-Blane killed that sepoy, or do you not?"

"Ogilvie met his eye. He said squarely, "I have that impression, sir—now."

"Now?"

"It was in my mind earlier."

"Then why did you arrest the havildar, Lal Binodinand?"

Ogilvie hesitated. "There were circumstances of guilt... and we were on the march in filthy and dangerous conditions of weather and likely attack—my mind was very full of that. Possibly I acted hastily."

"Or perhaps you were, even unconsciously, acting to safeguard the good name of your regiment? I'm not making an accusation—it's a fine thing in any officer that he shows consideration for his regiment. But in a case of murder..." He shrugged.

"I admit my regiment was in my mind, sir, but I don't believe that would have caused me to—to—"

"Commit a miscarriage of justice? Well, possibly it's no miscarriage at all. I suppose only a Court Martial can decide that. Or a man's own conscience."

"It *is* on my conscience, sir, I'll admit, but—"

"No, no, not *your* conscience, Ogilvie! Taggart-Blane's conscience."

"Sir?"

"Come, now! You're not grass-green, Ogilvie. A man's conscience can get to work on him, can it not? He can be made to see the importance of keeping the regiment's honour intact, of safeguarding, as you tried to safeguard, the good name of Her Majesty's service. That's of tremendous importance out here on the Frontier, Ogilvie."

"I still don't quite see, sir—"

"Then I'll be more explicit. Ogilvie, I have an idea Division doesn't want a Court Martial of either Taggart-Blane or Lal Binodinand. I also have an idea they don't want it because of Taggart-Blane's improper involvement with Mulata Din and because of his apparent homosexuality —*not* because they doubt his guilt. And I have no doubt that

Taggart-Blane is in danger, if the General should find himself forced to bring *him* before a Court Martial, of being found guilty. There is the fact of the thrown-away revolver, just to mention one thing only. If found guilty, he will of course hang. He'll first be dismissed from the Queen's service with disgrace, and stripped of his rank, and then he will be hanged in the civil jail at Nowshera. The implication for the army will be terrible, really terrible! He must be made to see this. I am asking you to put it to him, Ogilvie." Wilkinson paused. "You see, if he is guilty, there is a better way of settling this than with a Court Martial and an execution."

Ogilvie felt the blood drain away from his face, leaving him white-lipped and trembling. He said, "Do you mean, sir ... that he should be his own executioner? Is that what you're suggesting?"

Wilkinson nodded. His eyes were hard now, his expression implacable. In a clipped voice he said, "Yes, it is. An admission of guilt so that Lal Binodinand may be released, and then a finish. After that, there will be ways of ensuring silence—you know what I mean. It's a neat way to end it all, and very just. In my view—like the Captain who goes down with his ship—it's the *only* way for an officer and a gentleman."

*　　　*　　　*

The bullet through the temple, fired by the self-inflictory hand of the suicide! Yes, it was the traditional gentleman's way out when all was lost and black. Although everybody might be well aware of the reason behind the act, it left no dishonour in its wake. The dead man was in a sense respected, for he had, after all, done the decent thing; and in so doing had redeemed himself in the eyes of his fellows, all of whom were naturally gentlemen too. And afterwards, his name would simply be no longer spoken in the Mess. It was neat.

It was far, far better than the common hangman in the civil jail. It would not—and Wilkinson was indeed making much of this point—it would not take long for the Queen's

Own Royal Strathspeys to live down a suicide, especially that of a hero; in this particular case the real reason need never emerge, always provided no time was lost. There might be suspicions; but no decent man would ever voice them. Taggart-Blane's terrible experiences in bringing through Gilmour's despatch could be tacitly held to account for a young officer's act of mental aberration.

"You must talk to him," Wilkinson said. "*He's* the only man who knows for certain whether or not he's guilty— and if he is..." He left the sentence unfinished.

* * *

It was an overwhelming responsibility, to talk a man into ending his own life; even to put the idea into his head was in a sense to usurp the prerogative of God. This was more a job for the padre; but, though a talk with the padre might well help him, Ogilvie felt that he could not, must not, attempt to shift the burden. Wilkinson had been right: this was better done as between two men of much the same age, two men of much the same experience in so far as both were combatant officers. Curiously perhaps in the circumstances, it did not seem the occasion for the often heavy and sanctimonious hand of the church, the moral strictures, the sermonising and the pained looks. Better it should be down-to-earth, clean cut and objective.

Slowly Ogilvie crossed the almost deserted parade-ground of the Royal Strathspeys. The whole area had an alien feeling, with the regiment away; it was like a school during the holidays, in the hands of the caretakers—or in this case, the base staff, the clerks and storemen and the natives who did the menial tasks around the cantonment. Here on this very parade-ground there had been a hanging, rather more than two years ago. Every detail was as clear in Ogilvie's mind as if the terrible business were taking place at that very moment. Here, his company of the Royal Strathspeys had been fallen in; here, had been the dais upon which had stood Lord Dornoch, Fettleworth, and his own father, the latter having just taken over the command of the Northern Army; in front of the dais, between the escort under the charge of the Regimental Sergeant-Major, had stood the handcuffed figure of the guilty man—another murderer—listening to the reading of the Court Martial findings and the sentence of death; there, had stood the gallows, and beside the gallows the empty coffin, waiting for its occupant, currently alive and well. The man, a private reduced from the rank of corporal, had a little later swung from the gallows and as the corpse had swung the companies had been marched away to a lively tune, a contrast from the crepe-muffled drums and the sadly wailing pipes that had been the murderer's accompaniment as he had been paraded before the regiment earlier.

It had been a horrible business.

Ogilvie moved on more quickly, with a shudder of distaste for what was past. He found Taggart-Blane in the Mess, thumbing through some old magazines from London. The subaltern had been to see him on two occasions while he had been confined to his bed; but on neither of those occasions had the murder of the sepoy, Mulata Din, been mentioned, though Ogilvie had noted the pallor of Taggart-Blane's face and the miserable worry in his eyes, signs that gave away the turmoil of the mind. Today the pallor and the worry were there in even greater measure, Ogilvie fancied.

He sat down beside Taggart-Blane. The subaltern asked, "Is there anything fresh from Kunarja, James?"

"Not that I'm aware of. I hope Fettleworth gets a move on, though."

"Yes. It was a rotten enough Christmas for us; God knows what it was like for those poor fellows in that filthy palace."

Ogilvie himself had been scarcely aware that Christmas Day had passed; there had been too many worries on his mind, and all he had registered had been a change in his invalid diet, and a visit from Fettleworth, and another from Taggart-Blane. Abruptly, his voice made unduly sharp by his distaste for what he had to do, he said, "Alan, there are things we have to talk about now. We can't delay any longer. It would appear that Lal Binodinand is likely to live— indeed, I don't believe there's any doubt about that. So..."

"Well? Go on."

"For God's sake, man, you know what I have to say! Can't you try to make it easier for me?"

Taggart-Blane shrugged and threw down the magazine. "Why the devil should I make it easy for *you*? It's not very easy for *me*, you know. Or has that escaped your bloody lofty notice?"

"Of course not. I know how you're feeling. On the other hand..."

"Well?"

"I rather wonder why it's *quite* so bad for you. That is, if Lal Binodinand is guilty."

Taggart-Blane stared for a moment, then laughed. "Oh, come, my dear fellow! You know very well why. If you want me to spell it out for you—because of what the man may say at his Court Martial—that's why!"

"Then you did—"

"No! James, I did not! I was only doing what I could for his frost-bite. *Nothing more.* I've told you that already... oh, don't worry, I know you've never believed me. You think I killed Mulata Din too, don't you?"

Ogilvie looked away across the anteroom. A shaft of sunlight had stolen in and had touched the comfortable worn leather of the chairs, the sketches of former Colonels, the group photographs on the walls. So many happy times had been passed in here; it was hateful even to think that this place could be touched by scandal. Bringing his attention back to Taggart-Blane he asked quietly, "Did you, Alan? Did you kill him?"

"No, I did not. But even if I had, James, I doubt if I'd tell you!"

"I suppose that's true." Ogilvie hesitated, then decided to approach the real point more closely. "I don't think I need stress the effect upon the regiment—"

"If anything comes out—if any damn lies stick? No, you needn't! Can we take the sermon as delivered, please, James?"

Ogilvie nodded, seeing the increasing distress in Taggart-Blane's face. "All right. But just for a moment, I want you to listen to a hypothetical case. Supposing an officer, any

199

officer from any regiment or corps, was compromised in a dishonourable way—"

"I—"

"Just shut up and listen. Believe me, I'm sorry for the word, but we must be realistic now. Let us make that supposition; and suppose also that no charge, no real accusation in fact, has yet been made ... but the officer concerned knows that he is in fact guilty. What—"

"I must say this is all rather pointed. Are you asking me to condemn myself out of my own mouth—and then you rush panting to Bloody Francis Fettleworth to get his signature on my death warrant?"

Ogilvie flushed. "Nothing of the kind. I asked you just now to try to make my job a little easier. Now I ask you again. Let us stick to the hypothesis. Let us go back to this officer. He knows he's guilty. What can he do?" He leaned forward. "What, in point of actual fact, has often been done in such circumstances?"

Taggart-Blane gave a cold, tight smile. "Easy! He shoots himself, doesn't he? Makes a bloody mess, but it's a better mess than the one he left behind. Well? Am I right? Have you come to advise me to put a bullet in my head, with my own hand? You—whose life you said I saved that night in the Khyber—you come to tell me this, James?"

Ogilvie looked away, his face deeply troubled. He didn't answer; but was surprised a moment later to hear Taggart-Blane's sudden loud laugh in his ears. The subaltern said, "Oh, really, James, you needn't feel quite so dreadful, for I've no intention in all the world of shooting myself! For one thing, it's too damn traditional, too much *expected* of the wrong 'un. I'm never much impressed by the right thing to do. And I'm damned, James, if I'm going out of this world like some rotten little regimental paymaster who's done a bunk with the funds and can't repay—I'm damned if I am! I'll be honest and admit I don't think I'd have the guts ... not even, dear James," he added with another laugh, "for the sake of the bloody regiment! Frankly, the regiment doesn't mean all that much to me. Sacrilege, of course, but honest sacrilege."

"So you're—"

"So I'm not going to behave like a gentleman, James. I definitely am not. What's the use of spilling all that beautiful blue blood?" Once more, he laughed. "Now I'll tell you what I *am* going to do: if ever I'm charged, I'll fight! And I'll regard the choice of weapons as mine, James. They may not be very nice ones, but that's too bad and must be accepted—for it'll be my life I'll be fighting for. I'm sorry, but the thought of scandalising the good name of the regiment quite fails to move me. Quite fails!"

"And in the meantime, you'll take the risk of Lal Binodinand hanging—for want of evidence against *you*?"

Taggart-Blane snapped, "If *he* hangs, then at least *I* won't —whatever else he cares to come out with before he dies! That, I can take—if I have to."

Ogilvie got to his feet. "You did this thing, Taggart-Blane. You and I ... I think we both know that now. I assure you, the matter won't rest here. When you're brought to a Court Martial, you'll not have a chance. You'll be found guilty, and you'll hang—"

"Aren't officers shot? Isn't that the privilege of our rank and class, James?"

"I wouldn't count on it, and if I were you I wouldn't sound too frivolous. No, you'll hang like a rat, for that's what you'll be, so long as you're prepared to chance an innocent man facing the penalty that should be yours."

"Damn it all, James, you're talking like a schoolboy's essay! *'Play up, play up, and play the game.'* Besides, I rather think you're acting utterly improperly by talking to me at all about what should be *sub judice*."

"I don't think it's yet reached that stage. Anyway, we're on the North-West Frontier of India, on what is considered as active service—not in the Old Bailey. There's a pretty big difference. Think about all I've said—and then ask yourself whether the gentleman's way isn't the best way after all!"

He turned away and left the Mess, fists clenched in impotent anger. The man was a cad. A sepoy might in some quarters—by such officers as Taggart-Blane perhaps—be regarded merely as a native, a lower order who could on occasion be a handy scapegoat for an officer's shortcomings;

but to James Ogilvie Lal Binodinand was a human life in shame and peril and ignominy, and as such was to be protected. As against that simple fact, the regiment could no longer be allowed to count. Leaving the building, Ogilvie strode once again across the parade-ground, making for Brigade, to report to Colonel Wilkinson. On the way, however, he was met by an orderly from the General's staff.

"Captain Ogilvie, sir! The General's compliments, and he wishes to see you immediately, sir."

"Thank you." Ogilvie returned the salute. "Any idea what it's about?"

"Not really, sir, no. But the General, 'e seems cock-a-hoop ... crowing about the Civilian gentlemen from Calcutta, 'e was, sir, and not being complimentary at all, sir."

Ogilvie grinned, and went on more quickly. Shown into Fettleworth's study, he found Bloody Francis in a most excellent humour. "Ah, Ogilvie, my dear fellow, I thought in the circumstances you should be among the very first to know, though of course this information is to be regarded as secret for the present: Major Gilmour's report, and naturally my own recommendations, have had their effect and by *God* it's a good one! Notwithstanding those blasted nincompoops of Government clerks, I've just received word by telegraph that Calcutta's approved the terms—*in full*, with no cuts, no counter-proposals! Gad, for once they've acted quickly enough—they'll no doubt have taken my point about the urgency in regard to Colonel Rigby-Smith's position."

"I'm delighted to hear that, sir."

Fettleworth nodded. "So you should be, my dear fellow. Now—there's much to do. A very great deal." He paused, pursed his lips, and sucked in air. "By the way, Ogilvie, I gather you've already been spoken to by Colonel Wilkinson of Brigade. What's the result?"

Stiffly Ogilvie said, "None, sir."

"None? You've talked to Taggart-Blane, have you—hey?"

"Yes, sir."

"Well, then?"

"Sir, it's as I said. No result."

Fettleworth looked dumbfounded. "You mean he won't—won't—"

"No, sir, he won't."

"Damn young blackguard! Why, it was virtually an *order*..." The General blew out his breath, lifting the trailing ends of his yellowed moustache. "No, not an order of course, I withdraw that. But really! Can you imagine it—feller can't be a gentleman, can't *possibly*. Oh, confound all this!" For a while Fettleworth huffed and puffed angrily, then said, "Well, we'll have to leave Taggart-Blane for the time being, there's more important matters to attend to, matters of action. I must send my acceptance of the terms through to Jarar Mahommed just as soon as it's humanly possible to get them there! Forced marching—forced marching, Ogilvie! A full company, I think, with an officer to take personal charge of the documents, of course." He drummed his fingers on the desk, staring at the photograph of his semi-visible Monarch. "It'll have to be the Duke of Wellington's—I'd hesitate to commit the 114th's half-company again so quickly upon their recent ordeal—no, no argument on that score, my dear fellow, I'm adamant. But that brings me to you. You personally."

"Sir?"

"Well now, you've had a most terrible time. I realise that. Really a dreadful journey. Indeed I do hesitate ... but after all, you know the present situation in Kunarja better than anyone else available to me—and of course it was you whom Jarar Mahommed sent as Gilmour's escort. You're *known* to the blasted rebel! Therefore it might be prudent to—er. Well now! No, it's asking too much altogether. I'm being unfair. But if you cared to volunteer, my dear Ogilvie... well..."

"I'll go, of course, sir," Ogilvie said with a sinking heart. Fettleworth was blandly disregarding the fact that he had had a longer total ordeal than his half-company. The prospect of yet another march through the Khyber appalled him, but duty was duty and it would be a foolish junior officer who failed to accede to the wishes of his Divisional Commander.

Fettleworth looked immensely relieved. "Thank you,

Ogilvie, thank you! You'll find me not ungrateful, my dear fellow. Your task will be simply to carry the terms as my representative—you will be doing Major Gilmour's job in reverse—I shall not expect you to bear the responsibility of commanding the escorting company. That will fall upon an officer of the Duke of Wellington's Regiment."

"Yes, sir. May I make one request, sir?"

"Oh, by all means, yes. What is it, Ogilvie?"

"I should like to take Mr. Taggart-Blane with me, sir."

"Taggart-Blane?" The General's eyebrows went up in astonishment. "What the devil ... may one ask, *why?"*

Ogilvie paused, and stared straight ahead, at a point over the summit of his Divisional Commander. "It's just an idea, sir. I'd like him to retrace that march ... and think about what happened. This is a difficult situation, sir, not least for yourself, if I may say so. It could be that the Khyber will clarify matters." He hesitated. "Clarify them ... in such a way that no formal charge will be necessary. I don't think I can be more precise than that, sir."

Fettleworth stared back at him with his mouth sagging open. After a few moments he closed it with a snap. "I, also, cannot be too precise. I shall just say this: you have my permission to take Mr. Taggart-Blane with you, but *on no account* is he to be entrusted with any knowledge of the terms agreed. If he should become a casualty of the march from any cause, it is perfectly possible that the affair will end. I take it I echo, to some extent, your own thoughts, Ogilvie?"

"Yes, sir, perhaps. But there would remain the question of Lal Binodinand, the accused havildar of the 99th."

"Yes, indeed. This has been much in my mind." Fettleworth cleared his throat rumblingly. "You may take it that in certain circumstances I would order an investigation to be conducted by Brigade, an investigation that would find the sepoy, what was his name—"

"Mulata Din, sir."

"That the sepoy was after all shot by the enemy, in which case Lal Binodinand would be at once released from arrest and reinstated in his duties as havildar. It would, of course, follow that you yourself, as the officer who placed him in arrest, would be reprimanded for misplaced zeal and failing to conduct a proper investigation—a difficult enough task whilst marching through the Khyber, in all conscience! You would not mind this?"

"Not in the very least, sir."

Fettleworth nodded. "Well said, Ogilvie, well said indeed. You are a good officer. You are also something else."

"Sir?"

"Damn it, man, you're as cunning and artful as a blasted monkey—and so am I when I need to be, so am I!" Smiling now, Fettleworth heaved himself to his feet and reached up to pat Ogilvie approvingly on the shoulder. "You've relieved my mind of a serious problem to a great extent, my dear fellow—I trust you will find yourself able to settle it finally."

16

Once again past Jamrud, below the fortress and into the horrible conditions of the Khyber. Once again the bitter penetrating wind, once again the snow—though not so much of the latter as they had experienced last time. Ogilvie, without the responsibility of command, and feeling the after-effects of recent experiences still, spent much of the march, as he had when wounded, in a commissariat cart under thick blankets and greatcoats and with a fur cap pulled about his ears. Taggart-Blane struggled along behind, on foot, full of bitter complaint. Ogilvie had determined to wear him down by the time they reached the place where Mulata Din had died and where Lal Binodinand had been placed in arrest.

Taggart-Blane had been indignant at the start but Ogilvie, finding a welcome backer in Major Arkwright of the Duke of Wellington's—a rock-faced company commander of the old school—had told him curtly that he was to do as he was told and march with the men. Arkwright, overhearing, had spoken to Ogilvie afterwards. "The army's getting too damn soft, Ogilvie. The very idea of any unwounded man expecting to *ride* through the Khyber in a wagon—deplorable!"

"I'm not exactly wounded myself, Major."

"Not now—not now—but very recently. I've heard about your march, Ogilvie."

"Then you'll have heard that Taggart-Blane brought the

despatch through on his own. He's not done so badly."

"True, true. I'm sorry, Ogilvie—I seem to have been critical of your own subaltern—too bad of me, and I do apologise. Only I cannot stomach namby-pambyism. I was used to better things—the lash, the field-gun wheel and all that went with that! It built men, by God, and we had officers to match." He moved away, going ahead along the line of march, leaving Ogilvie to his own thoughts and anxieties. If he had not the responsibility of the march, he had other responsibilities: the all-important agreement, signed and sealed by Lieutenant-General Fettleworth and Mr. Peabody from Calcutta; and to some extent he had the responsibility of one of Her Majesty's judges. In his hands now lay the life of Lal Binodinand, and in a different context that of Taggart-Blane. He had somehow, and currently he knew not how, to force the issue with Taggart-Blane. As a corollary to these life-judgments, he had also a personal responsibility towards Bloody Francis Fettleworth, who was trusting in him completely to settle the affair in such a way that would leave no embarrassing ends trailing behind it. Fettleworth, as one of Her Majesty's Lieutenant-Generals, in high Indian command, was a very important figure who must never be seen overtly to connive, to conspire, to attempt to influence the course of justice. Great care would have to be exercised throughout. No scandal must attach to the Commander of the First Division—if it did, the repercussions could be immense.

Fettleworth had said as much, with great stress. "If any act of mine should be called into question—or rather, in this case, if I should appear to have *in any way agreed* to an improper course of action, then I don't think I would exaggerate if I said that the whole of the sub-continent would be affected—as would the whole of the British Army throughout the world. Why, even Her Majesty's reputation might suffer—at all events in the eyes of such of the damn niggers as can read!"

Recalling this, Ogilvie smiled a little to himself; allowing for the pompous over-statements, some truth did in fact remain. Images must never be tarnished; and memories for things that were better forgotten were ever long. In a sense the Raj was perhaps more vulnerable to the breath of scandal and the hint of corruption in high places than it was to the force of arms and the pressures of the Frontier tribes. Yet there would, Ogilvie believed, be no scandal on this occasion; with absolutely no real reason so to think, he felt that the Gods were going to help. Even as he thought this, he looked at the hard-packed snow along the track, and felt the keenness of the funnelling wind, saw the icy-looking sky lofting above the peaks that closed in the pass, and knew that in all the world there was no more God-forsaken place than this, even though, out of all that world, it was the place that was physically among the closest to heaven.

* * *

"I suppose you're going to shoot me in the back," Taggart-Blane said coolly.

"What the devil d'you mean by that?"

"What I said, damn you!" There was a hard laugh from the darkness. "I know very well why you brought me on this wretched trek."

"Whatever the reason, it certainly wasn't that!"

"But you do admit, then, that there was an ulterior motive?"

"Not ulterior, of course not."

"Well, I suppose it's a matter of language—of what *ulterior* means to you, James. Did you hope I'd be polished off by the enemy?"

Ogilvie said, "I don't think this is going to get us any-where. Why not drop it?"

"Oh, but I don't want to drop it! I wish you'd tell me the truth—the real reason I'm here, which I'm quite sure isn't to hold your hand *or* to do another heroic solo dash through the Khyber! Which brings me, rather naturally, to another point: why haven't I been told the object of the mission, James?" The voice was high and accusing, almost petulant. "I'm only *assuming* you've got sort some of terms in your pocket—nobody's *told* me!"

"I'm sorry."

"Sorry! You mean you're under orders not to trust me, don't you?"

"I can't discuss that—I repeat, I'm sorry. But you mustn't imagine you're not here on a real job, because you are. I *could* get knocked off, we *could* be ambushed again, and every officer's needed. Those are real enough reasons for anybody, Alan. But I'll make an admission, if you like: I was hoping the Khyber would make you see things as they are. Out here a man has time to think, and space to give him perspective. I hoped you'd see..."

"See what?"

"Well, that conscience is important. You've a long life to live—"

"Have I?"

"You know what I mean. I think the time'll come when you'll condemn yourself for what you're doing to Lal Binodinand."

"I see. And you have the cheek to talk about a long life! Oh, don't worry, I see your dilemma! Anyway, you're still, in a sense, offering me the gentleman's way out—aren't you?"

"I'm only asking you to get your thoughts in order, that's all."

Taggart-Blane gave one of his high, semi-hysterical laughs. "God, but you're pathetic! If getting one's thoughts in order leads one to a bullet in the brain ... why, for Christ's sake, go to the bother? Do you know something?"

"Tell me."

There was another laugh. "Not what you want to hear! This: I've a mother and a father in England, and a brother, and two sisters. I've an idea I mean quite a lot to them, yet you're asking me to die by my own hand and bring misery and distress to all of them—all innocents. Have you ever thought of that? The telegram or whatever it is from the War Office ... arriving, probably in the middle of a New Year's party or something? *Your son's dead, in the bloody rotten Khyber.* In heroic action? Oh, no! He blew his brains out, that's all, rather than face a possible charge of—"

"It wouldn't be like that, I give you my word."

209

"Well, Judge Ogilvie, you really needn't bother," Taggart-Blane said viciously. "If you think I'm going to bring sorrow to my family, my own flesh and blood, just for some damn black havildar, you're very much mistaken!" Taggart-Blane moved away towards his own bivouac, vanishing into the darkness. Sick at heart, Ogilvie said nothing; but found sleep hard to come by that night. There were always the innocents to suffer. He tried not to see Taggart-Blane's parents in his imaginings. Next day, tired out, he resumed the march with the men of the Duke of Wellington's Regiment and by the following nightfall they had marched again into terrible weather, into a howling blizzard that sent slivers of ice flinging cruelly into the faces of the soldiers as they tried desperately to find shelter. It was nothing short of a nightmare, in which each man was sunk into a close, individual world of silent suffering.

*   *   *

The blizzard blew for more than twenty-four hours before any easement came. As the snow thinned Ogilvie, with Arkwright and Surgeon-Major Corton, made his way around all the men of the escort, checking on the fitness of the soldiers to march out. There were many cases of frost-bite, which kept Corton and his medical orderlies busy rubbing the afflicted limbs with snow, trying to thaw them gradually, and looking for any signs of dry or wet gangrene. Four men had died; Ogilvie and Arkwright found them, four corpses, frozen solid, mere snow-covered heaps upon the ground.

"They'll need to be buried," Arkwright said. "It'll be a hard task, will that!"

"Yes..." Ogilvie sounded preoccupied; he was looking all around the now visible landscape.

"What's the matter, Ogilvie?"

"Taggart-Blane. I've not seen him."

Arkwright frowned. "Come to think of it—no more have I! That's very odd, Ogilvie. What the devil can have become of him?"

"He could have gone into a frozen sleep, I suppose, and

is buried in the snow," Ogilvie said. "God knows, it's deep enough! We must mount a full search, Major."

"Of course—at once."

Arkwright gave the necessary order; all fit men were set immediately to the task of searching the whole area, which, with patient endeavour, was covered almost inch by inch.

Nothing was found, no evidence of Taggart-Blane at all.

He must have gone, Ogilvie realised, must have deserted the march. After the main search had proved fruitless, Ogilvie questioned each man closely in case any movement had been observed during the blizzard; but with no result. Nothing at all had been seen, nothing had been heard above the howling of the ferocious wind. The place where Taggart-Blane had made his personal bivouac was roughly ascertained and a specially careful probe was made beneath the snow. There was nothing; if Taggart-Blane had gone, he had left nothing behind him. He had gone with all his equipment, his blankets, his revolver, his ammunition— gone, Ogilvie was now convinced, like a ghost, a trackless thing, into the Khyber's snows and the wildness of those remote hills, the lonely places at the roof of the world. It would never be possible to trace him; any tracks would naturally have been covered by the falling snow, snow which even now was still drifting slowly down.

Ogilvie felt old and utterly weary, worn out. Was this a suicide, the outward stumble of a man driven beyond endurance—a stumble out into the cold to die? Had his, Ogilvie's, words been the last straw, had he at last driven Taggart-Blane to the gentleman's exit from life? Or—was it an escape, an act of outright desertion, a desperate braving of cruel weather and hostile tribesmen in order to evade military justice, the retribution of the British Raj? *Was it?* And if so, would Taggart-Blane, with a sinner's luck, win through and live on to become one of the world's outcasts, a man for ever on the run? The search had been very thorough; it was certain beyond all doubt that Taggart-Blane was not in the close vicinity. He must have had strength to put a fair distance between himself and his comrades. Of course, he could have the desperate strength of the madman, the suicide's will to do the thing properly; but somehow, to

Ogilvie who knew Taggart-Blane, it failed to add up to suicide. When later his thoughts were interrupted by Major . Arkwright, he knew that Taggart-Blane had indeed made a bid for escape. Some of the troops' rations had been purloined, Arkwright said, and a commissariat mule had vanished. Suicides did not take provisions or transport.

"Can we be sure it was Taggart-Blane that took the food?" Ogilvie asked.

Arkwright shrugged. "No. But in the circumstances it's a reasonable assumption, isn't it? I can assure you that none of *my* men would stoop so low—besides, not one of my men is missing, to have taken the mule."

"It could have wandered off..."

"No, no. It was tethered. The tether had been cut through with a knife."

"I see." Ogilvie's shoulders drooped. "Then in that case ...yes, yours was a fair assumption, Major. He must have gone with the provisions."

"I'm very sorry, Ogilvie. This is hard for you, I know." Arkwright coughed. "He struck me as an odd sort of fellow, though. Very odd. And to take the food from the mouths of men on the march through the Khyber—well, need one say more? What's his idea? Tell me, Ogilvie: had there been trouble of some sort?"

Ogilvie hesitated, then gave Arkwright a straight look. "Yes, there had been trouble, Major. But it's a regimental matter, and I speak for my Colonel when I say we would prefer it to remain so. I'm sure you'll understand if I say no more than that?"

"Of course—of course! I fully understand. I'll ask no more, naturally." Arkwright clicked his teeth in embarrassment. "Now we mustn't delay further, Ogilvie. The sick have been provided for, and as soon as the dead are decently buried we must move out. I need scarcely remind you, the General's despatch is most urgent."

"Yes, I know, Major. I'm ready to march." Ogilvie looked slowly around the hills, and gave a sudden shiver. "I'd like to think I would never see this place again!"

*   *   *

From the safe and distant cover of the rocky crag to which he had dragged himself, Taggart-Blane watched the British troops march out. Close to exhaustion, he was shaking violently. As the comparative warmth engendered by his desperate effort to get away was dissipated by the Khyber's terrible cold, Taggart-Blane began to feel frozen to the point of numbness. Knowing he must keep on the move or he would undoubtedly freeze to death, he turned away from the crag and stumbled on, leading the commissariat mule by its halter. He was crying now; the tears of weakness and desperation ran from his eyes, only to freeze instantly upon his cheeks. He scarcely knew what he was doing, had no idea where he was going, except that he must get away from his companions, from the regiment, from James Ogilvie, from disgrace and ruin and perhaps a hanging.

After a while, feeling his legs give way, he tried to mount the mule. The animal bared its teeth, kicked out at him savagely, obstinately.

"You bastard!" Taggart-Blane screamed. *"Bastard, bastard, bastard!"*

Taking his revolver from its holster, he lashed out at the mule with the butt, cruelly, senselessly, drawing blood from its rump. With another wild kicking of its heels, the terrified beast went ahead, jerking on the halter and sending Taggart-Blane flying on his face in the snow. The halter slid from his grip and the mule moved fast away from him, plunging through the snow, into the beginnings of another blizzard, until it was lost to sight.

Now there was no commissariat, and no blankets.

Picking himself up from the snow, Taggart-Blane moved on behind the departed mule. Slipping again and again, falling, sliding, picking himself up, his flesh torn by the rocks upon which he fell, face cut and tormented by the wickedly sharp slivers of ice that were flung upon him by a biting wind, he made his slow progress to nowhere, dangerously crossing his little sector of the world's roof. He had gone perhaps a couple of hundred yards from where the mule had pitched him down, before he realised he no longer had his revolver. Two hundred yards was little enough distance to have made good in the time; but he knew it would be useless to turn, and go back, and search.

He fell, this time on his knees, and prayed to a God to whom he had never prayed before and who seemed to have no interest in him now. After a time he got to his feet again, and lurched on, crying, calling out obscene nonsense, feeling his mind leaving him. When, after hours of almost semi-conscious effort, he saw the shapes of men ahead of him, he thought at first they were the British.

"No!" he called out in a thin croak. "Let me die here. You'll never hang me, you'll never do that!" Then he saw that they were not British, but Pathans, wild men of the hills, heavily armed with rifles and long, snaky bayonets. He gave a high, crazy cackle of laughter, and collapsed again in the snow. He felt the strong hands lifting him, smelt foul breath fan his face, and looked closely into the eyes of cruelty.

"A British soldier," he heard one man say in a dialect which he vaguely understood. "A British soldier, to be killed."

"No!" Another face peered at him, and a rough hand slid around his throat, the fingers flexing against his windpipe. "Not to be killed yet. To be taken by the short route to Kunarja, to His Highness Jarar Mahommed!"

Taggart-Blane was lifted, roughly. He was manhandled along the track upon which he had stumbled unknowingly, and pushed ahead of the bayonets until he could go no farther. Then he was lifted up and carried across the shoulder of a big-built Pathan, and in this fashion, within two days by the short route known only to the hill tribes, he was brought to the gates of Kunarja, and smuggled in almost before the eyes of the Royal Strathspeys, encamped at a distance to observe and await events.

*   *   *

On his first visit to Kunarja, Taggart-Blane had feared torture. But then it had been a mere possibility, something remote, something that would probably never really happen.

Now it was happening.

He was screaming under the lash, as he had screamed and

screamed again under the razor-sharp knives with their small but many times repeated cuts, administered in a dimly lit, airless chamber in the presence of Colonel Rigby-Smith and Jarar Mahommed.

Taggart-Blane's mouth was hanging open; spittle drooled from the corners, ran down his chin. His eyes stared redly. "I have told you everything," he said with difficulty. "There is no more to tell, I swear it!"

"Search your mind afresh, Taggart Sahib." Jarar Mahommed's eyes gleamed with blood lust. "Silence brings more of the lash, a fitting punishment for a deserter, Taggart Sahib!"

"I tell you, there is no more. *No more!*"

The lash, at a signal from Jarar, fell again, cruelly wielded by a man naked to the waist whose black skin shone with sweat, a man who looked like a Nubian. Taggart-Blane gave another shrill scream from the bottom of his throat, a cry that was flung back at him from the enclosing stony walls now spattered red with blood. Rigby-Smith's face was grey and working; he seemed on the verge of collapse himself.

"There is, I think, at least one thing you have not told me, Taggart Sahib, and this is what caused your act of desertion?"

The lash was lifted again. Taggart-Blane licked his lips. "I ... had killed a man. Shot him."

"A man, of your own men, not an enemy?"

Taggart-Blane nodded, tears running down his cheeks.

"Why did you kill this man? Tell me, for I am interested! Who was he, Taggart Sahib?"

Taggart-Blane blubbered like a baby. The lash rose and fell. Punctuated by screams, the story emerged. Held under strong guard, Colonel Rigby-Smith listened in tense horror. His face was a study in many emotions. And when the story was ended, when it was obvious to Jarar Mahommed that the man beneath the lash had genuinely no more to tell, the signal was given for the real and final torment to begin.

*   *   *

The small British force found the 114th encamped in uncomfortable conditions outside the walls of Kunarja. As the drums and fifes were heard and the weary English soldiers were seen, the Scots came to their feet, waving and cheering. Lord Dornoch and the adjutant, Andrew Black, rode forward with an escort to greet them.

Dornoch was overjoyed. "James! An unexpected pleasure, to be sure! Do you come with Calcutta's answer?"

"Yes, Colonel—or I believe a term more popular at Division would be General Fettleworth's answer!"

Dornoch smiled, but his face was anxious. "And the answer is?"

"Agreement, Colonel. Agreement in full."

The Colonel let out a long breath. "Thank God—thank God and General Fettleworth! That's a relief, James. I've been allowed communication with Colonel Rigby-Smith inside the palace, up to ten days ago at all events, and I think you've reached us just in time. The princely patience, by all accounts, was wearing a little thin! Poor Rigby-Smith feared torture, and he and his officers had been subjected already to a degree of starvation." He glanced at the adjutant. "Captain Black, if you please—stand the regiment to at once. You and I and Ogilvie shall ride under escort to the gates, and demand an audience. I wish the main body of the regiment to be fallen in by companies and to be ready at a distance, ready for anything that may happen—though now I expect only peace!"

"Very good, Colonel." Black wheeled his horse, and rode down towards the encamped Scots. Courteously, Dornoch greeted Major Arkwright; and then, with a wave of his hand, indicated that he wished for a word in Ogilvie's ear. The two officers moved a little apart from the escort.

"Well, James?" There was sharp anxiety in Dornoch's voice.

"Taggart-Blane, Colonel?"

"Yes, yes—"

"He was ordered by General Fettleworth, on my own suggestion, to accompany my mission. Colonel, he left the column in the Khyber."

"Left?" There was a sharp intake of breath. "D'you mean —*deserted*?"

"In effect, Colonel—yes."

"You didn't find him?"

"No, Colonel. We tried, but it was no use."

"So he's still at large?"

"If he hasn't been frozen to death, Colonel."

There was a silence. "By God, James," Dornoch said after a moment. "You come with both good news and bad, do you not! What's the end of all this going to be!"

"Bad, Colonel, for the regiment. And for the havildar, Lal Binodinand, it could be fatal." Ogilvie paused. "And yet, perhaps not. General Fettleworth believes in his innocence..." He reported, briefly, his talks with Fettleworth and Wilkinson. "And to some extent, I suppose, Taggart-Blane has now incriminated himself by leaving the column ... by deserting."

"Murder and desertion—and worse! We shall not live this down James—never! This is a sad day for me, and will be so for your father also. The regiment ... it's his life, James, as it is mine."

"Mine also, Colonel."

"Yes, my dear boy, I know. I know!" Lord Dornoch looked away, his eyes shadowed—looked towards the regiment now falling in under the orders of Captain Black. He gave a deep sigh; then his back stiffened like a ramrod and he said, "Now we must go forward. There is much of importance to do. We shall talk fully about this later."

"Yes, Colonel."

Ogilvie followed on as Lord Dornoch rode towards the Highland line. A few minutes later, with the Queen's Own Royal Strathspeys in column of route behind him, and the pipes and drums of the battalion in front, Dornoch headed for the gates of Kunarja. The primitive, stirring wail of the pipes, and the beat of the drums, echoed off the age-old walls standing up from the cruel snow out of Himalaya. The Scots went forward with rifles and fixed bayonets and frost-stiffened kilts to the tune of 'The Campbells Are Coming', and as the head of the column drew nearer to the gates of savagery, Ogilvie could almost fancy himself to be one of those warring clansmen of old, bearing down with the threat of fire and sword upon Loch Leven, cold and lonely between Glen Nevis and Glen Coe.

*   *   *

"So you've returned at last," Colonel Rigby-Smith said disagreeably. The audience with Jarar Mahommed concluded to the satisfaction of both sides, Dornoch and Ogilvie had been taken to where the Colonel of the 99th Rawalpindis was being held in solitary confinement. The room stank, and so did Rigby-Smith—it was a smell of a lack of washing and hygiene, a horrible cold fug that sickened Ogilvie. Rigby-Smith himself had aged ten years; his cheeks were sunken and grey and his whole body was shaking. His uniform was awry and dirty and covered with blanket fluff; but he seemed to have lost none of his pernickettiness. "I trust you appreciate you've now returned to my command, not that of Lord Dornoch?"

Ogilvie caught Dornoch's eye and saw the fractional lowering of an eyelid. "Yes—sir," he said.

"Then kindly do me the courtesy of reporting in a proper manner."

"Yes, sir. Captain Ogilvie, on secondment from the 114th Highlanders, reporting back from escort duty, sir—with the terms fully agreed and the agreement delivered to His Highness Jarar Mahommed. Sir!"

Grunting, Rigby-Smith returned the salute that Ogilvie gave him. Then, turning to Lord Dornoch, he said, "I suppose you know why Jarar Mahommed had you brought here, Dornoch?"

"He said you had something to show me, Rigby-Smith."

"Yes, I have!" Rigby-Smith lifted a hand and rubbed at his eyes. To his astonishment, Ogilvie saw that those eyes now held tears. "Do you know, that man's the most *barbaric* monster I've ever come across in all my years in India? I've had the *most terrible* time—so have we all, all my officers and men. And now this. It took place ... oh, two days ago, perhaps three. Damn it, I've lost count of time ... I'm in no fit state for all this, I tell you! Horror has been piled upon horror, and this is the culmination of that brutal man's wicked cruelty ... that I should be made to show you what he has done!" He lifted one of his shaking hands and pointed. "Do you see that hatch in the floor, there?"

Dornoch nodded. "Yes."

"It leads to a hole, a mere hole gouged out of the earth and lined with some hard substance, I don't know what. There's something in it. If I were you ... I'd not look."

"I think I must look, Rigby-Smith."

Rigby-Smith gestured wearily, and brushed a shaking hand across his eyes. "If you must, then you must. Possibly ... yes, perhaps it would be better to do as Jarar Mahommed wants, since we're still in his power—"

"We are not! I have my regiment here, in readiness at the gates—you know this. We're in nobody's power, Colonel, I assure you of that!"

"I'm glad to hear it," Rigby-Smith said perfunctorily. He was shaking more than ever. "I shall tell you what's in ..." All at once, he staggered. Ogilvie caught him before he fell, and held the inert body in his arms.

"He's fainted, Colonel."

"The devil he has! Lay him on the floor—gently—and we'll open up that hatch. God, but I can't get away from this place quickly enough!"

Ogilvie lowered Rigby-Smith to the floor and then, with Dornoch, bent to the hatch and lifted it by means of a small ringbolt set into the wood. At first they saw nothing; then they made out a pile of sacking, as it seemed. Ogilvie dropped through the hatch into the hole, and poked at the sacking. There was a soft feel, almost a squelchiness, and more prodding resulted in some wetness, and a stain—a stain of blood.

Ogilvie flinched away from it, as the truth, the terrible truth, came to him. He looked up at Dornoch. "Colonel, it's a body. A dead body, I think."

"We must bring it up—or examine it *in situ* would be easier. Can you strip away that sacking, James?"

Ogilvie got to work. It was a horrible and gruesome business, but he did it. The opened sacking revealed a body, complete but dismembered, a torso with its limbs severed

219

and laid by its side, a torso wearing the uniform and insignia of a subaltern of the Royal Strathspeys, and the head of Taggart-Blane grinning, the teeth bared in the agony of death, from its position, like the crown and sceptre on the coffin of a dead monarch, in the centre of the gutted stomach.

Retching violently, Ogilvie straightened and lifted his shoulders through the lip of the hole; Dornoch bent to him, and helped him through. All Ogilvie could do was to point down, and utter the dead man's name. Dornoch's face was grim and set. He said, "There'll be work for my regiment to do before we leave Kunarja!"

"*No!*" This was a violent interpolation from Rigby-Smith, who had come round from his faint and was staring in fearful agitation towards the open hole, and at Lord Dornoch. "No, Dornoch, *you must not attack the town!*"

"My dear Rigby-Smith, you forget yourself. I must—"

"No! I beseech you!" Rigby-Smith moved across the floor on hands and knees, like some grotesque and enlarged beetle, then got to his feet and stood swaying before the Scots Colonel. "The moment your regiment approaches the gates, all the hostages will be slaughtered. I ask you to think now, not of one man who is dead, but of several hundreds who need not die!"

"Including you, Colonel Rigby-Smith." Hawk-like, Dornoch stared into his face, and he looked away.

"Indeed including me. But I am not asking for myself. Think, Dornoch, think!" Rigby-Smith reached out and clutched at Dornoch's arm, his fingers shaking as though with a fever. "A whole native regiment butchered as that unfortunate young man was butchered—and the agreement abrogated by your own act even before it has begun to take effect! You cannot, you *must* not, throw all that away! That subaltern of yours was captured by Jarar Mahommed's men, men from one of his outposts—the subaltern having deserted your regiment, Dornoch, whilst on service in the Khyber Pass! To avenge such a death is not a fit and proper premise upon which to build your own war, Colonel!"

"This act of desertion ... how do you know this?"

Rigby-Smith said hoarsely, "Why, because the subaltern was tortured in my presence—was eventually butchered in my presence, God help me! He said all this, do you not see!"

"Said—precisely what?"

Rigby-Smith lifted his hands to his ravaged face. "He revealed that he had killed a man of my regiment, my own regiment. A sepoy named, I think, Mulata Din. Before this ...he had committed an act of the grossest indecency, by his own confession. Your subaltern was a murderer, Dornoch— a murderer and a sodomist! You shall not start a war on his behalf, *you shall not!*"

Dornoch caught Ogilvie's eye. He asked Rigby-Smith, "Who else, beside you and Jarar Mahommed, was a witness to all this?"

"No-one else, at least no-one else of my regiment. Only the natives who were carrying out that maniac's orders on Taggart-Blane."

"I see. Give me a moment," Dornoch said abruptly. He strode up and down the stinking room, deep in thought, deeply agitated. There was a silence from the other two, as they both watched the Colonel. Then, at last, he stopped. Facing Rigby-Smith he said coldly, "There is possibly a way in which this can be resolved. I see no purpose in further killing, and am certainly not anxious to endanger the hostages. Rigby-Smith, I will withdraw my regiment upon certain conditions, the first being this: you will repeat my subaltern's words to General Fettleworth *and to no-one else* except upon the General's own order. This will save the life of one of your own havildars, currently in arrest in Peshawar. You promise this?"

"Yes, yes—"

"And secondly: how did this officer die?"

Rigby-Smith covered his eyes. "He died screaming— screaming. Oh, it was horrible."

"But he died well?"

"He died screaming, as I have said. No, he did not die well ..." Rigby-Smith's voice faded as he saw the look in Dornoch's eye. "He ... oh, very well, then. Yes—he died well. Yes."

"And this you will say in Peshawar?"

"Yes—yes, I'll say it. It's a lie, but—"

"Let the lie be on my own conscience, not yours, Colonel Rigby-Smith. *He died well.* I have your word?"

"Oh yes, yes."

"Keep your word," Dornoch said quietly, "or by God above, I'll see that you are relieved of the command of your regiment, Colonel Rigby-Smith!" He turned to Ogilvie, and put a heavy hand on his shoulder. "I think it's all right now," he said. "I have a very deep knowledge of the workings of the Divisional Commander's mind. And..." he gestured down into the hole with its horrible content. "He died on active service, James. On active service for the Raj. I'll guarantee no questions'll be asked about that, though it's possibly more than he deserved. But he's paid—he's paid in full."